DETROIT PUBLIC LIBRARY

P9-DNO-246

KEISHA & TRIGGA 4:
A GANGSTER LOVE STORY

A Novel By
LEO SULLIVAN
PORSCHA STERLING

CHASE BRANCH LIBRARY
17731 W. SEVEN MILE RD.
DETROIT, MI 48235
313-481-1580

© **2016**

Published by Leo Sullivan Presents
www.leolsullivan.com

All rights reserved.
This is a work of fiction. Names, characters, businesses, places, events and incidents are either the products of the author's imagination or used in a fictitious manner. Any resemblance to actual persons, living or dead, or actual events is purely coincidental. Unauthorized reproduction, in any manner, is prohibited.

PROLOGUE

A bright sun shimmered on the south side of metro Atlanta over a modest two-story home where the neighborhood was luxurious, something you would see straight out of a *Better Homes and Garden* magazine. The lawns were trimmed and well-kept, expensive automobiles lined the driveways. Majestic royal blue clouds floated high in the sky like cotton candy, bringing forth the promise of what should have been a glorious day but would end in cold-blooded murder.

A dark blue BMW pulled up to the side of the house with the blare of rap music pulsating so hard from the speakers in the trunk, that you could hear them rattling from the back. The occupant removed a .9mm handgun from the glove compartment, along with a pair of black gloves, and then exited the vehicle after doing a second scan of his surroundings to make sure no one was watching before walking to the front of the home. There was a soft knock on the front door as a wind chime serenaded a gentle breeze.

The moment lingered like heightened heartbeats of anticipation.

Finally, the door opened with a squeak, a gospel song could be heard coming from inside the house. The occupant of the home, seventy-eight-year-old Louise Mitchell, answered the door.

"May I help you?" she asked, then her eyebrows knotted up into a frown.

"Yes, I came to see Dior and my daughter," Lloyd said as he finger-fucked the trigger of the .9mm snuggled in his pocket, prepared to come up shooting at any minute.

"I...I don't know 'bout that. Dior said you and her been havin' issues." The old woman began to fidget with her dress hem.

"We ain't got no issues. Those issues have been resolved," Lloyd responded and peeked over his shoulder. A postal truck was passing.

"Who is that at the door?" a throaty, deep voice asked. The voice belonged to Ed Mitchell, Dior's father.

"It's—"

Before the old woman could get the words out her mouth, Lloyd pulled out the gun and shoved her in the house.

"Who is it?" her husband asked, annoyed.

What was the sense spending nearly eight hundred dollars of our social security savings on a hearing aid and she still couldn't damn hear? he thought as suddenly his wife stumbled into the living room.

He looked up from the paper, about to ask her if she had started back drinking again, when the man he hated more than anyone in the world came and stood in the living room doorway. His heart thumped in his chest and instantly he was furious to the point that his entire body began to tremble with rage. He reached for his walking cane on the side of the La-Z-Boy chair, prepared to get up and start swinging.

"Boy, is you done lost your fuckin' mind? Coming up in my home when I can't stand the sight of your ass!" Ed exhorted, getting up from the chair.

At seventy-nine years old, he was a fragile old man, a mere husk of himself in younger days but you couldn't tell him that. The thing was, he never liked Lloyd dating his daughter and he had no problem letting Lloyd know. On more than one occasion, he had openly expressed his hatred for Lloyd.

But their hatred was mutual.

The last time Lloyd had tried to come to their home to get Dior was after a bitter argument. The old man tried to spit on Lloyd and strike him with the cane for just knocking at the door. On the strength of his feelings for Dior, Lloyd gave the old man a pass.

This day would be different.

"If you don't get the fuck outta my house!" the old man said with grit and reached back to whack the shit out of Lloyd with the cane.

It was as if Lloyd had lived for this very moment, savoring it. In a swift motion, Lloyd reached out and struck the old man across his cranium with the .9mm, opening up a deep gash and causing him to crumble onto the floor in a heap as blood spilled from his head.

"EDDIE!!" his wife screamed as she raced over to him and was met with Lloyd's vicious backhand which sent her sprawling to the floor, dazed and semi-unconscious.

"Where is Dior and my muthafuckin' daughter at?!" Lloyd growled menacingly as he turned towards the woman, prepared to kick her in the face.

Lying next to her, her husband struggled to get back up but he was disoriented.

"She is not here! I promise. Please, don't hurt us, pleeeaaaassse!" The old woman began to cry. Mr. Mitchell managed to sit up with the help of the wall he clung to.

"I'ma kill your ass," he said in slurred words as he wobbled back and forth with blood streaming down his forehead, turning his face a horrific sanguine red.

Lloyd wasted no time. In two quick strides, he was upon the elderly man and struck him with his fists, twice, breaking his nose and opening a deep gash underneath his right eye. The injury caused him to groan in agony. From somewhere in the house, a gospel melody, a Mahalia Jackson song, crooned as the old woman cried pensively for Lloyd to stop his brutality.

"Where the baby at?!" Lloyd yelled as he frantically looked around the handsomely decorated home.

"She is asleep over there in her pen," the woman pointed with a shaking, gnarly finger.

Lloyd reached down and snatched the old woman up by her long hair, pulling brittle strands and flesh from her delicate head and causing her to shriek in pain. Once she scrambled to her feet, he relaxed his grasp, and chunks of hair, in large tresses, fell to the floor.

"Show me!" Lloyd barked and marched Louise to the other side of the room.

In a pink bassinet was the baby, just as sweet and adorable as she could be. Her short legs and arms flailed as she goo-gooed, smiling to herself as if the angels were playing with her.

She looked just like him. Lloyd's heart swelled with joy, then suddenly with dread when he thought about the drastic mistake he had almost made, placing the child in the oven, prepared to burn her alive because he'd thought she wasn't his. He reached his hand inside the bassinet as the child cooed. She grabbed onto his finger and wouldn't let go.

Unbeknownst to him, Ed had began to scoot to the other side of the room. In a desk drawer near the corner was his military .45 Colt. It was old but it would shoot. Lloyd was so preoccupied, he never detected the old man's movement.

There was an old stereo playing an album with a nickel on the turntable, causing Mahalia Jackson's record to replay. The music was terrible but, suddenly, Lloyd had a bright idea. He strolled over to the ancient record player and snatched the electrical cord out the wall socket as he continued to hold on to Louise's long hair.

As soon as he turned back around, shots were fired, the bullets just missing his head. He whipped Louise by her hair and placed her in front of him, using her as a human shield as he ducked and placed his banger to her temple.

BOOM! BOOM!

Ed fired several more shots, causing the jerk of the large pistol to almost knock him over as he stood on wobbly legs. Blood continued to spew down his face like a faucet. This was something straight out of a horror movie. Only this was real.

"I'ma splatter this bitch's brains all over the wall if you shoot one more time," Lloyd threatened, almost tripping over a table leg as he moved backwards.

"Let her go and get the fuck outta my home, you crazy muthafucka!" the old man said and tried to wipe his face with the back of his hand..

"Fuck dat! Drop dat muthafuckin' gun or I'ma spray this bitch's brains across the room."

"Eddie, pleeeaaassse! Just do what he says!" she cried frantically as Lloyd continued to press the cold steel of the gun to the side of her head. He yanked harder on her long hair.

"ONE!"

Lloyd began to count as his eyes skirted around the room in search of a quick exit. He was about to abandon his plan if he couldn't accomplish what he set out to do fast enough.

"TWO!"

Lloyd yanked Louise's hair back, causing her to cry out in pain as his eyes frantically looked around the room.

"Eddie, goddamnit fool! Drop the gun so the boy can leave! LET HIM GO!" she yelled so loud, veins protruded from her neck and forehand as she waved a frail hand at him.

Due to his wife's pleading, reluctantly Ed hunched his shoulders over as if the last sap of his vanity was unmercifully lost from his soul. He tossed the gun, and it flew across the floor and came to rest only a few feet away from where Lloyd stood. By then, Louise was hysterical.

Lloyd released a protracted sigh that merged into a chuckle of satisfaction. He retrieved the gun off the floor and examined it with a gloating grin of triumph.

"Get yo' asses in them chairs!!" Lloyd shouted, pointing to the dining room chairs to the side of them.

"I thought you said you was going to LEAVE?" Louise said, gesturing with her hands as if ushering him out the door.

WHAM!

He struck her across the head with his fist. When Ed moved like he was about to try to come to her rescue, Lloyd leveled the gun barrel at his chest.

"You better sit your old ass down. Both of you!" he barked. It was as if the fight had been knocked out of him. Ed sat in the chair and hung his head begrudgingly.

***

With the electrical cords from the record player, Lloyd was able to tie each of his elderly victims securely in wooden chairs. They sat only inches across from each other as Lloyd walked over and played with the baby. The couple stared at each other perplexed as to what he was going to do next.

It didn't take long for them to find out when Lloyd strode back over. His appearance was meek as a kitten, but dangerous as a lion as he spoke in a sinister tone.

"Now that I have the full attention of a captive audience," he paused to snicker at his own clever play on words and continued in a mocking voice.

"Your daughter stole my money and drugs. I came to kill her but not you—"

"Man, have you lost your fucking mind? We ain't got nothing to do with her taking your shit! And you ain't going to touch a hair on her head unless it's over my dead body!"

"Okay, we'll see 'bout your dead body, but for now, I need to know where Dior is. See, I ain't got all damn day."

Lloyd had begun to pace the floor. Occasionally, he would peer outside the curtains; he was getting nervous and antsy.

"She told us she had an appointment, we—"

"Shut up, Louise!" Ed grumbled at his wife with a stern look.

Lloyd stormed over and punched him so hard in the face, his false teeth nearly fell out his mouth. Louise shrieked in horror as Lloyd continued to pummel him in the face with the gun.

"I ain't neva liked yo' old ass! Muthafucka, don't think I forgot you tried to spit on me one time. I should go get a hammer and beat your old ass to death with it," Lloyd threatened with grit in his voice.

Then he turned back to Louise, "Tell me...what time does Dior return home? I just want my dope and money back."

"She...She..."

"Goddamnit, Louise! Shut the fuck up. The boy done already told you he came to murder our baby!"

Lloyd cut his eyes at Dior's dad and made a mental note to kill him good and slow, like maybe beat his ass with a hammer, cut his shriveled up balls off. Both of his eyes were nearly shut, swollen and discolored and Lloyd had to admit, as much as he hated to, the old dude was tough as nails.

"What were you saying, Mrs. Mitchell?" Lloyd asked politely, taking a few steps closer, the entire time his heart drumming in his chest.

Louise looked at her husband, then up at Lloyd with an apologetic scrawl on her face. She bunched her lips up and pursed them in a tight, straight line across her face, like 'mums the word'.

"Talk!"

She shook her head, then glanced over at her husband for his approval. Lloyd could have sworn he saw a smile tug at the man's bloodied face. A face that for some unknown reason taunted him because he couldn't break Ed's stubborn will, even in the threat of immediate death.

That was it, Lloyd completely lost it. His civility went out the window, only to be replaced with stark brutality. He rushed over and kicked the chair over, sending Ed sprawling on the floor in agonizing pain before Lloyd commenced to beating and punching him some more.

Then he rushed back over to the wife. On the table was a plastic Publix shopping bag with a few items inside. He dumped the items on the floor and looked Ed dead in his eyes to let him know how serious he was.

"You don't wanna talk, don't wanna tell me nuttin'? Say goodbye to your wife then, fuck nigga!" Lloyd exclaimed and placed the plastic bag over Louise's head as she thrashed and tried to resist.

Exasperated, Lloyd tightened the bag back on the old woman's head and held it tightly and began to suffocate her. It was as if Lloyd got some personal sadistic satisfaction out of suffocating the old woman. He choked her with the bag wrapped around her face until she stopped breathing and her body was limp. With a satisfied sneer on his face, he looked over at the old man, his face had paled ashine. Storming over to where he lay, Lloyd kicked and punched him.

"Hey! Get your ass up! I got something special for you!" Lloyd was prepared to beat him to death.

But Ed didn't move.

"Get the fuck up! Move," Lloyd shouted even though he knew that Ed couldn't get up even if he wanted to because he was still tied to the chair.

Then something suddenly dawned on him as he looked down at the body. The old man was dead. It looked as if he'd died of a massive heart attack.

"Fuck! Fuck! Fuck!" Lloyd cursed.

Suddenly, he heard something. At first, he thought it was the baby in the crib. Then he realized the noise was coming from outside.

Police! was his first thought.

He walked over to the window and peered out. A car had pulled into the driveway and just sat idle. Lloyd's nerves were on edge. He waited, undecided on what to do next as he stood by the window.

Then, the passenger door opened and low and behold, Dior stepped out looking all suspicious.

"Yes! Yes!" He pumped his fists in the air vigorously, then rushed over and dragged the bodies into the closet in the master bedroom and wiped up as much blood as he could.

"Show time!"

ONE

Keisha's heart beat so hard in her chest that she could hear it in her ears, thumping louder and louder as her brain tried to comprehend what was happening before her. Struggling to her feet, she ran through the sea of people who had surrounded Trigga and fought through them with tears in her eyes.

"Sir, are you okay? Can you hear me?" someone asked Trigga as she continued to push through the crowd. When he didn't answer right away, Keisha began to feel panicked and her throat tightened to the point where she thought she would suffocate.

"I'm good. Shit...step back a little so a nigga can breathe, damn!" Trigga snapped but it was clear he was in obvious pain as he stood bent over, lips pressed tight. He drummed his fingers on his pants leg and pinched his eyes closed, as if he was summoning the courage to walk.

Keisha's heart leaped for joy when she heard his voice, just as she passed through the last person that was blocking her from her view of Trigga. When her eyes landed on him, he was struggling to stand up. An older man with a stocky, muscular build reached out and grabbed his arm to help him up, but Trigga gave him a look that made him step back.

"I was only trying to help!" the man explained with his hands in the air. "I really don't think that you should be moving until you're examined though."

"I ain't gettin' examined," Trigga grumbled under his breath and wince in pain. "A nigga done spent more time in the hospital than the damn doctors...I can't go back there," he said with a shrug and winced again.

"Baby, are you okay? I think you need to go in and let someone look at—"

She glanced down and saw blood oozing from under his pants leg.

"I'm good, Keesh," Trigga said, brushing her away gently and shaking his head as he nibbled on his bottom lip, attempting to fight the pain. "I jumped on top of the hood and tried to roll off. The car managed to partially hit my leg but I'm lucky it was just the bumper. It's not smashed..."

"We got to get you in the hospital. We gotta get you help," Keisha said with a plea in her voice. If felt like he was putting more of his weight on her as he tried to stand straight.

"Keesh, drop it. I ain't goin' back in there!" Trigga cut her off and attempted to walk on his own and nearly fell once more. She reached out and grabbed him in a bear hug.

Just then, a woman ran towards them with two men behind her who were pushing a stretcher; they were dressed in medic outfits.

"Sir! You shouldn't be standing. Let us check you out!" one of the men said as he glanced down looking at the puddle of blood streaming from his leg. The woman standing with them frowned and then looked at Keisha with a quizzical expression.

"I saw him get hit so I called for help! Is...is he okay?"

"I appreciate it but I'm good!" Trigga said sternly once again. With a nod of his head, he backed away from the two men who were pulling out instruments, some type of medical gadgets.

"Sir, if we can just—"

"Ho, ho, ho, hold da fuck up. I said I was good," Trigga boomed while holding up his hands. He then turned to Keisha.

"Bae, let's go." Trigga turned and painfully hobbled off leaving a trail of blood and several people staring at him.

Keisha watched him stagger away and it felt like her heart was hemorrhaging. The entire time she could feel eyes boring through her. She turned and it was the medics and the nice lady that had tried to help.

Keisha read their thoughts and with a subtle shrug, she said, barely above a whisper, "I'ma watch him and I'ma take care of him. I'll make sure he gets to a hospital," her voice trembled. Then something occurred to her and she took off after Trigga, like a bolt of lightning.

As she rushed to catch up, walking behind him, she was consumed with seething rage and overwhelming hurt. She couldn't take it anymore. They had been through too much.

Just as he reached for the car door to the driver side of his Audi, she grabbed his arm and yanked him forcefully.

"Ouch! Fuck, Keesh!" he cried out in pain and nearly stumbled into the street. She hadn't meant to be rough with him but, in her anger, she had.

"What is your problem, man?"

"You're my fuckin' problem!" she yelled back in his face and chest bumped him. Trigga expelled a deep sigh and leaned on the car door.

"You trippin'."

Keisha sucked her teeth. "Oh, I'm trippin'? We are married now. I have your baby and you still runnin' around like you don't want to be a part of our life. Like you don't even care! You're acting like, fuck me! Fuck the baby! Fuck being married."

"Keesh, why you saying that, bae? I'm doing everything I can for you and the baby," he said in a softer tone.

"No, you're not. You're still running around like you're Rambo, nigga. You need to go to the hospital. You need to get some help and I'm starting to wonder if you need mental help, too."

"What kinda fuck shit is that to say to a nigga?" he interjected, narrowing his eyes, like she had struck a serious nerve.

"You walking around here with your leg bleeding, the bone could be broken, God only knows, and you won't take your ass to the hospital. That's retarded."

"Retarded?" he repeated, blinking back at her as if she was speaking another language.

Trigga turned facing the sun, causing his gray eyes to shimmer. "I have a warrant out for my arrest for failure to appear in court after that time NeTasha bonded me out. It showed up a few days ago, I got a call about it."

"Are you serious? How did you miss your court date?"

"A court date was the last thing on my mind when I was searching for you! I just lost track of it. I didn't care about anything or anybody. I know that sounds lame but it's the truth. Now, if I go to the hospital there is a chance my name might show up somewhere. If I go back to jail this time, I won't be able to get bonded out. They will let my ass sit."

"Ohhh, Lord, this can't be happening," Keisha droned and grabbed her forehead like she was catching a major migraine headache.

"I'm sorry," Trigga finally said, solemnly, and reached out for her.

She took a timid step and melted in his arms like butter, nestling in the crook of his shoulder and, for that infinite moment in time on a desolate street, they held each other like nothing else mattered. It was just them in a secular universe of their own. Them against the world.

"Baby, there's no need to apologize for somethin' you can't do anything about," she said, while caressing his back. "I just need to get you home and take care of you."

"Okay," he agreed happy she'd dropped the hospital talk. "I'll drive."

Jovially, she flashed a mischievous smile as her eyes sparkled in the bright sun.

"Not happening," she chimed, snatching the keys from his hand. "You got a fucked up leg and a warrant for your arrest. With the kind of luck we have, your ass would crash into the police and both of us would either be dead or in jail. I'll pass on lettin' your one legged ass drive me around."

Trigga folded his arms and frowned at her as she waltzed over to the driver side of the car, pretending not to notice his stare.

"You know what, Keesh?" Trigga grumbled as he grabbed the door on the passenger side. "I got something that will fit perfectly in that slick ass mouth you got."

TWO

What did I do?

What did I do?

WHAT did I DO?!

The question circled round and round in Dior's head as she drove at top speed the entire way to her parents' home, with tears running steadily down her cheeks. With each passing second, she tried to bring herself to terms with the horror of what she'd done.

What the fuck is wrong with me?

Of all the things Dior had done in her life, killing someone had never been one. She'd arranged for people to be killed but she hadn't ever actually delivered the shot that ended it all. She left that kind of stuff to the pros.

But now she was possibly a murderer, incited by incense, rage and hatred. She had slammed her car into Trigga by accident. Who she intended to kill was Keisha.

"Fuck! Fuck!" she cursed as she slammed her hand on the steering wheel.

After witnessing the most selfless act of love that she'd ever seen when Trigga tossed Keisha to safety so that he could take the hit, Dior mashed the gas and kept going. She had no idea what the hell she could have been thinking, doing something so stupid in broad daylight. There were people outside, cameras, her tag wasn't covered...it would be easy to track her down.

There were so many reasons why what she'd done was stupid that there was no reason to even bother counting. The last thing she'd wanted to do was to murder someone who was innocent.

That poor, innocent man with Keisha probably hasn't done a single wrong thing in his life other than get caught up with her hoe ass! she thought as she bit her lip sadly and glanced behind her for fear that someone had followed her and called the cops.

When Dior crept steadily down her parents' street, slowly approaching their home, she sucked in a sharp breath when she saw that they were home already. She still didn't want to let her parents know that she could walk and now, it was for good reason. Since everyone thought she was paralyzed, she had the perfect alibi if anyone came looking around after they started checking cameras for who had murdered that man.

Dior parked and turned off the car, then waited and looked through the windows for a while before rushing to get her wheelchair. There wasn't any movement inside so most likely her parents and the baby were down for a nap. She rushed out of the car and into the house, happy to be home and ready to take a long shower and wash off the guilt that she felt about what she'd done. But after about two seconds after entering the house, she knew something was wrong.

Very wrong.

Dior stood up and started walking slowly into the living room with her lips quivering, from the thick sense of danger she felt looming in the air.

"Where da fuck is my muthafuckin' money, Dee?" an all too familiar voice resonated in the dark, causing a timorous shiver to run down her spine.

All of a sudden, the urgent sense of alarm and panic overcame her and nearly made her return to her crippled state, as she keeled over and had to grab on to the back of the chair next to her to keep her balance. Her eyes widened in horror when she saw Karisma in Lloyd's arms. It was like déjà vu. Her legs wobbled and her bottom lip quivered as she had quick flashbacks to the day when Lloyd had almost killed both of them.

"Wha...what are you doin' here?! Put her down!" her voice screeched with a falsetto of fear.

"Bitch, shut up! Yo' ass walkin' around and some mo' shit and you supposed to be paralyzed. Get the fuck outta here." Lloyd waved her off as he balanced Karisma in one arm. Dior started to tremble as she watched her child began to stir in her father's arm. Then something occurred to her.

"Where are my parents?" she asked looking around the room for any sign of her parents or worst, evidence of their demise. Then her eyes fell on droplets of blood on the floor. Suddenly, she began to feel cold. She wrapped herself in her arms and took a step towards Lloyd, but stopped when his hand moved to his hip where she knew he had a banger stashed.

Just then, Karisma began to wail in his arms as if she could sense the disharmony in the room.

"Waaaaaaaaaaaaaaaaaaaaaaaaaaaaaaaa!   Waaaaaaaaaaaaaaaaaaaa!" Karisma screamed, loudly voicing her irritation.

With his lips pulled up as if disgusted, Lloyd frowned at the infant in his arms and tried to shift the baby around to the crook of his other arm awkwardly. That's when Dior noticed the large .44 Desert Eagle in his other hand, gleaming off the light. Her heart did a somersault.

"Lloyd...Please...Lemme have her!" Dior begged with her hands clasped as if she was in prayer. "Please don't hurt her. I swear she's yours!"

"I know she's mine! Any muthafucka can tell after lookin' at her in this ugly, gypsy-clown, lookin' ass dress. All you wear is expensive shit and got my shorty wearing these cheap ass shits." Lloyd grabbed and threw one of Karisma's shoes into Dior's direction. She winced when it just narrowly missed her and pelted into the wall behind her.

"L—L—Lloyd, please..." her voice quavered.

Dior sunk down into the chair that she had been using to steady herself and she began to cry hysterical, pungent sobs that rocked her body as she looked into his menacing eyes. They were dark as coal. She had seen that look before. It was death's stare. She began to babble uncontrollably as a stream of snot and tears ran down her face. She muttered a silent prayer and reached out for her baby. Lloyd backed away from her as if she was filthy.

"Dis how we gone do dis shit," Lloyd started as he cocked the gun, the sound echoing as a glitter of light gleamed ominously off the gun. He took several steps closer to her; the sound of his Jordans squeaked on the old wooden floor.

He had a feral grin on his face that signaled he was getting pure satisfaction out of what was doing. With startling quickness, he placed the barrel of the gun firmly against her forehead, so hard that it broke skin, and he seemed to get enjoyment from watching her cry out in pain. A teardrop of blood slid slowly down her face and mixed with the beads of sweat and tears that lie in its path.

Soon, there was a harmonic sound of the symphony of horror as Dior and the baby both cried in unison.

"Pl—pl—pleeeeaaase, don't do this. The last time you nearly killed her! Your own flesh and blood!" Dior begged but she knew it was in vain. Whatever Lloyd wanted to do, he would do.

"If you tell me where all my dope and money is that you took with that fuck nigga, Kenyon, I might spare your life."

"That was so long ago, I—" Lloyd clocked her in the head with the gun and she cried out.

"BITCH, I KNOW YOU STILL GOT MY SHIT!"

Dior looked up at him as a trickle of blood cascaded down her face. She mopped it with the back of her hand and thought to herself.

Perhaps, maybe there was a ray of hope. Perhaps he won't kill me if I give him the money and dope. Over one million dollars is in my stash, she contemplated. After all, she was still his wife and the mother to his child.

"Waaaaaaaaaaaaaaaaaaaaaaaa!! Waaaaaaaaaaaaaaaaaaaaaaaa!!" the baby continued to cry.

Annoyed, Lloyd looked at the infant in his arm like he wanted to toss her across the room. Dior trembled as if she'd read his thoughts. Victim turned vixen, she mustered the courage to face her fears. She had no choice.

"You ain't gotta die dis evenin'. You can just give me my shit you and that nigga stole." Lloyd paused when Dior's sobs began to subside as she fought with her emotions like she was trying to bridle her fear.

"Lloyd, listen, I never told the cops on you when you tried to kill me and your child, I've always been by your side—"

"Bitch, you stole a nigga dope and money, fucked my cousin, then tried to send a nigga to the chain-gang for life. The only reason you didn't tell on me is because your conniving ass was the mastermind behind a lot of shit I've done and there was a chance you might catch a case with me."

"No! No! Don't say that," she pleaded with melancholy as she continued to fumble with her hands. She was a bundle of nerves.

"Don't say what?" Lloyd's body went rigid, stiff as a board as he got visibly angrier. Dior knew he was about to do something crazy. Suddenly, he tossed the baby across the room.

"LLOYD!!" Dior screamed out. The baby landed on the couch and bounced, nearly falling on to the hard wooden floor, but she was unharmed.

"Waaaaaaaaaaaaaaaaaaaaaaaaaaaaaaaaaaaaaaa!!!!"

Dior prepared to rush over to her baby, but Lloyd grabbed her neck with one hand in a vice grip, using so much force that Dior found herself on her tiptoes, struggling. All the blood raced from her face.

"You...hurting...me."

Lloyd choked her harder and she began to gasp. Her hand, with fingers like talons, reached out to scratch his face. Then he leveled the gun at her head.

THREE

Keisha and Trigga drove down the road back to their home in silence, both of them deep in their thoughts. Keisha turned slightly and stared at Trigga from the corner of her eye as he sat with his seat reared all the way back. They'd found a white T-shirt in the back seat of the car to wrap his leg with, to help stop the bleeding. Even though his eyes were closed like he was resting in peaceful bliss, she could still see the pain etched in his face like a hard rock with a scratch on the surface.

She reached out and grabbed his hand in hers when they stopped at a light. He squeezed her hand and Keisha felt a pang in her chest as she watched him, knowing that everything he'd said about leaving the game alone was now officially off the table. She'd seen the expression he had on his face, while at the hospital, many times before. It was the expression a man made when he'd resolved to murder.

Someone had tried to kill her, and one thing that she knew for sure was that Trigga wasn't about to let that shit slide. She knew from just looking at his countenance that Trigga was feigning sleep and, in reality, was next to her planning and plotting on how to wreak havoc on his enemies.

"God help us," she muttered to herself as the light turned green and she pulled off. For some reason she rubbed her belly, wondering if their child could hear what she said.

She just happened to glance down at the floorboard of the car and noticed the white T-shirt that was wrapped around his leg had turned bright red.

"Did you see who it was that hit you?" she mustered the courage to ask right as she pulled into their driveway.

"Nawl," he answered stoically, but something in his tone told her that he was lying. She watched him intensely as he struggled to get out the car. Just that fast, his leg was starting to swell and he grumbled his discontent.

"Let me help you, bae," she said, knowing damn well that his male ego was not going to let him help her. Ignoring her, he continued to wrestle with his leg.

"You put the T-shirt on too tight and it must have cut off my circulation," he grumbled some more stalling for time. She looked over and he was sweating profusely.

"Either that or that speeding *CAR* that hit you and damn near left you a cripple," she shot back sarcastically and cut off the engine.

"Man, whateva... I'm good!" he continued to struggle.

With a frown on her face, Keisha jumped out of her side and stormed over to watch Trigga struggle. He avoided her eyes, clenching his jaw to hide his pain from showing up on his face. But Keisha took notice anyways and she couldn't decide if she was furious or humored by it. After all, it was Trigga's stubborn attitude that she fell in love with in the first place.

"Oh, I see you got it. Are you gettin' out the car now or you want me to come back and help you in the morning?"

"You got a slick ass mouth, Keisha," he said with a painful frown and finally pulled himself up.

As they walked to the door, Trigga leaned over and mumbled into her earlobe while reaching down to squeeze her backside.

"Let a nigga get a shot of ass, some Cîroc and a nice, fat blunt and I'ma be good to go."

Rolling her eyes, she removed his hand and said, "You probably can get the Cîroc and the blunt, but I don't know where you gonna get a shot of ass from."

"Why you acting like that, shawty?" Trigga gasped. "That pussy officially mine now."

"Yeah but remember, I got a slick ass mouth."

"Baby, I was just playin'."

"Humph," Keisha grunted.

Trigga reached out to unlock the door but before he could, it swung open. In the entrance stood Gunplay and LeTavia holding their suitcases and other belongings in their hands. The two dogs were standing at attention at their feet.

They both took one look at Trigga and both of them drawled at the same time in chorus. "Dayum, nigga, what happened to you?"

"Minor accident," Trigga explained, shrugging it off like it wasn't anything.

"Minor?" Keisha repeated with a roll of her eyes and sucked her teeth.

"Okay, I'm fucked up. But it's only temporary until Keesh hook a nigga up with some ass—"

Trigga stopped and doubled over after Keisha punched him in the gut. Once he recovered, he sat down in the closest chair in the front room, while Keisha left to grab some medical supplies from the kitchen.

"Nigga, you look like you need to be in the emergency room," Gunplay said and LeTavia seconded it with an officious nod of her head.

"I'm good. You know a nigga got nine lives," Trigga laughed.

"My nigga, if you had nine lives, you just lost about six of them shits. You fucked up," Gunplay said with his face screwed up.

"I'm good," Trigga repeated as Keisha returned. He watched as she knelt down at his feet and eased his sock off with her face balled up with apprehension.

With dread, everybody watched in silence like they were looking at some cinematic horror show. Keisha removed the bloody sock, then pulled his pants leg up.

"Uh, huh, hell-to-the–muthafuckin'-nawl. It looks like a train ran over your leg," LeTavia said with a frown and hesitantly took a step back. She reached for her stomach like she was about to vomit.

"Tavi, shut your dramatic ass up. It's just a lil' bit of blood. Stop bein' such a fuckin' female, damn!" Gunplay playfully pushed her to the side.

Trigga shifted some more in the chair trying to get comfortable.

"Keesh, can you go get that shit I asked about earlier?" he asked. She shot him a look.

"You mean the blunt and Cîroc?"

Trigga nodded his head. "Unless you want to give a nigga the other thing first." He smiled and gave a Keisha a pointed look, but she only rolled her eyes and walked away.

"So what is the word on the streets? What's up with that nigga Lloyd, any word on him and his crew?"

"Yea, my nigga, I wanted to holla at you about that," Gunplay said and gave Trigga a warning glare.

"Like what?" Trigga asked with interest, giving Gunplay his full attention.

"I'll tell you later. Now ain't the time to talk," Gunplay responded sharply, his eyes glancing down the hall where Keisha had disappeared.

"Shawty been with me through a lot of shit. She even took a bullet for a nigga. So if you got something to say you can say it. Keesh is my ride or die."

Just then, Keisha reentered the room carrying a bottle of Cîroc and a blunt. She pushed it at Trigga who smiled and attempted to soften her up by reaching out to slap her on her ass. She blocked and reached back like she wanted to pop him one good time. Her ill temperament was still present.

"Stop all that damn playin'!" she scoffed.

"Anyway, you can say whatever it is. Keesh just in her feelings but she knows I love her evil ass."

Ignoring him, Keisha poured alcohol onto a clean towel and dabbed at his wound. Trigga raised up from the chair like it was on fire as he reached for his leg.

"Goddamnit, girl! Fuck you doin'?!"

Despite her discontent, Keisha couldn't help but chuckle at his antics. Even LeTavia cracked a smile.

"The fuck that was you poured on my damn leg? Sulfuric acid? It's burning my shit up," he said as he writhed in the chair.

"No, it's alcohol, it kills germs," she responded tersely. Trigga grumbled something under his breath and then turned back to Gunplay.

"As I was saying, my nigga, you can talk in front of her," Trigga repeated not paying the slightest attention to his warning.

Gunplay just stared at him with his lips pressed tight with an expression like mum was the word to be quiet. He glowered at him with contempt then, in agitation, he stepped forward, popped his knuckles, rolled his neck and suddenly let it all out.

"Dig this, that nigga Black ain't playing right. We might have to get ghost and abandon this whole operation. This shit looking crazy."

"Man, fuck that bitch ass nigga. I'll abandon the mission when I feel it's time to muthafuckin' abandon the mission. Fuck he up to now?"

Gunplay primed his lips to speak. The entire time LeTavia stood over by the window, quiet as a kitten.

"Now instead of a hundred-thousand-dollar bounty out on you, it's two million dollars, dead or alive, for you or Keisha."

"Whaat?!" Keisha exclaimed, petrified. The towel that she was using to clean Trigga's leg with, fell onto the floor as she stood and looked between the two men in consternation.

"Where the fuck he get that kinda money from?" Trigga said, mumbling to himself.

"The nigga also saying that Keisha is pregnant with *his* baby and that the entire time he had her kidnapped was fake. He says Keisha was down with the lick."

Shocked into silence at what she was hearing, Keisha looked over at Trigga and didn't like what she saw smoldering in his eyes as he gulped his drink straight down and glanced at the swell of her belly.

"I guess this gun shot to my leg is fake too?" Keisha lashed out sarcastically.

Trigga didn't answer. He just turned and began to stare at the unlit blunt between his fingers as if he'd forgotten it was there. Her heart sank and it didn't make matters better by looking at the pained expression on Trigga's face.

Gunplay tried to defuse the moment as best as he could when he spoke brazenly.

"Man, fuck dat nigga and his lies. He's just sayin' that shit to make himself feel good. That nigga got a personal vendetta and it's all bullshit. Me and Tavi headed out to grab a bite to eat and get a room so we can give y'all newlyweds some space."

"Where y'all headed?" Trigga asked as he reached out to give Gunplay dap. There were duffle bags behind him. Trigga hadn't even taken the time to notice they were in the process of leaving when him and Keisha entered.

Gunplay dropped the bags he was holding and reached out to return the greeting.

"We gone check into a nice spot. I gotta find something good enough for her bourgeois ass so I guess we'll be downtown or some shit," Gunplay said with a straight face as LeTavia sucked her teeth and rolled her eyes. "Call a nigga if you need something."

"Actually, I do. Get settled in and then I'll meet up with you in a few hours."

Keisha fought the urge to roll her eyes and bite her lip instead. It took everything in her not to lose it as she stood there and watched the superficial exchange of words spoken just for the sake of conversation. Words said only to avoid the real danger that lurked underneath the surface like a poisonous snake about to pounce.

"Okay," was all Trigga said with a nod of his head in response to Gunplay. As they spoke, LeTavia patted her foot and stared at something on the wall. She looked uncomfortable.

Pregnant with Lloyd's baby? Keisha's mind couldn't help repeating.

There was too much shit going on around them and sooner or later, someone was going to be killed. The only way to make sure it wouldn't be one of them would be to get the fuck out of the city. She was over it all. If what happened earlier didn't show him how badly they needed to leave, nothing would, and now this.

Unable to stand listening to their conversation any longer, Keisha gritted her teeth then pushed past Gunplay and LeTavia and stomped down the hall. Frowning, Gunplay lifted one brow and looked at Trigga with irritation.

"See, man? I didn't even want to bring that up in front of her," he bristled.

"Well, why did you? I wasn't expecting you to say that shit!" Trigga whispered back in a rough tone.

"You fuckin' told me to, saying it was all good and all that other blah, blah shit!"

"My nigga, I wasn't prepared for you to say some shit like that, especially with the fucked history Lloyd and Keisha have...now I'm just hoping..."

"Hoping what?" Gunplay asked and reached for the blunt that Trigga had finally lit. Trigga passed it to him. A large ash fell on the white carpet.

"Hoping it's my baby."

Silence.

"Uh...ay, Tavi, get the keys out the bag. I'll meet you at the car," he stammered. He could tell Trigga was starting to take the news hard. Things were looking like they were about to get out of control.

LeTavia bent down, unzipped one of the bags and reached in. When she pulled her hand out, she was holding about five bands...all crispy hundreds.

"Nigga, you been holdin' out!" she exclaimed loudly, frowning up at Gunplay.

"That's the wrong damn bag, Tavi!" he said, snatching the money from her hand.

He stuffed it back in the bag, zipped it up and then retrieved the keys from the bag next to it. When LeTavia hesitated to walk away, he turned and frowned at her.

"The fuck wrong with yo' feet, nigga?" Rolling her eyes dramatically, LeTavia stomped away loudly as Gunplay watched her leave.

"Always rollin' yo' eyes and shit. That's why I hope them muthafuckas get stuck lookin' up at yo' damn forehead!"

Gunplay turned to Trigga as he stared at the vacant window. He saw a placid ray of white sunshine gleaming in his eyes, along with something else.

Treachery.

FOUR

"Gone head! Scratch me, bitch! I'ma splatter your brains all over dis muthafuckin' room. Now tell me where my muthafuckin' dope and money at, bitch, or I'ma kill you *and* ya mama and pops. But, first, I'ma kill dem so you can be a witness to it all as I strip they ole asses naked and carve they ass up with a butcher knife. It'll be good and slow. Just like I did Munchie," Lloyd revealed, loosening the grip he had on her neck just a little.

Dior gasped and put her hands to her mouth as fresh tears came to her eyes. "YOU KILLED MUNCHIE?!"

She looked at Lloyd as he grinned, revealing all of his gold teeth, and nodded slowly. Dior felt like she would faint. Munchie was her cousin but they'd been raised like sister and brother. One day, a few weeks after Dior and Lloyd started dating, Munchie was murdered. The police had said Munchie was murdered by a rival gang, shot in the head and stripped naked. His body had been butchered, fingers cut off and his penis had been severed and shoved in his mouth.

Munchie and Lloyd never got along which made Dior all the more confused when Lloyd appeared to be so torn up at the funeral as if his own brother had died. The emotion he'd exhibited that day made Dior grow closer to him, thinking that he'd let her in to see a part of him that no one else ever had. Now she saw that it was all an act.

As the full realization of Lloyd's confession settled on her, Dior grew enraged and started thrashing and flailing her fingers towards Lloyd, scratching and pulling at whatever piece of his body she could come in contact with. Lloyd responded by tightening his grip on her neck to the point where his knuckles grew white. Dior's eyes bucked wider as she continued to thrash and struggle against Lloyd's hand tightening around her neck, cutting off oxygen to her windpipe.

"It's...It's...it's...in...the closet. Please don't kill my parents," she managed to say as she struggled to breathe, sipping air like she was sucking it through a straw. Her lifeline was winding down.

"Fuck 'em! They ain't never had respect for a nigga anyways! I knocked both of they ugly asses out and tied them up in the room. If you don't tell me where my muthafuckin' shit at, I'ma murk they ass in front of you and then you next! Now which closet?" he choked harder with a fiendish scowl on his face.

For some reason he was getting a slight erection. Dior's eyes began to roll to the back of her head. She was about to lose consciousness.

"...the money...dope. That closet," she gargled minced words, as red and white stars exploded in front of her eyes.

He let her go. She fell to the floor in a heap, gasping for air. Her skirt had driven up her thighs, and she wasn't wearing any panties. Lloyd stole a glance between her legs and shook his head dismissively.

"All that good pussy you done fucked up," he said disconcertingly. "Austin told me yo' ass wasn't nothin' but a hoe back when we first started fuckin' around. I shoulda listened to dat nigga."

"Austin?!" Dior piped up once she heard Austin's name. "You can't trust him. He's a liar. He's the one who got you in this shit with Queen, he—"

"Who told you dat shit?" Lloyd shouted, cutting her off. "Dat loose-lipped nigga Kenyon? Save da bullshit before I make you swallow dis shit." He lifted his gun in the air.

Dior's mouth clamped down shut and she backed further away, until her back hit the wall. Lloyd looked at her as she shifted, exposing more of her pink pussy. Then he glanced over at the baby, her crying was starting to subside and she began to coo sweetly on the couch. Lloyd couldn't help it. His mind took an unwanted trek down memory lane as, unconsciously, he chewed on his bottom lip.

"You fucked my cousin...stole my fuckin' money and tried to send me to prison for the rest of my life," he said with a glitter of hurt in his voice, momentarily showing off the man with emotions that was hidden behind the mask of a thug.

"I'm sorry! None of this would have happened had you not had your whorish ways," Dior raised her voice as she rubbed her sore throat.

Lloyd flinched like he had been slapped and rushed over to her, rearing back his leg as if he was about to kick her in the face. She coiled up, flailing her arms to ward off his attack.

Stopping suddenly, he stood over her, towering and fuming mad with his nostrils flaring. His lips moved but no words came out. The gun was still at his side. Then with capriciousness, he suddenly turned and stalked over to the closet. He opened the door wide so he could keep his eyes partially on Dior.

The closet was littered with clothes strewn everywhere, along with just about every expensive handbag and shoe you could name. At first, Lloyd had to strain his eyes. But then he saw it. His Gucci luggage was in front of him and he knew without a shadow of a doubt his product, the dope and money her and Kenyon had stolen from him, was in there.

He rushed in and dragged both luggage bags to the middle of the floor just as Dior sat up. She continued to massage her neck and wince in pain. The entire time she watched Lloyd intensely.

"Old habits hard to break, huh, bitch? This the same spot I always keep my stash," he said with a gloating sneer.

Silence.

He popped open the baggage and a smile tugged at his lips. The dope and money were there. He grinned sheepishly as he rubbed his hands together anxiously.

Dior's voice cracked with emotion when she spoke passionately. "Lloyd...we don't have to do this...I love you and I know you still love me. I hurt you...I apologize. Let's give it a second chance."

Dior scooted up to a sitting position. She was conscious that her legs were open and she was showing him more than peek-a-boo cleavage. She wanted him to see her pussy lips; it was her invitation, her bargain at a new lease on life.

Lloyd picked up a kilo of cocaine and examined it to check if the neatly wrapped plastic was open. Then he got up and casually strolled over to her. The baby continued to coo on the couch. Dior leaned forward; he hadn't recalled her blouse being open with her succulent breasts fully exposed. His erection grew bigger in his pants. He wanted to pull his eyes away from her voluptuous body, but for some reason he couldn't. His mind went primitive in the cranial place of thug masculinity, where fucking and fighting were just as much a part of their ritual as living and loving.

He walked over to her as if his mind was in a trance, and squatted down between her legs. The entire time, Dior held her breath as she absentmindedly wiped at a ringlet of hair on her forehead. She spread her legs wider. She couldn't help but notice the huge bulge in his pants and the wanton lust gleaming in his eyes. He wanted her and she knew he would. Pussy was Lloyd's downfall. Always had been and always would be.

Lasciviously, she turned on all her enchantress charm and licked her hand like licorice, then slid her finger into her vagina, caressing herself. Secretly, she enjoyed the lustful expression on his face when he leaned forward, teetering on his knee with his erect penis only inches from her hands.

"I'm sorry baby..." she whispered as melodious as a love song.

She then began to unbuckle his belt. He assisted her by taking the belt all the way off. Then she unzipped his pants and pull out his penis. He was ramrod hard with corrugated, thick veins pulsating. She took him in her hands, stroked him vigorously and felt him shiver seismically as pre-cum sparkled from the mushroom head.

"I'm sorry too," he responded looking down at her like he was having an outer body experience.

His dick was the hardest he could ever remember as he watched her with hooded eyes. She scooted forward and squeezed his dick in her hands making the head swell, then she went into her freakish ways...ways that always turned him on. She spit on his dick and massaged him with vigor, like she was putting out a small fire.

"Oh shit," he groaned. He reached out and forcefully grabbed the back of her head then shoved his dick into her mouth. Gluttonously, Dior sucked like a starved baby with a pacifier.

"Bitch, suck it. This how you like it, huh? Raw dick in the back of your throat?"

Dior nodded her head and responded with a garbled, "Yes."

Truth be told, this *was* how she liked it. Rough sex was the best sex and it was normal for them to fuck after an Earth shattering fight. That reality made it all the easier for her to play her role. Then, with both of his huge hands, he held on to her head roughly, manipulating her strokes as the wet sounds of slurping and sucking grew louder and louder with a fervid pace, near a frenzy.

Then it happened. Lloyd's body began to tremble like he was having a seizure as he jerked and moaned. A trickle of slob ran from the corner of his mouth as he gripped Dior's head, forcing himself deep down her throat.

"Ohhh, sheiiiiit, bitch! Suck all dat shit up!" he groaned while he came in her mouth and, like a vacuum, she sucked every drop of his semen until she saw his body grow slack.

She still continued stroking him and caressing him. She licked up and down his shaft and smiled with gaiety, slyly, as she thought to herself, *all men are the same. Some crocodile tears, good head and a shot of ass will get him every time.*

Just then, Lloyd did something unexpected. He pulled her face away from his dick and looked at her with a deep crease in his face as she massaged her sore jaw.

"Are you ready?" he asked in husky voice lisping with sex.

She couldn't help but smile. She knew what he wanted next. To take her to the bed and bang her back out. Lloyd liked anal sex and she did too every now and then. It was still painful but she was more than willing to endure the pain to get him back into her life. Or at least to be able to escape with hers.

"Yeah, sure baby. I'm ready but what you wanna do?" she asked quizzically as she beamed with a smile already knowing what he liked.

"I wanna send you with him...so you two can be together," Lloyd said with a stone cold, black expression on his charcoal face.

"With him? What are you talk—"

Dior's words were cut off when she suddenly felt his pants belt lassoed around her neck so tight her neck snapped back. Instantly, she couldn't breathe. She was paralyzed with fear as she struggled to get loose...struggled not to die.

With the belt buckle in one hand and the end at the other, Dior never had a chance as all the blood drained from her face. Lloyd began to choke her so hard that his own eyes bulged and large veins protruded from his forehead. He looked insane. Almost demonic.

"Bitch...I'm sending you...federal express...to hell to meet up with dat fuck nigga, Kenyon..." Lloyd growled as he choked with all his might. He used every fiber, every strength within him to kill her. In jail, he had dreamed about this so many times. His dick started to get hard again.

Dior resisted with her face inches from his, eyes locked in mortal combat as he choked the life out of her. Then she stopped moving. Her body went limp. A jagged breath escaped from her mouth. It was her last breath.

As her life fled, she lost her bowels and shit all over the floor. Feces splattered his shoe. The stench was so overwhelming he had to let her go. Her body keeled over on her back and onto the shit-stained floor.

"Punk ass bitch! Thought a nigga was pussy-whipped. Thought I was gone go for dat 'sucka for love' shit. I just wanted some of dat smokin' head before I murked your hoe ass," Lloyd said, talking animatedly to the dead body.

His dick was back hard and he was tempted to roll Dior on her back and hit her in the ass while she was still warm, but she had shit on herself. He shivered with disgust at thought of what he'd just contemplated doing.

Quickly abandoning that thought, he scrolled his eyes over to the baby...his baby. She was still lying on the couch, cooing jovially, as her tiny fists moved. He walked over and looked down at her; a baby that, at that moment, suddenly looked even more like him.

"What I'm I going to do with your lil ass?" he said aloud.

The little girl giggled lovingly and then yawned wide. She was adorable in his eyes. Just as he reached for her she smiled wide, her beautiful eyes focused on him. He picked her up and stared into her eyes, giving her a return smile. Her doe-like eyes focused on his gold teeth and they widened with fascination.

"Yo' pretty ass," he beamed. "Well, daddy been murked yo' fat ass grandma and grandpa, as you already know. And mama don't look like she gone be a problem no mo'. So what you think about bustin' out this muthafucka?"

Karisma giggled, her eyes glittering as she enjoyed the sound of her father's voice.

"Yo, dat's funny to you, huh?" Lloyd asked her with a soft chuckle. "Daddy's little girl."

FIVE

After closing the front door behind him, Trigga walked over to his car while Gunplay followed behind him. He wanted to make sure Keisha was definitely out of earshot before he spoke.

Gunplay shielded his face from the ardent sun and looked at the bandage on his leg.

"Fuck happened to your leg anyway?"

"A bitch tried to hit Keesh after y'all left us at the hospital. I pushed her out of the way so I could take the hit and the car hit me instead."

"Hit Keesh? Who da fuck would hit a pregnant chick? That was cold. You think it was Black's bitch ass? I ain't gone even front, with a two-million-dollar reward a nigga mama will turn on a nigga, so it could be any damn body. Feel me?"

"Nawl man, chill. A bitch tried to hit Keesh with a car. Black might be behind it but I think this might be some other shit..."

Gunplay's eyes shot open.

"A whaaaa....? The fuck we standing here for? Who was it?"

Trigga paused for a minute as the image of the driver ran through his mind again. He was sure of it, there was no mistaking it. He knew exactly what Dior looked like from all the digging around he'd done on Lloyd and there was no mistaking it. He knew it was Dior who had been in the car but still, something wasn't right.

He looked back at the house, an image of Keisha's angry face as she stomped into the house coming back into his mind. They'd been married less than two damn hours and in the short amount of time, his world had been rocked with devastation beyond compare. She was his woman and he loved her more than his own life, but if that was Lloyd's seed inside of her, he was going to have to walk.

He'd almost been killed trying to save her ass and now she was mad as hell.

"I can see your brain over there working overtime. Tell me what's next. What you goin' to do?

Trigga shook his head. "I don't know...I just know it was a bitch. But fuck it. Minus her stank ass attitude, Keesh is good and she'll be better as soon as I get her ass out of this city. This shit ain't worth it and I can't keep takin' Keesh through it.."

Dumbfounded, Gunplay stared at Trigga as if he'd grown an extra head out of his neck. "You sure 'bout dat? You been my nigga a long time and I ain't never known you to back down from shit!"

Trigga shook his head gently and looked off in the distance. A vivid and beautiful image came to his mind of Keisha sitting in a big ass house, happier than he'd ever seen her as she held their baby in her arms. The longer he kept her here in the midst of danger he'd created for her, the more he risked never being able to experience that reality.

"I'm not backing down from shit. I'm making a decision to go after what's most important to me. The second I left Keisha alone, dis nigga caught me slippin' and scooped her ass up. He did shit to her dat she'll probably never talk to me 'bout. Dat shit fucks with my mind every time I think about what she probably went through...all because I wasn't there. All because I didn't handle shit the way I needed to. I can't risk no shit like dat happening again."

Trigga stopped suddenly when his eyes teared up. He clenched his jaw tight as he fought to control his emotions. This was new to him and he still wasn't sure of how to deal with the level of passion that he felt for one person. He'd never loved a woman ever before...not the way he loved Keisha.

"Shit."

Blinking back the tears in his eyes, he cursed at his frustration of being betrayed by his body's automatic response to what he was feeling.

Gunplay smirked as he watched him with a knowing look in his eyes.

"Don't hold that shit in, nigga. Let it all come out," he joked, playfully punching Trigga in the shoulder. Trigga laughed and sucked in a breath, trying his hardest to keep himself calm.

"Man, fuck all dis love shit," he laughed. "And I'ma fuck yo' ass up if you tell somebody you saw me gettin' all soft and shit over a chick."

"Dat ain't just a chick no mo', nigga. Dat's yo' wife. You get a pass so I'll let you keep yo' Black Man Card for now."

Trigga shot Gunplay a look and snorted out a chuckle. "I appreciate dat, man."

"My pops always said dat a woman would change ya," Gunplay chuckled as he looked at Trigga and shook his head, making his shoulder-length brownish-blond dreads dance around his head. "Dat old ass muthafucka right about some shit sometimes. Tavi damn sho'll changed a nigga because if any other bitch put me through what she does, I woulda been choked her ass. But...well, you see she still livin' and shit."

On cue, LeTavia opened the car door and popped up with her hand on her hips. "De'Shaun, can't you joke and play 'round with Trigga on the phone? My stomach growlin' and y'all out here just kee-keeing and shit!" she groaned loudly, before sitting back down in the car and slamming the door closed.

Gunplay crossed his arms in front of him and sighed as he scowled at her. Then he shot a look at Trigga who was damn near laughing his ass off.

"Damn, nigga, don't choke laughing. Shit," he grumbled with narrowed eyes. "Ain't shit funny about her disrespectful ass."

"You know you like dat crazy shit or else you wouldn't still be dealin' wit' her ass. How long you and Tavi been together?" Trigga asked.

A subtle smile passed across Gunplay's face as he ran one hand over his low-cut goatee. "It's been some years...She been ridin' with a nigga for a minute now."

He looked over at LeTavia with a look in his eyes that showed every bit of love that he felt for her. She caught his glance and took the opportunity to widen her eyes with her hands up as if to ask him 'what was takin' so damn long' and then pointed to her stomach. Gunplay chuckled and shook his head before turning to Trigga to give him dap.

"Let me tend to her greedy ass. Give me a call when you ready to ride out. I'll be waitin'."

"A'ight," Trigga said, tapping his fist with Gunplay's. "Lemme get in here and get my wife out her feelings first, then I'll hit you up."

"Bet."

Gunplay started walking to his car as LeTavia glared at him the entire way. He mean-mugged her and shot her a bird before walking around to the driver's side of the car. After watching them drive away, Trigga exhaled heavily and then turned to walk into the house when his cell phone began to ring. He grabbed it and checked the caller ID. It was a local number.

"Yeah," he answered.

"Hello, is this Mr. Maurice Blevins?" a woman on the other side asked. With one brow lifted, Trigga frowned. The last few times a local number called his cell phone, it had been bad news.

"I'on know. Who is dis?"

"My name is Sarah Timbels and I'm calling on behalf of Emory Medical Center. We have Maseyon Maxwell Blevins here and he's in critical condition. He has you saved in his phone as his emergency contact."

"What?!" Trigga nearly shouted as he held the phone in his hand with his face balled up. "You might have the wrong person. My brother is—"

He stopped short when he thought back to the night when Mase 'died'. He had thought he saw movement from him the last time he saw him but he didn't go back to check because the police were coming. He called Detective Burns to ask about Mase's body but he'd been informed that he was on leave. Trigga's next step was to show up at his house but he hadn't had a chance to do that just yet since he'd been with Keisha.

"No sir...I believe we have the right one. We have his license. He had it on him. When you come down to the hospital, you can check to be sure. We need you to fill out some papers on his behalf. He's unable to, at the moment. We can explain once you get here."

"Okay..." Trigga sighed and ran his hand over his face.

He looked towards the house where he knew Keisha was most likely lying in the bed sulking. If she found out that his brother was still alive and he was actually going to see him at the hospital, she might get in the car and run him over again her damn self.

"Great! We'll see you here soon! You can come to the Critical Care Center and check in at the desk."

Trigga ended the call and pushed the phone into his pocket. As he walked to the door, he pushed the thoughts of Lloyd, Mase and Queen from his mind so that he could focus on Keisha. They'd only been married for a couple hours and already, it was turning into one crazy ass day.

SIX

The grisly sight of Dior's dead, bloody body sprawled out on the floor with her eyes wide open in horror was enough to make the normal person shudder, but to Lloyd it was just the body of another dead bitch who deserved what was coming to her. Walking away from Karisma, Lloyd bent down and took one last look in the terror-filled eyes of the woman he'd once loved and was willing to give it all to.

Stricken by an emotion he couldn't explain, he reached out and pulled her eyelids closed before standing up and walking away. Although he knew it had to be done, it didn't take away from the fact that he still had feelings for Dior and in the smallest, weakest part of his heart, he still loved her.

Lloyd walked out of the house with the portrait he'd found of Karisma and Dior tucked under his arm, and his mind set on fixing the outlying issues in his life as soon as possible so that he could get back on top. Now that he had his dope and money back, he had a leg up on what he needed to do.

For a few minutes as he drove down the road away from Dior's parents' home, he mulled around the idea in his mind of legitimizing his money and pulling out the dope game so that he could live his life with his daughter without constantly looking over his shoulder. Even after he was able to get Trigga out of the way, he knew as long as he stayed in the dope game, he would always have to worry about some bold muthafucka who would be trying to take away his throne. That meant he'd always have to watch his back.

"What you up to, nigga?" Lloyd asked once Austin picked up the phone.

Austin exhaled sharply as he held the phone to his ear and looked at the beautiful brown-skinned beauty next to him wearing only a thong, nestled up close with her booty tooted in the air towards him.

"Ain't shit," he answered as he patted NeTasha softly on her plump ass.

She moaned and snuggled up even closer against him, in a way that silently begged him not to leave but she knew he would anyways. He rarely handled his business in front of her. Austin had feelings for her to the point where he felt he was in love. But still, his number one rule was to never trust a bitch when it came to his business or his money.

Austin stood up, wearing nothing but his boxers and walked through the glass doors that led to the balcony outside of the master bedroom of the penthouse he'd rented at The W hotel. He leaned out on the railing and looked out at the city. His city. Or at least it would be as soon as he was able to get rid of Lloyd, which he planned to do soon. He couldn't stand playing the subservient role to another nigga. But he kept telling himself that it was all a means to an end. As soon as he got all his shit in order and won over the loyalty of the EPG crew, he wouldn't have to play this position ever again.

"Thanks, fam, for dropping on me that knowledge earlier so I could handle shawty and get my shit back. I got lil' bit too," Lloyd spoke in a cryptic way, letting Austin know that Dior was dead and he had gotten back his money and daughter. "How you came up on dat addy anyways?"

"A bitch I'm fuckin' wit' at da hospital gave me some info along wit' some other shit, if ya' know what I mean," Austin lied and faked a laugh, although his face was expressionless. "Said ole girl's folks had moved closer so she could keep the same doc and shit. But what you got on the agenda for today?"

"Right now, ain't nothin' on the muthafuckin' agenda but to murk dat long-neck ass nigga, Trigga. But I don't even wanna focus on dat shit because I know dat nigga after me so dat means he'll show his muthafuckin' ass soon enough and we just gotta be ready to wet his punk ass up when he does. So for now, I wanna get my squad right. I'ma meet with all my team dat's left and get shit back in order. My money been held up for a minute and I need dat shit back in order."

"Bet," Austin responded. "You tell me the location and I'm there, fam."

Lloyd didn't respond before hanging up the phone. The line went dead and Austin dropped the phone to his side but it started ringing again almost immediately.

"You got good or bad news?" he asked into the receiver after checking the caller ID.

"Good news. We got everything in order and we should be good to go by next week."

"That's what I like to hear. And I don't want shit to look like it did before. This is my spot now and I want everything muthafuckin' thing in there to remind niggas that this spot ain't shit like it used to be. I don't do nothin' halfway. Ya feel me, Ced?"

"I understand, sir. We have laid off all the girls that you didn't like and hired new talent to take their place. We have all new wait staff on deck that meet your requirements, and the construction workers are ahead of schedule on the remodel. You should be open for business in no time."

Austin nodded his head and smiled to himself as he thought about how fast his dreams were becoming reality. As soon as he learned of Cash's death, he made moves to buy the strip club. Cash's spot was more than just a strip club. It had been the unofficial headquarters to Lloyd's crew and it was where every bad bitch and nigga with money in South Atlanta went to have fun, conduct business or get word on what was happening in the hood. He knew that buying the club would piss Lloyd off, but he was prepared to deal with that. And soon, him buying the club would be the least of Lloyd's worries.

Owning the club was his first move in taking over Atlanta because word would spread fast that he was the new owner and, along with the news, his legacy that was known so well in Dallas would spread as well. Anyone who didn't already know him and respect him would begin to see that he was a force to be reckoned with; even more so than Lloyd, which would make it easy to push his ass out the way.

"One more question," Cedric said before hanging up.

"What are you goin' to call the place?"

Austin turned around and looked through the glass at NeTasha sleeping peacefully in the large, beautiful bed, with her ass slightly tooted up in the air. She was even more so angelic asleep then she was awake, and everything about her made him wanna wife her up quick with a fat ass diamond ring that captured the sparkle in her eyes when she looked at him. In fact, 'Sparkle' was the nickname he'd given her because of the twinkling of her eyes that he adored. The name fit her perfectly and he bought her a new piece of diamond jewelry every time he thought about the way she looked at him.

"Diamonds," Austin said with a smile just as NeTasha opened up her eyes and look at him through the glass. He licked his lips and wished he could get a taste of her before he had to run and take care of business. But according to her, she was still on her period.

Two more days, he thought to himself, mentally counting down the remaining days.

"Yeah...let's call it Diamonds," he repeated.

"Okay," Cedric replied. "Diamonds it is."

NeTasha watched through the glass door as Austin spoke, hoping that it would end up being the nice, long conversation that she needed in order to get what she needed done. Peeking under the covers, she dialed Trigga's number and prayed he would pick up. The line rang continuously and then she heard the automated message pick up.

Austin turned back around and shot her a smile that sent a bone chilling sensation down the middle of her spine. NeTasha mustered up the best smile that she could and tossed it back in his direction, fluttering her eyes slowly and feigning a yawn so that he would think she was still sleepy. When she peeked through her eyelids again, he'd turned around and was continuing his call. NeTasha tried the number a few more times but each time it went to voicemail.

"Shit!" she whispered as she deleted the number from her outgoing calls.

She already knew that she was reaching for straws by trying to call Trigga, but the situation with Austin was getting worse and, for some reason, she felt like he was the only one she could turn to. She'd gathered enough from overhearing a few of Austin's conversations to know that Trigga and Austin's cousin were attempting to kill each other, and NeTasha thought that just maybe reaching out to Trigga could help her handle her issues with him.

Suddenly, NeTasha saw movement come from Austin's direction. She tucked the cell phone under her pillow and closed her eyes, pretending to be asleep. A sense of dread passed over her when she heard the sliding glass door open and Austin walk inside. It was getting harder and harder for her to pretend to be content in his presence. There was something sinister about him and it was almost like she couldn't put her finger on it. Yeah, there was an attraction but being attracted to Austin was like being infatuated with a ticking time bomb. At some point, she knew he was going to explode and she wanted to be out of dodge when he did.

"Ay, wake up, pretty lady," he said in a gentle voice as he slid in the bed beside her and kissed her on the forehead.

NeTasha moaned softly and stretched out, allowing Austin to wrap his arm around her and squeeze her ass. She giggled and stared into his handsome face, trying to ignore the feeling of warning that rose up in her. He was going to mention sex and she was running out of time for using her current excuse.

"I'm up, baby," she cooed and snuggled into him. "What's up?"

"I got you a surprise," he whispered.

NeTasha looked up at him and saw that he was holding something out to her in his outstretched hand. A small cell phone. With her brows furrowed, she looked up at him with question in her eyes. Although he had a smile across his face, his eyes were black as coal and held no humor, love or care in them.

"What's this? I got a phone," NeTasha said, slowly grabbing the phone from Austin's hand.

"About that..." he reached under her pillow and took the phone from under there.

NeTasha's stomach twisted into knots as she watched him press a few buttons and start scrolling through it. She said a prayer of thanks that she'd been smart enough to erase the calls and prayed that Trigga wouldn't call back in that moment. It would be the end.

"I'll be taking this one," Austin informed her with a sigh after he was satisfied with what he'd seen in her call log. "You take that one for now."

NeTasha scrunched up her nose as she looked at it.

"But it has no buttons to call—"

"I have my number programmed as the first speed dial button, my second phone as the second speed dial button and the last will stay free for now until I program a number there. That's all you need. Right, Spark?" he leaned over and kissed NeTasha on her lips lightly.

Reaching over, he pinched her nipple and then bent down and started sucking on it gently which sent tingles through her, despite the fearful feeling that had her on high alert. Austin had a way of perfectly missing his charm and threatening demeanor in a way that captivated people and frightened them at the same time.

It was the way that he was able to run the streets in Dallas and how he planned on running them in Atlanta. He had charisma with a threatening flair. People were drawn to him automatically, but there was something about him that told you to fear him because he wasn't all there. It worked with everyone he dealt with and NeTasha was no different. She was pushed away from him by her fear but when he put on his charm, she couldn't help but to be aroused.

"Lay with me for a little before I go," he whispered, putting his hands in between her legs so he could rub on her thigh. She nodded and relaxed on the bed, placing the phone on the nightstand next to her. She watched as Austin tucked hers into his pants and a tremor traveled up her spine.

Please don't let Trigga call back, she thought to herself as Austin wrapped his arm around her.

SEVEN

Karisma gurgled and stuck her fingers in her mouth as she slid sideways on the backseat with the seatbelt wrapped around her small body. Lloyd lifted a brow and stared at her through the rearview mirror. The idea of having possession of his daughter seeming more and more surreal to him by the second. He watched as she munched on her two little fat fingers so intently that her brows formed a deep frown on her chubby, brown face as she slobbered liberally.

"What the *fuck* am I gonna do wit' a kid?" he said more to himself as he continued to drive to his newly purchased condo and stash spot that he kept downtown. Then the thought occurred to him who could help. Reaching into the seat next to him, he grabbed his cell phone and pressed the button to call a number.

"What?" the female on the other line answered with a poorly hidden attitude.

"That's the way that you speak to yo' nigga now?" Lloyd teased with a smile. She sucked her teeth loudly and smacked her lips. The sound of it wiped the smile right off of Lloyd's face because he knew that when those sounds came from a Black woman, it meant there was about to be some shit. *Bull*shit.

"Nigga, what you mean *my* nigga? I ain't heard from your ass in months!"

"That's too long back for you to remember how a nigga's dick feel between them fat ass cheeks, huh? Maybe yo' smart mouth ass needs a quick reminder," Lloyd teased as he ran his finger back and forth across his bottom lip. He heard her suck in a breath and he knew he had her.

Bitches so damn predictable. Dick 'em down just right one time and you got they asses right where the fuck you need 'em, Lloyd thought to himself.

"But why you ain't been 'round no more? You got out and shit then forgot about me," she whined.

"Toy, you know I can't forget about that sweet pussy," Lloyd said into the phone, feeling himself get even harder than he'd already been.

He was still nearly rock hard from that shit that Dior had tried to pull earlier.

"Well, you can come through if you want to but I gotta go to work in a lil' bit."

"Call in. I got shit I need you to do," Lloyd said, then he was hit with an awful smell as he realized the baby must have taken a dump in her pamper and, even though she was just a small baby, it smelled like adult shit.

"Phew!"

He let down the window and glanced back at Karisma, suddenly remembering the reason for his call. "I'll be there in ten minutes so start taking that shit you wearin' off and put on somethin' sexy."

He hung up the phone and made a U-turn to head down Memorial Drive towards where LaToya stayed. The last time he'd seen her was when he was leaving the jail, right before he hooked back up with Luxe. LaToya was a decent bitch with a bad ass body, but she was still the Feds in his eyes and he didn't wanna fuck with her on no permanent level. However, until he could figure out what he was going to do with Karisma, he was gonna need her help.

***

"Nigga, what the fuck is that?!" LaToya asked once she answered the door and frowned down at Karisma who Lloyd was holding in one arm like a football.

LaToya was standing in the doorway wearing an open pink silk robe with nothing but a thin pink lace thong and a matching see-through pink lace bra, but when she saw Karisma in his arms, she clutched the robe tightly closed as if the baby would judge her by her clothing.

Lloyd scowled at her and pushed through the entrance of her apartment forcefully.

"The fuck you mean?! It's a baby! And watch yo' muthafuckin' mouth in front of my damn daughter!" he scolded her.

"YOUR DAUGHTER?!" LaToya exclaimed as she shut the door behind her. "When the hell you get a daughter? Shit, she looks brand new!"

LaToya walked over to Lloyd, still clutching her robe closed, with her eyes focused on Karisma who had her fingers in her mouth as she chomped ferociously on them with slobber spilling down her arms from her pouty lips.

"Aww, she's hungry and her pamper needs to be changed," LaToya said as she pried Karisma from Lloyd's arm and held her. Her robe fell open, exposing her large, voluptuous breasts. Lloyd's eyes slid down her body, starting at her breasts and ending with the space between her thighs. He rubbed his erection through his pants and licked his lips hungrily.

"Ay, Toy, what's up?" he asked with his eyes still attached to the imprint of the fat lips poking through her lace panties.

LaToya glanced at him and then did a double-take when she saw what he was looking at.

"Hell nawl, nigga, I ain't fuckin' you wit' yo' baby over here. Where is her mama?"

"On vacation," he answered quickly with a straight face. "I need you to take care of her for me for a minute."

"Oh, heeeeellllll nawl," LaToya shook her head and handed Karisma back to him. "I don't do kids and I gotta work and shit. What I'ma do wit' a baby?"

"You gone do what da fuck I say, that's what. And you quittin' dat job because I'on want my lady workin'. You can live in my spot downtown and I'll take care of both of y'all." Lloyd pulled out three bands of hundred dollar bills and dropped them on LaToya's coffee table as she watched him with her eyes nearly bulging out of her skull.

"That should hold you over for a couple days so you can get whatever da hell babies need and a lil' somethin' for yourself," Lloyd said, his eyes returning to her chest as he licked his lips.

"Weeeeelllll...I guess I can help you out a little bit," LaToya said, eyeing the cash. She reached out and grabbed Karisma from his hands. "She needs to eat. You got bottles and formula?"

Shrugging, Lloyd handed her the baby bag that he'd taken from Dior's house. LaToya rummaged through it and grabbed a can and a bottle from it.

"Distilled water?" she asked.

"Who-da who?" Lloyd responded with a frown.

"Did you bring water for me to mix the formula with, and where is her pampers?"

"Nawl...why? Yo' shit turned off? Damn, you doin' bad. And pampers in there somewhere, Toy."

LaToya rolled her eyes. "Never mind."

She walked over and laid Karisma out on a blanket while she prepared the bottle in the kitchen. Then she found the pampers and changed the baby. About a minute later, she came back in the living room, shaking the bottle in her hand and then propped it up on a pillow so that Karisma could drink from it as she lay down. Lloyd watched as she greedily gulped up the liquid as if she hadn't eaten in weeks.

"Look at her lil' chunky ass." Lloyd smiled as he watched her drink. "She good now?"

LaToya nodded her head.

"She was just hungry," she told him with a shrug.

"Shit...I am, too."

Lloyd walked over, grabbed LaToya up by the ass and she wrapped her legs around his waist. Balancing her with one hand, he brought his other hand forward and dipped a finger deep inside her warm, wet folds.

"We can't do this in front of her!" LaToya shrieked while giggling as Lloyd bit her on her neck.

"Why not? Don't you know babies blind when dey dat small?! Plus, her greedy ass ain't focused on shit but that bottle."

"Lloyd!"

"Fuck...a'ight," Lloyd cursed.

He walked, while carrying LaToya over to a small area set off to the side of the kitchen where she'd placed a small wooden dining room table. He laid her on top of it and pushed the thin layer of her lace thong to the side, exposing her swollen, throbbing pink nub. As soon as he saw it, his mouth began to water.

He normally didn't put his mouth on random broads, but LaToya was a clean chick and he could tell that when he first saw her back when he was in lock-up. He hadn't hesitated back then to suck on her sweetness and he wasn't going to now. She had the prettiest pussy he'd ever seen and it tasted like tropical fruit. How he'd managed to write her off so quickly was beyond him.

"Sssssssssss," she whistled through her teeth as she tossed her head back and opened her legs wider to give him more access.

Lloyd massaged the head of his dick through his pants and then pulled it out. After sucking up her sweet nectar a few seconds longer, he couldn't take anymore. He stood up, pressed her thighs further apart and pushed himself in, deep and forcefully. She sucked in a breath and leaned her head even farther back and pushed herself even more into him. Her perky nipples were high in the air and hard as could be, as her chest rose and fell along with the rhythm of her jagged breaths. Lloyd leaned over and pulled one of her chocolate morsels into his mouth, then began working his tongue around it in circles as he rammed himself harder and harder into her.

Suddenly, LaToya did something she'd never done before. She sucked in a breath and clenched her pussy muscles tight around the shaft of his dick, holding him as tight as a virgin. Lloyd frowned and stared at her as she suctioned his dick and began working her hips at the same time. A smirk crossed his face as he watched her in action, twerking on his long pole in a way that made her pussy smack against his skin as she worked him over.

"Oh shit, bitch!" Lloyd groaned with his black face twisted up in sheer pleasure and his eyes twisted to the back of his head.

In less than a minute, Lloyd could no longer compose himself and he couldn't take no more. He grabbed her by her ass and began slamming her into him so hard that the table began to rock.

"Aaaaaaghhh, shit!" LaToya gasped as he went harder and harder. She reached behind him and dug her nails deep into his flesh, pulling him deeper into her and trying her hardest to open her legs even more so that she could take in all of his dick. She arched her back with her legs wide open which gave him direct access to her G-spot and instantly, she went crazy.

Lloyd watched her as she bucked wildly on top of the table while he rammed inside of her. She was cumming and as she cried out in pleasure, Karisma began to cry out in anguish but he didn't care. He was so close to an orgasm that he could feel it in his toes.

"Fuuuuuucccccck, shit!!!" Lloyd yelled out to the top of his lungs as he slammed one final time inside of LaToya and released his seed inside of her. He closed his eyes and moved slowly in her, working his cum over and over again in her pussy as he allowed the feeling to wash over him. When he opened his eyes, LaToya had fallen back on the table with her eyes closed as she enjoyed the aftereffect of her climax.

"Shit, that was good," she whispered as Lloyd pulled out of her.

She rolled over on the table and continued to lay there with her eyes closed as if she was going to sleep. Lloyd patted her on her ass and then grabbed the hem of the tablecloth to wipe his dick.

"Get your ass up. Don't you hear the baby crying?"

Sucking her teeth, LaToya peeked at him out of the corner of her eyes and then rolled them before lifting herself off the table. She grabbed up her robe and pulled it around her to shield her naked body from Karisma, as she walked out of the dining room and ran down the hall.

"Where the hell you goin'? The baby *that* way!" Lloyd yelled out over Karisma's shrill cries which were getting louder and louder as each minute passed.

"I know! I need to wash my ass before I get her...damn!" LaToya shot back and then Lloyd heard water running in the sink.

He pulled on his clothes and then checked his phone. There was a message from a potential new supplier that he wanted to meet with who supposedly had a better product. It looked like the possible new connect was in town and wanted to meet with him soon. He needed to speak to his crew to let them know that there would be some changes.

Bout fuckin' time, he thought to himself.

It was about time that he got on top of his shit. Dior's words about Austin were agitating him in a way that made him feel the same eerie feeling he'd felt after seeing his mother's reaction to Austin while on her deathbed. Something wasn't right and the sooner he could get on his shit and send his cousin's ass back home, the better.

"Ay, I'ma be back later on tonight. The money on the table. Grab some baby shit," Lloyd yelled down the hall.

He heard a grunt that let him know that LaToya heard him. When he walked past Karisma, he looked down at her, noticing for the first time that her sobs had stopped. A smile crossed his face when he saw that she was lying on the blanket with her thumb in her mouth, sucking vigorously as she drifted off to sleep. She was a beautiful child, complete with his dark chocolate brown skin and her mother's curly hair. She stirred in her sleep as if she could feel her father watching her. Lloyd backed away slowly before walking out the front door.

Now that he had her taken care of, he could get to work rebuilding his empire, so he could get the hell on with his life. His phone started to ring and he answered it as soon as he got inside the whip.

"Yo, I wasn't late about the muthafuckin' money I paid you. Why da hell you late callin' me?" Lloyd informed the person on the other line after checking the time on his watch.

"I got held up with somethin'. My bad, Black," the voice said on the other line.

"Fuck all that apologizin' shit. Where you at on what the fuck I'm payin' yo' ass to do?" Lloyd snapped as he backed out and tore off down the road. "I need dis shit with ya boy taken care of ASAP, ya feel me?"

"He ain't my boy. But I got you."

"I ain't fuckin' around wit' you. I told you dat I got mo' money for yo' ass but you gotta give me somethin' and it gotta be quick. Dis bitch ass nigga got my team stressin' and shit. Den his lil' bitch stole my money for the second time in a row. I'ma fuck both dey asses up."

"Money? Keisha took money from you?"

"Hell yeah, dis'll be the second time that bitch done tried me with dat shit." Lloyd glowered as he thought about how Keisha had managed to make away with his money and dope not once, but twice! "Dat ole rooster neck ass hoe! One thang for sure, she got some good ass pussy. I fucked da walls out dat bitch last time I saw her. Had her ass my way like a muthafuckin' Burger King. She liked dat shit, too."

Lloyd wasn't even aware of the wide grin plastered across his face as he thought about all the things he did with Keisha before she got away. One thing he couldn't turn down was good pussy. That was the reason he had dealt with her all those years before, gave her money and had her living up in his stash spot watching after his dope and cash. Her shit stayed wet and was tight as hell. And when she was high, she got extra freaky just like he liked it.

"Anyways," he continued, bringing himself back to the matter at hand. "I'ma call you again and when I call you, you better be able to tell me somethin'. I'm ready to get all dis shit behind me and move da fuck on. You want da rest of dis money, right?"

"Yeah," was the response. "I'll get you what you need."

Lloyd hung up the phone and continued driving towards his destination, his mood the best it had been in a long time. Dior was dead, Kenyon was gone, he had his daughter in his possession and the plan he had in place to get to Trigga and get at Queen was being carried out perfectly. As soon as he found himself in a position that allowed him to give someone close to Keisha and Trigga an offer that couldn't be refused, he seized the opportunity and was confident that in a matter of days, all of his current concerns would be old news.

Enough money makes a nigga invincible, was his belief. *The next thing I need to do is find a new spot to handle business*, he thought to himself as he looked around at his surroundings.

He was in the heart of the ghetto, which wasn't anything foreign to him, but Lloyd liked to conduct business in the lap of luxury which, in his case, always included bad bitches, liquor and some bomb ass head to end the night. But since Trigga gunned up Cash's ass, his club remained vacant and he had to find another place to meet up with his team.

Yet another reason Trigga was a thorn in his side.

Lloyd dialed a number and waited once the line began ringing.

"Hello?" the soft, sexy voice answered on the other line.

"Send me a pic of dat juicy pussy, nigga."

"BLACK! You so damn crazy. What you want?" she laughed in his ears.

"Shit! Dat is what a nigga want. But I do have another request, Minnie."

She was a thick chick, big-boned with a flat stomach and thick thunder-thighs but her voice was high-pitched and squeaky like a mouse which is how she earned the nickname Minnie.

"What is it?"

"I need you to check on a property for me. You know da club *Pink Lips?* Hit me back and lemme know how much it's up for sale for."

"Got it," Minnie agreed immediately. "I'll call you back later on today with all the details."

"Good," Lloyd responded as he bent a corner. "Now send me dat pussy pic, nigga."

"BLAAAAAAACK!" she squealed and Lloyd hung up the phone.

Less than a minute later, his phone chirped with a photo of her fat pussy with her fingers holding the thick, juicy lips wide open so he could see every pink detail of her feminine anatomy. Lloyd licked his lips and then stuck the phone in his pocket.

I'ma have to make some time to tear that ass up, he thought to himself as he felt himself begin to rise. *But lemme handle this business first.*

EIGHT

Wiping the tears from her eyes, Keisha sat down on the king-sized bed in her luxurious master bedroom and laid down on the long, fluffy body pillow that Trigga had bought for her in order to help her sleep more comfortably at night. She circled her arms around her body and held her tiny stomach in her arms while she willed herself to stop crying. She wasn't sad, she was more frustrated than anything. After everything that she'd been through with Trigga, it had seemed as if she was finally about to get her happy ending and now it had been snatched away from her only seconds later.

She heard the front door open and slam, followed by the heavy sound of Trigga's footsteps down the hall to where she lay. She'd made sure to close the bedroom door in hopes that Trigga would take the hint that she wanted privacy but, in reality, she knew that a closed door didn't mean shit to him and if he wanted to come inside, he would come inside. Just as he did.

"I know you ain't in here crying and shit," Trigga said once he walked in through the door, his limp only barely visible. "Crybaby ass."

Keisha avoided his eyes and watched as he came towards her. He was working hard to mask the limp that interrupted his once casual saunter across the room, but Keisha picked up on it. She pulled her lips into a straight line and fought the urge to beg him to go to the doctor to be seen. It was a worthless argument because he was too stubborn to listen.

Trigga sat down on the bed behind her. Keisha waited for him to say something but he didn't. She couldn't decide whether she was grateful for that or not. She wanted him to say something but she knew he wouldn't say the words that she wanted to hear. Instead of speaking, Trigga flipped around on the bed and laid down behind her, spooning her while wrapping his arms around her midsection. They sat there for a while saying nothing, listening to each other breathe while Trigga stroked back and forth over Keisha's belly.

Each motion across her stomach made it easier for her to forget why she'd been upset to begin with. When Trigga began kissing her down the side of her neck and rubbing the inside of her thigh from under her skirt, the anger disappeared completely and left passion and desire in its place. Keisha loosened the tension in her thighs and allowed Trigga to push his hands up even further in between her thighs, until he was gently massaging the outside of the thin material of her panties. She got wet instantly and almost immediately, the seat of her panties were soaked and the material was sticking to her skin.

Trigga pushed gently on her thighs and she shifted to let them fall to opposite sides, allowing him room to slip his fingers inside of her. Her lips parted and her breathing slowed as she allowed him to stir her insides gently while he massaged her clit with his thumb. Suddenly, he lifted up and positioned himself over her, still keeping his fingers deep in her soft warmth.

Keisha kept her eyes closed as she enjoyed the feel of him pressed against and in her. She began twerking her hips subtly against him with her lips parted slightly as she enjoyed every sensation. Trigga leaned down and sucked her bottom lip into his mouth before dipping back down and pressing his mouth against hers in a passionate kiss. Keisha opened up and allowed him to roam her mouth, and he worked his tongue around her just as freely as his fingers did below, each motion bringing her closer to absolute pleasure.

When he finally entered her, the sensation almost sent her into an instant orgasm, but she bit her lip and told herself to slow down and enjoy every bit of their love making. This was the first time he'd entered her as her husband; she didn't want to rush any of it. Keisha wanted this moment to last for the rest of their lives.

Gritting his teeth, Trigga pushed more forcefully inside of Keisha as she moaned softly in his ear. Being inside of her gave him peace. Every single thing that had been going on in their lives was no longer relevant in this moment. The only thing on his mind was how good her body felt pressed up against his and how much he wanted this moment to last forever.

***

"You've gotta go, don't you?" Keisha asked softly the next morning.

Her voice invaded the silence around them as she and Trigga laid in the bed, side-by-side with their eyes focused on the ceiling above them. Her body was sore but in the best kind of way. The room still smelled like the beautiful mixture of the scents of their bodies after making passion-filled love.

Keisha's thigh was pressed against Trigga's as they lay on the bed. She wanted to enjoy being able to feel him next to her because she knew that he would leave soon to go, and there was always the possibility that he wouldn't return. Until he got them out of this life, that was always a real possibility.

"Not yet."

Trigga stood up and walked to the adjoining bathroom and closed the door behind him. Keisha laid in the bed and listened to the sound of the shower running. Trigga's cell phone chimed on the table beside the bed. She turned over to look at the screen as the text message flashed across.

Call.

It was a message from Queen.

Keisha grabbed the phone and went to the message. She long-pressed it to bring up the option to delete it, but she couldn't bring herself to delete the message. They'd already had one run-in with Queen and the last thing she wanted was for her to bring her ass back to Atlanta with her goons.

Pursing her lips in frustration, Keisha was about to put the phone down when her hand grazed the button that sent the screen to Trigga's recent calls. He had about four missed calls from a number that looked very familiar to her. After thinking for a few seconds, it suddenly came to her who the calls had been from.

NeTasha? Keisha thought with a frown on her face. *This bitch is crossing the muthafuckin' line!*

The only thing that calmed Keisha was that Trigga hadn't answered any of her calls, but it still pissed her off to the max that she'd even tried calling him. She was thirsty as hell.

The door to the bathroom swung open, startling Keisha who still had Trigga's phone in her hand. She pushed it under the covers and lifted her head to look at him as he walked towards her. He had on sweatpants and no shirt. His rock hard abs and muscular arms glistened with moisture.

"Get'cho fine ass up out dat bed, girl," Trigga ordered with a sexy smile on his face that made Keisha laugh.

Pausing mid-step, he bit his lip and squinted his eyes at her playfully, as if she was the sexiest thing he'd ever seen. Then he reached his hand out and she placed hers in his. Her heart fluttered when he helped her up gently by the hand and then swooped her up into his arms, cradling her like a small child as he walked towards the bathroom.

The lights were off inside and candles were lit. The Jacuzzi bathtub was filled with water and bubbles. Trigga lowered her slowly so that she could dip one foot in to test the temperature of the water.

"Good?" he asked her with a lifted brow. Keisha nodded her head.

Once she was in the water, he put a pillow behind her head and knelt down beside her. Trigga bathed her gently while she took in the aroma of the lavender candles and bubble bath.

"Listen," he started. Keisha's heart dropped. Whenever he said that, whatever followed was never something she wanted to hear.

"Neither one of us planned dis shit, Keesh. I ain't come to ATL to...find love." He chuckled a little and shook his head as if he couldn't believe what he was saying. "No one on Earth could have told me dat when I saw your ass ducked up underneath an SUV, high as hell in the middle of da night, dat you would be my wife and pregnant with my baby months later. But it is what it is."

Feeling slightly mortified at Trigga bringing up their first encounter, Keisha nodded her head and peeked at him out of the corner of her eyes. As he spoke, his head was down while he ran the washcloth along her body, as if he was talking more to himself than to her.

"So Dior...Lloyd's chick tried to run your ass over, huh?" he asked suddenly, his tone more of a statement than a question. "She got beef wit' you for some reason?"

Stunned into silence, Keisha's eyes shot up and she noticed that Trigga was looking right at her with his piercing gray eyes. She ducked away from his stare, unable to hold it any longer. The idea of Trigga knowing anything about her past with Lloyd shamed her; especially the fact that he was well aware of her role as Lloyd's side bitch, among other things. She wondered how much he really knew about her past with Lloyd. He had been watching him for a while as he planned out his attack, after all.

"My point is, I got a past and so do you. Just like you gotta deal with da shit dat came along wit' your past, I gotta deal with mine. Once we get dis shit together, we can live life like I said. Until then, you gonna have to suck in yo' lil' attitude while I straighten dis out, a'ight?"

The warmth of the water, coupled with her shame, made perspiration cover Keisha's face as she nodded her head slowly. Washing his eyes over her, Trigga's shoulders dropped as he relaxed and then took a deep breath.

"One more thing...when you get mad at a nigga, don't go stomping yo' ass off and shit," he added, which lightened the tension in the room just as he intended.

Keisha sucked her teeth and rolled her eyes. "Oh does that bother you?"

"Hell yeah!" Trigga replied as he looked at her like she was asking him something she should have already known. "You ain't gotta act up and shit just because we beefin'!"

"You mean like how you send me those short ass, abbreviated texts when you get mad at me?" Keisha asked with a smile.

Trigga's face went blank and his eyes lifted to the ceiling as he tried to figure out what she meant. Seconds later, he shrugged and shook his head.

"I'on know what da hell you talkin' 'bout."

Keisha laughed and pulled herself up so she could look Trigga straight in his eyes.

"When your ass gets mad at me, if I text you, you always abbreviate every damn word in your reply. Half the time I can't even tell what the hell you trying to say. Letters be missin' and shit. You act like it hurts your ass to text me back."

Instantly, his eyes lit up and Keisha's grin grew wider. He knew exactly what she was talking about.

"Hell the fuck yeah it does!" he responded. A smirk crossed his face which made one of his dimples poke out. "If you done pissed a nigga off...shit, you lucky I'm textin' ya ass back. So gone ahead and decipher that shit because that's all you gone get."

They both started laughing and Trigga playfully mugged her in the face. Once the laughter died down, Trigga checked his watch and reality set in. When he looked up, he could see the disappointment in Keisha's face.

"Call Tavi to come over here so you won't be alone."

With a frown, Keisha shook her head. "I can't deal with her dramatic ass today. I love her and all but she's too much sometimes."

"What you mean? From how you almost knocked her ass down and stomped your short, pregnant ass in da house, I think you might be pretty damn dramatic, too," Trigga laughed as Keisha pursed her lips at him before shaking her head and rolling her eyes.

"You know what I mean. She's just so damn extra and I don't want all that right now. I wish Tish was here..." Keisha's voice trailed off when she sensed Trigga tense up beside her. "What?"

Trigga paused before answering her. He couldn't put his finger on it but there was something about Tish that he didn't like or trust. It all started when he went to her apartment while Keisha was in the hospital to ask her to sit with Keisha for him. She didn't trust him when she saw him and, in his experience, when a person who used to be a friend all of a sudden acted like they were afraid of you, it was for a damn good reason. It usually meant they had been doing some shit that merited an ass whooping or worse.

"You been talkin' to her?"

Keisha nodded her head sheepishly, although she didn't know why she felt guilty about admitting that she had been speaking to a friend.

"Yeah...why? What's it with her anyways? Why can't she be here?"

"I don't want anyone knowing where we lay our head unless I know they can be trusted," Trigga told her. Keisha frowned.

"Why can't Tish be trusted? She's my friend."

"Somethin' ain't right 'bout dat bitch."

"Something like what?" Keisha quizzed. Trigga paused. Then he leaned in close and whispered like he was telling her a secret.

"I ain't wanna tell you dis but da last time I saw her, I caught her lookin' at my ass. You know niggas don't like dat shit," he joked with a serious face.

"MAURICE, that girl wasn't looking at you or your ass at all. Please! Be for real!"

"But dat's da type of shit I'm talkin' 'bout, Keesh," he explained. "You can't trust no muthafucka who can't look you in yo' eyes. Her ass ain't right."

Keisha rolled her eyes and shook her head. "Trigga, no one feels right to you unless it's someone you know. But remember, it was *your* twin brother who tried to kill both of us. Tish hasn't done anything for you to treat her like she's the enemy. You can't just isolate me from everyone just because your ass is paranoid. I have no family that I know of. All I have is my friend."

Poking out her lips in a soft pout, Keisha crossed her arms in front of her chest and rested them lightly on her tiny baby bump. Trigga cut his eyes at her and couldn't help but laugh. Picking up the damp washcloth, he threw it playfully at the top of her head and stood up to grab her towel.

"Get your spoiled ass up. You can call her and see if she can come over to keep you company. I'll wait for her to get here before I leave."

Keisha tried to hold down the smile that started to grace her face but she couldn't. Trigga looked at her and shook his head.

She's so damn sexy with her spoiled ass, he thought to himself. She reached out to grab the towel and his eyes fell on the big ass diamond ring on her finger.

And she's all mine.

He let his eyes wander over her body as she stood up and then he checked his watch.

Gotta finish this shit up quick so I can come back, kick Tish's ass out and get back up in that sweet pussy, he thought as he licked his lips and rubbed them together.

What Keisha had been through and the scars on her body, didn't take away from her beauty. In his eyes, she was perfect and he vowed to remind her of that fact every single day that he spent living on God's green Earth.

NINE

"Baby, do you have to go?" NeTasha whined as Austin started putting on his clothes. He pulled his t-shirt over the top of his head and then shot her a look followed by his signature sexy smirk that made her smile.

"Yeah, I got bidness to handle." He buttoned his jeans and then walked over to where she sat in the bed with the thin sheets partially covering her beautiful, flawless mocha-colored skin on her bountiful bosoms.

Austin winked at her as he stood up and walked over to the balcony. He pulled the dark satin blue curtains apart and showed off their beautiful view from the penthouse room.

"I'ma make you the Queen of dis city. Believe that," he promised. "And we'll be in our new house soon. I just need to get a few things done with it."

NeTasha stood up and wrapped the sheets around her then walked over to him. He pulled her into a deep kiss, complete with plenty tongue, before he pulled away and stared at her lustfully, biting his bottom lip.

"I gotta get out of here so I can get back. I can't wait 'til I can get a sample of dat sweet, tight pussy." He licked his lips.

Smiling sweetly, NeTasha watched him walk to the elevator and get on. The doors began to close and she blew him a kiss right before they closed in front of his face. As soon as they shut, she dropped the sheet to the floor and ran over to the bedroom to grab her clothes. She started putting them on as fast as she could, her breathing coming in rough jagged spurts. She had no idea where she was going or how she would get there but, one thing she knew was that she had to get the hell up out of there and away from Austin.

The more she hung around him, the crazier she began to notice he was. He never allowed her to have money; everything he needed or wanted he preferred to buy for her himself. She hadn't noticed it until she looked in her purse the day before and saw her cash was gone. When she asked him about it, he'd nonchalantly said he would buy whatever she needed.

Now there was this issue with the phone. He was escalating, steadily trying to make her his prisoner and it was too much. Lying in the bed, she tried to plead her case with him on why she should keep her old phone, and he gave her the most menacing and threatening look. In an instant, he became the same Austin she'd seen that night at the club when he had nearly beat the guy to death for staring at her. Sensing that she would be next in line for a brutal ass-kicking if she didn't change her tune, she changed courses quickly and pretended that she loved the phone in order to calm him down.

Now he was talking about this house they would be moving into and NeTasha knew that she had to figure out a way to get away before they moved in. Austin thought that she couldn't hear him when he spoke from the balcony, but the glass was thin and she could make out just about all of his conversations. Earlier that day she'd heard him telling a contractor that he needed the basement to be soundproof and the door leading to it should have a door lock that locked from the outside and couldn't be unlocked if you were in it. There was no doubt in her mind that he was making that room especially for her.

"SHIT!" NeTasha cursed when she grabbed the hotel phone and heard nothing but dead air. The line wasn't working. She ran from room to room and checked every phone but none worked.

"Fuck it," she concluded. Grabbing her purse, she ditched the play-play phone in case he had a way of tracking it and ran over to the elevator. Holding her breath, she pressed her finger into the button to call the elevator.

But it didn't light up.

"What the fuck?!" she exclaimed with a frown.

She pressed the button again. And again. And again.

Nothing.

Gritting her teeth, she pressed her fingers to the opening of the doors and tried to claw them apart, using all her might, but they didn't budge. The dreaded feeling of disappointment, fear and anxiety compounded her as she tried over and over again to press the button with no luck at all.

The power to the elevator was off. She was stuck. Somehow, Austin had gotten one of the workers to cut the power to the penthouse elevator and the service to all the phones in the room. And since he had money, she was sure that it had been easy to find a low-paid hotel employee who was ecstatic to comply with his request, thinking it was a harmless way to earn a little extra cash.

Strength completely depleted and hope shattered, NeTasha sunk down to the floor collapsing into a fit of sobs.

The phone rang.

NeTasha stopped crying instantly and a shimmer of hope ignited in her body as she dashed through the living room to answer it, praying it was someone she could ask for help.

"Hello?" she answered with a shaky voice, perspiration beginning to form on her brow in spite of the frigid temperature in the room.

"Ay, you good?" Austin asked in a way that sent chills down her spine.

Can he see me? NeTasha asked herself. She lifted her head and allowed her eyes to dart around the ceiling in the room, scanning quickly for any kind of device that Austin could be using to spy on her.

"Y-yes, I'm fine. Just...hungry," she lied. "I—I need to go down to the restaurant downstairs or...maybe I can call room service to get some food."

"Nawl," Austin said monotonically.

NeTasha frowned into the phone, unable to readily respond. Her bottom lip began to quiver.

"B—but I'm hungry..."

"Check the fridge. I got you some food in there," he informed her. NeTasha dropped down and sat on the sofa next to the phone. He had thought of everything. He wasn't going to let her go anywhere.

"I'll be back soon," he told her. His words sounded endearing but his flat, emotionless tone made it seem more like a thinly veiled threat. "Eat, sit down and watch TV or something until then. Don't tire yourself out."

NeTasha's head snapped up as an icy feeling traveled down her spine. He was watching her some way. Had to be.

"O—O—Okay," she stuttered as tears came to her eyes once more.

"A'ight," he said and then the line went dead. Absolutely dead. He hung up but there was no dial tone. NeTasha placed the phone back on the stand, took off her clothes and laid back down on the bed.

There was nothing she could do.

TEN

Trigga had his eyes on Tish from the moment her car turned in through the gates and pulled down the driveway. The last thing he wanted was to allow someone he didn't trust to be sitting her ass in the same place him and his wife laid their heads. But after Keisha guilted him into having Tish come over by reminding him of his error in judgment concerning Mase, he couldn't find a real reason to stand on that would explain why he didn't trust her.

Squinting through the partially open blinds, Trigga watched as Tish slowly stood up outside of her car and looked up at the house. There was a flash of an emotion that passed through them and Trigga recognized it instantly; envy. He'd seen Mase look at him in the same way many times when they were younger. Knowing that his brother was jealous of him and his achievements made Trigga overcompensate by feeling that he had a duty to take care of him and to make sure he was able to enjoy the things that Trigga worked hard for. Even if Mase didn't deserve it. Still, it seemed that his efforts did no good.

Under Trigga's watchful eye, Tish seemed to shake off the envy and neutralized her expression, but something about the way she did it made Trigga feel as if it were all an act; as if she were forcing herself to seem caring and friendly.

This bitch ain't right, he thought to himself as he watched her.

Without waiting for her to get to the door and knock, Trigga walked over and opened it up just as she walked up the front stairs. A startled expression crossed her face as she looked into Trigga's glowering eyes and her lips parted although no sound came out. Her eyes were wide open and her face was pale in a way that wasn't normal, even for someone with a complexion as light as hers. The forced composed vibe she'd tried to give off gave way to one of worry and trepidation that made Trigga feel unsettled. She wasn't at ease, like someone should be if they were simply visiting a friend. She seemed to be on edge for some reason. Trigga crossed his arms in front of his chest and watched her acutely without saying a word as he waited for her to speak.

Tish swallowed hard as she looked at Trigga. Then her eyes traveled down to his bandaged leg and back up to his face. His piercing gray eyes searched her face in a way that made her feel naked, as if all of her secrets were bared for him to see. His usual, cheerful and joking expression that he reserved for his friends, was replaced by the accusing, untrusting, penetrative stare that he reserved for niggas he came across in the streets.

"Hey Trigga," Tish started, her voice sounding coarse and dry although she was trying her hardest to seem like there was nothing wrong. "Keesh called me and—"

"Ain't shit happening around here that I don't know bout," Trigga informed her with a thinly veiled warning. He continued to stand, blocking her entrance until Keisha suddenly came up from behind him.

"Maurice! Move out the way, damn! HEY, GIRL!"

Trigga watched with the edge of his upper lip turned up as Keisha scooted past him and pulled Tish into a big ass bear hug, rocking her from side-to-side as they embraced. Then both women turned around and walked through the door, one after the other. Trigga made sure to keep his eyes on Tish as she walked through. She cast a weary glance in his direction and then turned sharply away and focused on Keisha, as she talked on and on about her pregnancy cravings as if she'd been living a normal life for the past couple months.

"Whoa...wait!" Trigga heard Tish yell out all of a sudden.

He turned around quickly to see what all of the alarm was about. Tish grabbed Keisha's hand in hers and lowered her face down so that she could inspect the rock on her finger.

"Is this an engagement ring?" she squealed as she admired the diamond. Keisha joined her and started jumping up and down about as much as she could while holding her belly with her other hand.

"YES! And *this*—" she pointed to the other ring on her finger, "—is a wedding band! Bitch, I'm married!"

Trigga stood by and watched as they screamed, shouted and embraced each other as they walked into the master bedroom. A smile crossed Trigga's face as he examined the expression on Keisha's face. He couldn't remember the last time that she'd been this excited and carefree. He knew that she was happy with him, but there was something different about the joy a woman felt when she was surrounded by one of her girlfriends. That screaming and shit definitely wasn't something that she did when they were together.

Trigga closed the front door and grabbed his phone as he listened to Keisha and Tish continue to speak to each other with excitement, as they updated each other on what had been happening in their lives. He noticed that Keisha was careful to skip what had happened after the wedding ceremony at the hospital when she ran through their special day.

Maybe I was *being paranoid*, Trigga thought as he scrolled through the phone to Gunplay's number. He hit the button to dial and walked to the living room so that he could let Gunplay know it was time to move. The quicker he could get things wrapped up here, the sooner he could make sure the happiness in Keisha's voice never left.

***

"Shit...that's crazy, Keesh," Tish said after listening to Keisha's run-through of Trigga's vows and the promises he made. "He's willing to give up everything just to be with your lil' ugly ass. And here I am, willing to fuck with a bitch *or* a nigga and my ass still ain't found the one."

"Maybe that's your damn problem. Stop lookin' for a nigga. I damn sure wasn't lookin' for his mean ass," Keisha pointed behind her towards the door. "And now I'm knocked up and married. Life is crazy as hell."

"It is. And y'all livin' in this big ass house!" Tish turned her eyes around the room. "Shit, can a bitch get a room? You know I ain't workin' at the club no more and since your ass livin' big, I ain't got nobody to split rent with!" Tish spoke in a way that sounded like a joke but Keisha instantly felt guilty.

"You told me you moved into a smaller place..."

"A smaller place still costs. I gotta find me a job or I'll have to take my Black ass back home to my mama. Last fuckin' thing I wanna do. My life is all fucked up." Tish looked off in the distance.

Silence hung in the room. Keisha began to feel uncomfortable. Deep down, she faulted herself for Tish's situation because being involved with Trigga is what got her shot by Lloyd, made her lose her job, and her roommate who had been helping her cover part of the rent. Keisha had been so caught up in her own life that she hadn't taken the time to really think about how much everything had to be affecting Tish, the one innocent person in the situation who was left with nothing.

"Let me talk to Trigga…I'ma make sure we get you some money to help you out. I'm sorry, Tish. I've been so worried about the baby that I wasn't thinking."

"Yeah, I know," Tish responded. A slight frown crept across Keisha's face as she tried to figure out whether or not she should ignore the feeling that Tish was taking lil' slick jabs at her.

"You know, Luxe called me the other day," Tish said in a quiet tone. "She's in Miami, stripping at the club down there. She got money and shit but still hittin' the pole. That's why I love her crazy ass. She don't know nothing but hustle."

"Love?" Keisha asked with a smile on her face. She leaned in closer and waited until Tish lifted her face and looked her in the eyes. Then she blushed and ducked her head once more.

"I knew it! Y'all asses been doing more than just catchin' up, huh?"

Biting her lip, Tish tried to hold down her smile but she couldn't. "She calls me every now and then but that's it. She's asked me to come down there to see her but I can't bring myself to do it. For someone to say they love you and then drop you just because a nigga dangles some cash in front of their face…I can't just get over that shit. Bitches always choosin' niggas over the ones that were there for them." Keisha flinched as she wondered if she were included in the group of 'bitches' who did that.

"Well, Lloyd isn't exactly someone that a bitch can just up and say no to. I've seen what's happened to people for trying it." Keisha lowered her voice and glanced towards the door even though she knew Trigga had left out already. When she looked back at Tish, she saw that her eyes were pointed downward and her brows were furrowed as if she were deep in thought about something.

"You okay?" Keisha asked with a frown.

Something hadn't been right with Tish since she'd come over. She seemed like she was trying to be her old self but every now and then, Keisha would see her looking off in the distance as if she had a lot on her mind.

"Luxe told me something...I wasn't sure if I should tell you," Tish started. She shifted uneasily as she sat on the bed, then began fidgeting with her fingers.

"What is it?" Keisha asked and leaned closer.

She placed her hand on Tish's thigh in an attempt to comfort her so that she could say whatever it was she wanted to say. What she really wanted to do was grab her by the neck and shake her ass until she started speaking.

Tish wiped away a loose strand of hair from her face, exposing the scar on her face that she normally kept hidden by her long mane.

"I spoke to Luxe...and she mentioned everything that happened to you when Lloyd took you. She—she said that he drugged you so badly that she thought you would overdose. A few times she had to sneak away to check and make sure you were still breathing because you would be unconscious for hours...days."

Tears came to Keisha's eyes and she snatched her hand away from Tish's thigh angrily.

"Is there a reason you're bringing this shit up? I don't want to remember what happened! I'm trying every day to forget the little bit of it that I do remember."

"I'm sorry! We were just talking about the baby and all...I was just curious about if you told him."

"Told who what?" Keisha snapped, crinkling her nose at Tish. "What the hell this gotta do with my baby?"

This bitch done lost her damn mind with her crazy ass, Keisha thought to herself as she observed Tish a little closer. She definitely looked like something was off about her and the more she seemed to visibly struggle with what she had to say, the more it angered Keisha.

"Luxe told me that h—he...Luxe told me that Lloyd raped you repeatedly after he drugged you. She told me that she thought the baby might be his—"

"SHUT UP!" Keisha yelled, standing up off the bed. "He did *not* rape me! Shut the fuck up!"

Tish's eyes widened and her mouth dropped open. Her lips began to twitch as if she was trying to say something but couldn't find her voice at the moment.

"I—I'm sorry, Keesh! I just thought maybe you were going through something and needed me to—"

"To what? To be a shoulder for me to cry on? You just can't stand that I'm happy with him, huh? You never liked Trigga from the beginning and you let all that be known loud and clear. And now you wanna bring your creepy ass over here and—"

Eyes stretched wide, Keisha's mouth shut instantly when she heard the sound of a heavy door closing. She listened intently for the sound of his heavy footsteps coming down the hall but the next sound that she heard was a car engine starting, followed by the sound of it tearing out of the driveway.

Trigga had been in the house the entire time. And he'd definitely heard everything.

The tears that Keisha had been holding in her eyes finally ran down her face, as she stood in place and tried to convince herself that Trigga hadn't heard their conversation. But she knew that wasn't the truth at all. He'd heard it all.

"Keesh, I'm so sorry…I didn't know he was here," Tish apologized.

When Keisha didn't respond, she started to walk towards her with her hand out-stretched to console her, but stopped short when Keisha flinched out of her grasp.

"Just leave," she told her quietly. "Go."

After casting one last apologetic glance in Keisha's direction, Tish exhaled heavily, grabbed her purse and then turned around and walked out of the room. Keisha stood in place, unmoving, until she heard the sound of the front door closing and Tish getting into her car. Then she collapsed onto her bed with her head in her hands, but the tears had stopped. Her mind was consumed with so many thoughts that she couldn't even begin to cry. Her emotions were so fucked up she didn't know how to act.

But the most powerful emotions of all was shame and guilt.

Shame because Trigga knew something more about her experience that she'd never wanted him to know. And guilt because she'd know everything that Lloyd had done and convinced herself that it hadn't happened so she wouldn't feel bad for not telling Trigga.

Trigga treated her as if she was precious and pure, regardless of what happened before him, and Keisha wanted to always keep it that way. That was why there was so much of her past that she'd kept from him. If he knew that Lloyd had fucked her in every hole on her came over every inch of her body, there was no way that he would look at her same.

Lloyd raped you repeatedly...she thought the baby might be his...

Tish's words echoed in her brain so loudly that it seemed as if she were still in the room. Grabbing her cell phone, Keisha pressed the call button next to the contact *"My Always"*. She placed the phone to her ear and waited as she held her breath. But the phone rang and rang until the voicemail picked up. She dialed it again and this time it went straight to voicemail. Trigga was ignoring her calls.

Sucking in a breath, Keisha wiped the hair away from her eyes and dialed another number. She bit her lip as she waited for the line to pick up.

"Nigga, ain't you had enough?!"

Keisha's heartbeat sped up. She'd never been so happy to hear LeTavia fighting with Gunplay in her life.

"Nawl, I ain't had enough. Get'cho fine ass over here, gul," Gunplay said in a way that almost made Keisha laugh despite her situation.

"Nigga, bye! Hello?"

"Y'all crazy," Keisha tried to laugh but the pang in her heart made it catch in her throat. She swallowed hard and let out a long sigh.

"Keisha...something wrong? What's going on?" LeTavia asked. Keisha heard a slapping noise followed by Gunplay grunting in the background.

"D—Did Trigga call Gunplay to meet up with him yet?" she inquired trying to ignore the scuffling noise on LeTavia's end.

"Hell nawl, but I wish he would so he could get off my ass. What you need?"

"Tish was over here and she brought up that I had been raped while I was...she said that the baby might not be Trigga's and he heard it." Keisha gritted her teeth together and tried to will herself not to cry.

"Oh shit! Why the fuck did that bitch say that shit while he was there?" LeTavia damn near shouted through the phone.

"She didn't know that he was in the house. We both thought he'd left."

"Listen, Keesh," LeTavia said in a matter-of-fact tone that she used when she knew she was about to spit some real knowledge. "If yo' nigga *ever* tell you that a bitch ain't your friend, BELIEVE THAT SHIT! Most times he's tellin' you that because she done tried to fuck him, he done fucked her or, in Trigga's case, he knows that her ass can't be trusted and just don't want to tell you why. I don't care what you say, her ass is bad news. She shouldn't have brought it up *at all.* Whether he was there or not, if you ain't mention it, she shouldn't have opened her big ass mouth about it."

Keisha nodded her head, not even thinking about the fact that LeTavia couldn't see her.

"I'm going to come over. De'Shaun on the phone talking all low like he on a top secret mission, so I guess he's talking to Trigga. If I didn't know him like I do, I'd think he was talking to some bitch..." she paused for two beats. "DE'SHAUN! WHO THE HELL YOU WHISPERIN' TO ON THAT PHONE?"

Keisha shook her head and waited for LeTavia to come back on the line.

"Sorry about that. I'll be over there in fifteen minutes. We not that far."

Before she could answer, LeTavia hung up the line. Keisha clicked through her phone and sent Trigga a text. She knew he would read it even if he was ignoring her calls.

I love you.

Seconds later, a return message lit up on the screen.

ilu2. 4e

"The hell, Trigga?" she squinted at the text. "I love you too...forever?"

She started laughing as fresh tears came to her eyes. It was obvious that Trigga was definitely pissed off to the max. But a weight was lifted off of her because of the fact that, even in his anger, he still couldn't ignore her when she told him that she loved him.

ELEVEN

"The *fuck* you mean you bought my muthafuckin' club?" Lloyd asked Austin with his lips pulled into a tight sneer. "That's EPG property, nigga!"

They were standing in front of a row of dilapidated two-story apartments where a few members of the EPG crew hung out to serve drugs. It was the place where Lloyd decided to meet up with Austin so he could catch up on a few things he'd been working on for Lloyd while also ensuring that it was only his crew still on the block.

Austin stared back at him blankly with a poker face but his jaw was clenched, showing off his irritation at Lloyd raising his voice. He stretched out his fingers by his side, silently willing himself not to grab his banger and bash it against Lloyd's face repeatedly until he drew blood. It was an instant reaction to what he considered blatant disrespect. The only thing that stopped him was the fact that Lloyd was his cousin and, more importantly, he had an agenda with a big plan, so it was important that he played his position with Lloyd until the time was right. That was easier said than done.

"Ay, nigga, I ain't know that shit was a sore spot for you. I saw an opportunity so I jumped on it. Better that than it go to somebody else that we gotta pay off in order to do biz," Austin said through his teeth as he stepped a little closer.

Lloyd narrowed his eyes at him but held his ground. He hated when Austin walked up on him and Austin knew that shit but did it anyways. The closer he got, the more Lloyd had to lift his head to look him in his eyes and that pissed him off to the fullest.

"Nigga, fuck wrong wit'chu, all in a nigga grill! Back the fuck up!" Lloyd pressed his hand against Austin's chest and tried to push him back.

Austin countered and grabbed Lloyd's arm at the same time, pulling him close as he reached for his banger and kept his eyes on him. Lloyd did the same, only he removed his strap from his waistband, cocked it and held it to his side. They were only inches apart, face-to-face. Just that fast, the moment had become lethal, like fire and gasoline, as they looked into each other's eyes. Austin's stare, with his obsidian, black eyes, would have been enough to make the normal nigga fold, but Lloyd wasn't threatened by Austin in the least. In fact, he was about to fire a shot in his dome if Austin didn't back the fuck up.

Austin could sense his dilemma with each passing second. He knew his trigger-happy cousin was about to start bustin' shots and the only way to thwart that was to fire first, resolving the immediate threat with the quickness. Or he could be tactful and bid his time wisely until the moment was right. Then he'd be able to seize control of what he needed and right then he needed Lloyd in order to pull off his multimillion dollar scheme.

So he swallowed his pride, thus placing his ego to the side, the same way he used to do when they were little kids about to fight over toys at his auntie's house. Even then, he avoided kicking Lloyd's little ass when they scuffled because he didn't want to draw attention to the fact that when he left to go home, he stole as many toys as he could hide. This was the same scenario, different objective, only now the stacks were bigger...much bigger.

Crooking his brow, Austin feigned a smile as he took a step back and threw up the palms of his hands in mock surrender.

"Come on, lil' cuz. Shit ain't dat serious, my nigga, na'mean? We fam! Ain't nothing supposed to come between us."

Lloyd stood solid.

"Nigga, I was finna light your ass up and you playin'," Lloyd said, dead serious.

"Then who gone defend your ass on the playground the next time you get jumped on by big ass Shattoria and she sit her fat ass on your chest?" Austin cracked and burst out laughing.

Lloyd couldn't help but smirk despite his own chagrin. It had been an ongoing joke between the two of them for years, since they were in third grade. Lloyd had spit in Shattoria's face so they fought on the playground schoolyard. It wasn't even close; Shattoria beat him like he stole something. Luckily, Austin happened to show up and jumped into the fight to help him. Still, she nearly beat both their asses.

"Yo, now ain't the time, I got a lotta bullshit goin' on in my life," Lloyd said even tempered, as he eased his banger back in his pants. Then he added on a giddy note with a slight smile, "Besides, nigga, Shattoria tapped your ass up proper. too."

"Yes, 'cause I was trying to pull her big ass off you!" Austin interjected making a face and they both laughed. He then walked up to Lloyd and wrapped his arm around his shoulder in a half-hug and tried to change the subject back.

"C'mon, lil' cuz. You know I ain't mean shit by buyin' up the spot. A nigga just setting shit up for when I jump out the game, na'mean?"

"Nawl, I don't," Lloyd responded, suddenly serious again. "It's about time for you to start packin' shit up anyways. I'm good here. I got a new connect and I'm about to get my team back on top of shit. So you can start figuring out how you gone run yo' new spot from up the road, my nigga."

Lloyd checked his watch. It was almost time for his meeting with the new connect but he needed to stop by some of his trap houses before he went. It was his plan to pop up on them and make sure them niggas weren't slacking like they'd been doing in the weeks prior while he wasn't on hand like he usually had been.

Austin's dry laugh interrupted his thoughts and he glanced at him with one brow lifted high.

"What da fuck so damn funny?" Lloyd gritted, his agitation increasing.

Still laughing, Austin shook his head and started walking over to his dark blue Lamborghini convertible. "Nothing, nigga. I'ma holla at you later."

Lloyd watched him leave as he slowly crept down the street in his whip, making sure to greet and speak to every EPG nigga he passed on the set. Just watching the exchange between Austin and his crew made his blood boil. He'd crossed the line. Austin was driving through Lloyd's streets getting the respect that should have been reserved only for him; dapping up his crew, shooting the breeze and shit like he owned the streets.

With a scowl on his face as he watched Austin greet the last of the crew before tearing down the streets at top speed, Lloyd started his canary yellow Maserati and watched as every eye on the block turned to watch Austin speed away. Niggas weren't even paying attention to the fact that the boss was around because they were so busy gawking at his cousin. Lloyd pulled his banger out from behind him and set it on the passenger seat next to him as he rolled up on a few of his goons standing on the corner.

"Ay, nigga, why the fuck you out here showing dat off-brand ass nigga love? Don't you got enough shit to do?" Lloyd vented at a young cat everyone called Block, mainly because he was always on it.

No matter what time it was, Block was up and serving fiends whatever they needed. He'd been working with Lloyd since he was fourteen years old and now he was eighteen and making more money than some of his top men. But he still preferred to be on the block.

"My bad, Black. Austin came through to check on some shit he asked us to do," Block responded with both hands in the air as if to show he didn't mean no harm.

"When da fuck you started takin' orders from that muthafucka?!" Lloyd yelled with his eyes so wide they looked as if they would bug out of his head. "The hell he gotcho dumb ass workin' on?"

Block tensed up and glanced at his homeboys out of the corner of his eyes before speaking. His delay in response only infuriated Lloyd even more. Right before Lloyd moved to open up his car door so he could walk over and bust Block dead in his face, he opened his mouth to speak.

"He told me that the shit I had was weak and it was why niggas wasn't makin' the money we shoulda been. Muthafuckas in Dallas on some new shit. He had me try some for the last week and the shit been sellin' twice as fast," Block blurted out, uneasily.

Lloyd's eyes filled with rage and he nearly toppled over as he rushed out of the car with his banger in his hand. He left the engine still running as he ran up into Block's face. While holding his strap at his side, he cocked it and glowered at Block. His homeboys around him sensed the dangerous situation and backed away a few paces.

"What da fuck dat was you said, nigga?!"

"I—"

Lloyd knocked Block across the jaw with the butt of his gun, drawing blood. "I know yo' ass wasn't 'bout to open yo' mouth up and repeat dat shit you just told me! So Austin got you workin' on 'secret squirrel' missions and shit, huh? You sellin' for dat nigga now? On *my* muthafuckin' block?!"

Unable to determine whether Lloyd actually wanted him to answer or stay silent, Block kept his mouth closed and swallowed down the blood and saliva mixture in his mouth as he stared back at Lloyd.

"You want me to smash ya ass on the other side of ya fuckin' face? You ain't hear my question, nigga?!" Lloyd's voice boomed throughout the now nearly silent streets. Every eye was watching the altercation between him and Block.

"I—I...Austin said you put him in charge of shit because you was handling some personal shit wit' yo' baby moms," Block blurted out.

Here we go wit' dis Austin nigga doin' dis shady shit again, Lloyd thought to himself as he looked at Block.

"Y—you and him fam so we ain't think shit 'bout it when he mentioned it."

"When it comes to my money, ain't no niggas makin' decisions but me! I shouldn't have to tell yo' ass dis simple shit!"

"My bad, Black," Block apologized. "We'll swap up and go back to da shit we been usin'."

A dark look passed through Lloyd's eyes as he watched Block speak. Although his tone seemed harmless, it was the look in his eyes that Lloyd didn't like. The respect that should have been there was gone and in its place was latent hostility, doubt and distrust. He wasn't saying it but it was obvious that he was second-guessing Lloyd for delivering what he now thought of as a subpar product, thanks to Austin's willingness to show him the light.

Narrowing his eyes, Lloyd tightened the grip on his pistol as he addressed Block.

"My nigga, I'm lookin' at you right now and somethin' just ain't right. Is you feelin' some type of way 'bout some shit?" Lloyd asked with narrowed eyes. "I'm sensin' somethin' ain't quite right wit'chu right now. You wanna talk dat shit out wit' a nigga?"

Block's light brown eyes glanced down at the pistol and then back up at Lloyd. He teetered from foot-to-foot and slowly shook his head. The fire was gone from his eyes and was replaced by a new submissive stare as he spoke.

"Nawl, Black. Ain't shit wrong, my nigga. Just out here tryna get it like I know how, ya feel me?" he responded, a nervous smile crossing his face.

Lloyd continued to glare at him, pulling his lips up into a sneer. "You sho'? Ain't nothin' wrong at all? Nothin' I can help you wit'?"

Block shook his head once more just as Lloyd's cell phone started ringing. While keeping his eyes on Block's face as he shuffled nervously under Lloyd's glare, Lloyd answered the phone.

"Yo."

"Black, I ain't got no car seat," LaToya whined through the phone. Lloyd dropped the phone to his side and turned his attention back to Block.

"Listen, my nigga. If I ain't said it, it ain't been said, you feel me?" he asked him. Block nodded his head silently. "I'ma holla at y'all niggas later."

With that, Lloyd walked back to the car, got in and pulled off. He pushed the phone back up to his ear.

"What da fuck you want me to do, Toy? I left yo' ass wit' money. Shit!" Lloyd checked his watch. He had a few hours before he was going to meet with the new connect. Just enough time to check up on his trap houses to see what's been going on and to make sure Austin ain't have his hands in too much else.

"Yeah, but how the hell I'ma take the baby with me to the store without a car seat, Black?" LaToya said with her slick ass mouth. He could almost see her rolling her eyes through the phone.

"How the fuck you think I got her to yo' spot? Strap her ass in the backseat and drive yo' ass to the store!"

"What?! I can't strap no child in the back like that without a damn car seat! Nigga, is you insane?"

"Figure it out. I gotta go," Lloyd hung up the phone and ran his hand over his face, wondering, for the first time, how in the world he was going to do what he needed to do plus be a father to his daughter without Dior.

TWELVE

"Okay, so I know this is a sore spot and all for you right now but I gotta ask," LeTavia said as soon as she walked through the door. Keisha backed out of the way to allow her to enter.

"Is the baby Trigga's?"

Keisha slammed the door closed and then whipped around on her heels so fast that she almost lost her balance.

"Yes, the baby is his!" She crossed her arms in front of her chest and glared at LeTavia who only stared back at her with her lips pursed. Then she sighed and looked at her nails, picked at them and then turned her attention back to Keisha.

"You out yet?" she asked her.

"Out of what?" Keisha responded with a frown.

"Out your damn feelings!"

Keisha rolled her eyes and walked past LeTavia who followed right behind her, still talking.

"You told me that the doctor said you were possibly nine weeks. That means that you *may* have gotten pregnant before you were taken but it also means you *may not have*! Due dates and all that aren't exact all the time. Now, I know you want this baby to be Trigga's but it might not be and that's fucked up. You need to give him a minute to process that shit."

Keisha nodded her head, knowing that LeTavia was right. She hated to admit it but LeTavia was right more often than not.

"The hell you get all this wisdom from all the time?" Keisha asked as she eyed her up and down.

"A bitch done been through a few crazy ass situations. Trust." A look passed across LeTavia's face that piqued Keisha's curiosity. Beyond that, she was eager to get the focus off of her situation and think or talk about someone else's fucked up life for once.

"Like what?"

LeTavia frowned slightly and for the one time since Keisha met her, she seemed sincerely speechless. After a long pause, she finally spoke.

"That is actually the start of a long conversation." She sighed and grabbed her purse from the small end table that she'd placed it on. "Why don't you put on some shoes and fix that nappy hair? Let's go to the mall and hit up some baby stores or something. I know you feeling some type of way but I'm assuming you want to keep the baby so let's get out of here for a little bit."

Keep the baby? Keisha thought as she walked to her room to put on her shoes and grab her phone.

The thought hadn't occurred to her that she wouldn't. But LeTavia was right...she wasn't absolutely sure about when she'd gotten pregnant. There was always room for error. Just thinking about it made her wonder about Trigga and what he had to be thinking. Would he want her to get rid of the baby if it wasn't his?

***

Keisha was sitting in the middle of the food court shoveling ice cream in her mouth by the spoonful, as LeTavia watched her with an amused expression on her face.

"That must be some good ass ice cream," LeTavia laughed as she watched her. She took out her phone and started pecking away. Keisha watched her.

"You would know if you would take a minute to get off your damn phone for once in a while. Who the hell you talking to anyways?" Keisha sat up and tried to peer over at the screen on LeTavia's phone but she moved it out of the way.

"Nobody," she said but it was obvious that it was a lie. Not only was she definitely texting somebody, but whoever it was must have been someone important from the way she suddenly looked incredibly uneasy.

"Bitch, you're keeping secrets." Keisha pushed another spoonful of mint chocolate chip ice cream in her mouth.

"Everybody has 'em," was her response.

With her eyes on LeTavia, Keisha stood up and tossed the empty ice cream container in the garbage next to them and grabbed her purse.

"I wouldn't know because you been all up and through all my little business but now you wanna act all secretive and shit," Keisha huffed, walking away.

LeTavia stood up and followed behind her. "Yo lil' small problems ain't shit. My secrets could get me killed. It's not the same."

Keisha rolled her eyes and opened her mouth to remind LeTavia that she could see her dramatics, but stopped short when she saw someone off in the distance approaching her who took the words right from her lips.

"NeTasha?" Keisha whispered as she squinted at the woman ahead of her.

She staggered a few paces forward, keeping her eyes on the woman who seemed to be NeTasha, who was walking straight towards her wearing a beautiful olive colored long maxi dress with olive and gold gladiator shoes that looked much more expensive than anything she'd ever worn to class. She looked like new money and as beautiful as ever, which made Keisha feel somewhat self-conscious being that her hair was a mess, she could barely fit into her clothing and she felt like she weighed double her normal.

Keisha looked at the man standing next to her; he was incredibly handsome. Handsome to the point that Keisha felt the urge to fix her hair and her clothing just from looking at him. He had the prettiest brown eyes, shaped like almonds, and caramel skin that glowed. His complexion was smooth and, although he was dressed neatly, he had a thug swag to him that could be felt miles away. He was someone who you respected right away because he commanded respect just by his stance. But beyond that, he was the type of sexy that made you stare even if your man was looking you dead in your face.

And NeTasha was standing right next to him holding on to his hand and smiling like he was her prized stallion. The way she seemed to be soaking up the attention made Keisha feel sick to her stomach.

How the fuck this bitch sittin' here smiling up with this nigga and she been callin' Trigga?

Something told Keisha to leave it alone but she couldn't. She was getting a taste of her own medicine and she didn't like it. All the memories of how she'd played the side bitch to Lloyd while he laid with Dior at night and pretended she was the only one, came to her mind. It was like God was playing tricks on her. She was the one pregnant and now she was being faced with the same pain that she'd inflicted on another woman. And if Trigga was a lesser man, he'd already be fucking NeTasha and Keisha would be getting a big dose of her own medicine.

"Tasha!" Keisha called out, startling NeTasha who stopped in her tracks and turned in the direction of where she'd heard her name.

"K—Keesh...what's goin' on, girl?" NeTasha grabbed onto Austin's arm as they both turned and watched as Keisha walked over to them with a scowl on her face and her hands balled up at her side.

"Don't fuckin' 'what's goin' on girl' me! I want you to tell me this..." Keisha started as she pulled up right in front of NeTasha's face.

"Hol' up, ma," Austin said, putting his hand out to block Keisha from getting too close to NeTasha.

"Nigga, get yo' muthafuckin' hands—"

"Keesh, what the hell's goin' on?" LeTavia asked as she walked up and stood to the side, looking back and forth between Keisha and NeTasha.

Mortified, NeTasha grabbed Austin's arm and tried to pull him away but he didn't move an inch. She looked up and saw that he was looking at Keisha with a scowl on his face, the edge of his bottom lip twitching in a way she'd seen many times before. Keisha was in danger and regardless of their past, NeTasha didn't want her to get hurt.

"Keesh, please...we gotta go. I'm sorry for everything I did to make you angry with me but...please don't say anything. Just let me go," NeTasha pleaded. She looked back and forth from Keisha to Austin, wishing that she could deliver a mental message to her or at least hoping that Keisha would notice the rage building on Austin's face and move on.

But she did neither.

"What's wrong? You afraid I'ma tell yo' new boo how you been callin' yo' old boo?" Keisha spat with her hands on her hips.

NeTasha gasped and shot a glance at Austin whose focus had shifted completely. He was no longer looking at Keisha at all, his full attention was on her. He had his eyebrows crinkled and his lips pulled into a straight line. NeTasha could see the wheels in his head turning as he processed what was being said.

"Oh shit!" LeTavia commentated from the sideline. Then, without wasting a moment, she began taking off her earrings and dropped them in her purse before pulling her long weave up into a ponytail.

"And don't try to deny shit because I saw the calls coming from your cell phone! Now, I was wrong for kicking your ass the last time because you didn't know whose man you were fuckin'. But this time you know! Since I'm pregnant, I'm not goin' to drag your ass at the moment but you need to lose Trigga's muthafuckin' number! I'm not gonna always be pregnant, bitch!"

"Trigga?" Austin said, turning back to Keisha. "'Keesh'..." he repeated the nickname NeTasha had used. "You're Keisha?"

Something about the way he said her name made Keisha pause and squint at him as he looked her over. A smirk passed over his face and it was like a thousand warning bells went off in Keisha's mind.

"Who's asking?" Keisha inquired.

She saw LeTavia shift slightly, putting her hand behind her back and Keisha wondered if she had a gun stashed back there. It wouldn't surprise her. LeTavia seemed like the type of chick to know how to take care of herself.

Austin looked Keisha up and down slowly, his eyes settling for a few seconds longer than they should have, on her stomach. Keisha felt self-conscious and her eyes began to dart around behind him, checking to see where the nearest exit was.

Scrutinizing her, Austin couldn't help but be a little curious about the woman that his cousin wanted so desperately to kill but he knew he wouldn't harm her. The more that he heard about Keisha and Trigga from Lloyd, the more he realized that the issue his cousin had with them was a personal problem. It had nothing to do with him. Even still, Keisha was beautiful and he could see why niggas was tripping over her. He could see why Lloyd would be heated she wasn't still his.

"But that's not my beef," Austin muttered to himself.

Keisha frowned, hearing his words, although she had no idea what they meant.

"Ay, we gotta bounce," Austin said, grabbing NeTasha roughly on her elbow and snatching her away.

Keisha's frown deepened as she watched them walk away. NeTasha turned around one last time, shooting Keisha a look that seemed to be an unspoken plea for help.

"What is that about?" LeTavia asked, walking up next to where Keisha stood and scratching the top of her head.

Keisha shrugged as she continued to stare, feeling as if she had just narrowly missed out on a dangerous situation, although she didn't quite know why.

"I don't know..." Keisha shrugged with a sigh.

THIRTEEN

When Austin came into the room around 3am the next morning smelling like liquor and weed, NeTasha tried her best to pretend to be sleep. But when she felt him yank the cover from off the top of her body, she knew that her little act was over.

"Take all dat shit off," Austin ordered, belching loudly.

"W—W—What? NeTasha sputtered.

Not wanting to repeat himself, Austin leaned over her and grabbed at her lace panties then yanked hard.

"Owwww!"

"I said, take dat shit off!" Austin scowled at her. "I wanna fuck."

"I can't, I'm—"

"Bitch, don't fuckin' lie to me!" he yelled as he pushed her legs apart forcefully. "You can give another nigga the pussy but been makin' me wait and lyin' and shit!"

NeTasha gasped when he grabbed her around her throat and squeezed so hard that she saw stars. Her mouth gaped open like a fish out of water as she sucked for air, but Austin didn't loosen his grip in the least.

With a quick motion, he reached down and freed his stiff pole then pushed forward, roughly impaling her insides with his hardness. Tears ran down NeTasha's cheeks as he squeezed tightly on her throat and stroked repeatedly into her, harshly splitting her in two with every thrust. Then panic set in as her body continued to fight for the air that he was not allowing it to get. She started to thrash against him but it only seemed to excite him even more.

"That's right. Get nasty for a nigga, bitch!" Austin grunted as he assaulted her insides, forcefully, while gripping her neck.

All of the fight left NeTasha's body and she felt herself begin to pass out from the lack of oxygen she was receiving. And that's the exact moment that Austin let go. Taking a gulp of breath in, NeTasha heaved and gulped in enough air to fill her lungs and expelled it sharply as Austin kept going, his strokes becoming swifter and longer. He was about to come.

Austin pulled his dick out speedily, right as he was on the verge of an orgasm, lifted up and stuffed it into NeTasha's gaping open mouth, shooting his hot liquid straight down her throat. NeTasha, who had barely been able to catch her breath, gagged and felt as if she were drowning as Austin exploded inside of her mouth while running his hand up and down the shaft to make sure he released every last drop. With his other hand, he pressed NeTasha's head into him so that he was pushing past her tonsils.

This was the type of nasty shit that he hadn't felt he could do with her when he'd thought she was pure and fragile. Now he knew that she wasn't anything special like he'd been treating her. She was a regular chick who'd already been around the block and fucked with more than a few niggas, Lloyd's nemesis included.

"Shut up all that noise. I should kill your fuck ass for lyin' to me," Austin gritted as NeTasha gasped and gagged while holding her throat as if she still couldn't catch her breath. Her antics were annoying him.

"I didn't...I didn't lie," she finally managed to get out.

Austin reached back and came forward hard, right against the side of her face. He hit her so hard that she flipped straight out of the bed and tumbled onto the floor.

"You did fuckin' lie! Had a nigga thinkin' you was a fuckin' virgin and you been hoein' around the whole damn city. Don't wanna give me the pussy but you gave it up to another nigga who got a chick? Get da fuck outta here!"

Austin jumped out of the bed and walked over to the bathroom while NeTasha cried quietly and rubbed at the sore spot on her face from where he'd hit her. She heard the water running as he cleaned up. When he finally walked out of the bathroom, he was fully clothed and holding the phone to his ear.

"Ay, y'all can come on up," he said into the phone and then hung.

NeTasha stopped crying suddenly, wondering what it was that he was planning. She grabbed at the covers on the bed and used them to cover her semi-naked body.

"Ay, gimme that nigga number. You must know got that shit memorized since you been blowing his shit up and I know it ain't saved in your phone," Austin demanded as he looked at her with his eyes narrowed into slits that made him appear even more threatening than he normally did.

"Wh—whose number?" NeTasha asked slowly, her eyes flicking from left to right as she tried to figure out a way to get out of her current situation. But there was none.

Before she could open her mouth to say another word, Austin walked over and backhanded her so hard, she flew backwards and hit the table behind her. Blood rushed into her mouth and she spit it out onto the floor, using the back of her hand to wipe her mouth.

"Don't ask me no muthafuckin' questions that you already know the fuckin' answer to! What the fuck is that nigga's number?" he repeated, glaring down at her as if she were the scum of the Earth.

As her throbbing lip began to swell almost immediately, NeTasha rattled away Trigga's phone number, watching Austin as he locked into his phone. Then, as if thinking about something, he paused before pressing another button on his phone. NeTasha heard the phone began to ring.

"Who da hell is this?" a voice said on the other line. It was Trigga. NeTasha's heart thumped in her chest with disappointment at finally hearing his voice. He'd deliberately been ignoring her calls but had no issues with answering another random number.

Austin smirked. "Wrong number."

There was no response. The call simply ended.

"Good choice because if you'd given a nigga the wrong number, it wouldn't have ended well for you," Austin said in a way that sent chills up her spine. Then the elevator chimed and the doors opened.

"Actually, it's not goin' to end well for you anyways, ma," he added and then turned towards the elevator. "What's up, niggas?"

A group of nearly nine or ten men filed in the room all curiously taking in the scene. When they say NeTasha lying on the floor, partially naked and wrapped up in part of a sheet with a busted lip and bruised face, they all stopped in their tracks and shot confused stares at Austin.

"What's goin' on?" one of them asked him, scratching the top of his head in a way that made him look like a small, bewildered child.

Smiling, Austin stepped up and spread his arms wide in an inviting manner.

"Sup, Block? I'm here with a gift for you niggas. *Mi bitch es su bitch*," he told them, his grin growing wider and wider. "I've seen the way some of you have been looking at my bitch..."

Some of the men started shuffling their feet nervously when he said that, ready to deny that they had ever in their life looked at NeTasha.

"...Well, it's your lucky day because I'm in the mood to share. I just sampled the pussy...it's decent but I'll let you be the judge of that," Austin told them with a shrug. "Have her your way. Call that hoe 'Burger King'."

Austin laughed at his own joke and then chuck the deuces at the team before turning to walk away. NeTasha stared at the men before her, trembling viciously with terror as she digested Austin's words. The men started to lick their lips and mutter various perverted things about her body as they began to strip.

"I need ya'll to do a pump and dump," Austin said, using the code word meaning that he wanted them to fuck her, kill her and then dump her dead body somewhere it couldn't be found. "After you're done, I'll meet up with y'all on the block. We got some shit to discuss."

"Pleaaaase!" she begged as Austin stepped onto the elevator and pressed the button. "Austin, please don't do this!"

But when he saluted her just as the doors closed in his face, she knew all hope was lost. Biting her quivering bottom lip, NeTasha turned back to the group of men, her eyes singling out Block, the one who had spoken before, and seemed to be the unofficial leader.

"Ay, pretty lady," he cooed with a sickening smile on his face as he came closer.

Squatting down, he was level with her and able to look directly into her eyes. The intense stare in them scared her to the point that her breath caught in her throat and she couldn't utter the words she wanted to say in order to make one last attempt to plead for him to leave her alone. She saw him make a sudden movement and her eyes glanced to his right hand where he was holding a sharp hunting blade.

"This can go easily or it can be hard. You decide," Block told her as she began to cry.

"P—P—Please, don't do this," NeTasha begged.

She looked up and saw that one of the men, a young one, was looking off to the side instead of staring at her with hungry eyes as the other ones were. He was also the only one who hadn't taken off his pants.

"Shut up, bitch!" Block snapped and snatched away the sheet from her body, the lust in his eyes obvious. He licked his lips and grabbed at her breasts.

"I'm first," he told the ones behind him as though it needed to be said. "Don't fight it," he ordered her.

She didn't.

***

"Y'all muthafuckas took too damn long," Block muttered checking his watch. "We 'posed to meet up with Austin in thirty minutes."

"Tone the one who acted like he couldn't get his dick in her ass," one of them laughed at his own joke and the others joined in. All but one.

"That shit was tight," Tone explained, grabbing his dick through his pants as he thought about how good it felt. "I figured I had time since Nas acted like he ain't wanna fuck da bitch."

Nas shifted uneasily when everyone's attention went to him. He was fairly new to EPG and he knew that he was failing miserably at getting the rest of the crew to trust him. When it came to serving fiends on the block, he had no issues and excelled at it. In fact, he brought in more cash than any of the niggas standing around him. But when he had to do things that resulted in the innocent being harmed, he ain't have the heart for that kind of shit.

Even as he looked at NeTasha's body, nearly covered with dried cum as she lay on the floor, breathing so subtly that it was hard to tell if she was even breathing at all, he felt ashamed knowing that he'd taken part in it. Taking a sharp breath, he tried to play it off as if he wasn't unaffected so he wouldn't arouse suspicion.

"Naw'll it ain't like that," he replied with a smirk on his face. "My bitch was trippin' on a nigga this morning and I had to fuck all that shit she was talkin' out of her ass. I'm just tired as fuck, that's all."

Block's face went blank as he scrutinized him for a few minutes, attempting to decipher whether or not he was telling the truth. Then suddenly, his grim expression broke into a teasing smile as he reached over and punched Nas playfully on the arm.

"Yeah, nigga, I done had to do that shit a few times. Dick'll make a bitch shut da fuck up every time." He chuckled and checked his watch again. "Shit, we gotta get rid of this bitch."

"I'll do it," Nas heard himself volunteer before he even knew it.

Block turned and looked at him with one brow lifted. "You ever did a dump before?"

Nas shrugged fretfully and then quickly regained his composure. "Naw'll but I got this. I'm new so I ain't part of the meetin'. I'll handle this bitch with one straight shot to the dome and get rid of her."

Clenching his jaw, Block thought about it for a moment and then shook his head.

"No better time than now for you to prove you up for this shit. No need to shoot her though. Just toss her ass in her car and set dat bitch on fire. Hit me up when it's done."

And with that, Block signaled for the other men to follow him out of the room. As soon as they had left, Nas stared at NeTasha's body. She was wheezing out her labored breaths and he could tell she was in excruciating pain; her entire body was covered with bodily fluid as well as her own blood.

Walking into the bathroom, he turned on the shower and then walked over to her. Leaning down, he touched her face and felt her flinch slightly at his touch. Her eyes were closed but she was alert.

"I'm sorry for what I had to do," he told her. "I'm goin' to pick you up and get you cleaned up. Then I'ma take you outta the city. You don't have to die today but you have to promise to never, ever come back."

Nas was about to stand up and get to work cleaning her up so that he could get her out before something happened to run his plan, but he stopped when he saw NeTasha move her lips as if she were trying to say something. He leaned down once more and placed his ear to her lips, careful to be completely still so that he could hear the words she was trying to say.

"I promise," she said in a barely audible whisper.

And she meant it. Never again, for the rest of her life would NeTasha ever return to Atlanta.

FOURTEEN

Annoyed to the max, Lloyd hung up the phone and stuffed it in his pocket. It seemed that every muthafucka around him was incompetent when he needed them to get their shit together. Now, here he was about to meet with a new connect that he'd connected with and he had all this extra shit on his mind about Karisma and whether or not he was gonna be able to deal with LaToya, when he was supposed to be focusing.

On top of all that, his pockets was lighter than they'd ever been before, thanks to Trigga who had managed to tap out nearly every single one of his trap houses when on his rampage, searching for Keisha.

Keisha, Lloyd thought, her name bringing a scowl to his face.

One thing he knew for sure was that men ran the world but bitches ruled over the men. The fact that Trigga had gone so hard to get at him once Lloyd had taken Keisha told him that now shit was personal. Regardless to the bounty Queen had put on Lloyd's head, Trigga wouldn't stop until he was able to get to Lloyd himself or died trying. Lloud gritted his teeth as he thought about how he'd let Keisha escape right out of his grasp, thanks to that bitch, Luxe. The dumbest thing he'd ever done in his life was fuck with both of their asses and he was regretting it every passing day.

Shutting off the car engine, Lloyd got out of the whip and then looked up at the abandoned building in front of him. It looked like an old warehouse. Tucking his strap in his waistband, he proceeded slowly to the entrance, making sure to scan his surroundings with each step. There was no other vehicle in the area so either he was the first one there or the connect had parked around back.

Once Lloyd approached the entrance to the building, he grabbed the door handle to the front door and turned it when he heard a clicking noise as if someone had triggered the lock to unlatch. As soon as he pulled open the door, he heard two voices talking but he couldn't make out the words. Then there was a chorus of laughter. Lloyd reached behind him and placed his hand on his banger, as he walked cautiously inside. He was told he'd be meeting with one person; the connect himself. But now he was hearing two voices. Something wasn't right.

The inside of the warehouse looked nothing like the outside. It was luxuriously decorated with warm, earthy tones that seemed nice but a little too feminine for his taste. As he walked closer and closer towards the voices, he caught the scent of smoke from some high-priced, strawberry-flavored Kush. Just the scent of it made the hairs in his nostrils twitch.

"Black! Come on in," a voice called out to him. "And you can put yo' banger down, my nigga. Ain't no need for that shit."

With his brows furrowed as an uneasy feeling traveled down his spine, Lloyd sauntered casually towards the room ahead of him while tucking his pistol back behind his back. He lifted his eyes and glanced around at the ceiling of the warehouse. There were cameras positioned sporadically throughout. He had been being watched probably since he pulled onto the property. The voices in the room continued to speak enthusiastically about what sounded like a sports game but, although Lloyd could finally begin to make out the words, it wasn't the words he was focused on. It was the sound of one of the voices.

Clenching his jaw, Lloyd picked up speed and walked straight into the room, pushing the already ajar double doors even further apart with so much force that they flew back and bounced off the walls behind them. The two men in the room both turned to look at him, one wearing a shocked expression with his hand on his banger while the other one simply sat back and stared at Lloyd with a blank look in his eyes and his thin lips pulled into a sinister smirk.

Lloyd's eyes were pulled into slits as he tapered them and glared back and forth at the faces of both of the men ahead of him. Then, finally, he focused on the one with the smirk on his face and bared his teeth in anger.

"Nigga, what da fuck is you doin' here?!"

FIFTEEN

"I might be mistakin' but it looks like you got a lot on yo' mind, nigga," Gunplay finally spoke, pulling Trigga out of his mental haze.

With brows furrowed, Trigga looked up at Gunplay as if he was just seeing him for the first time.

"Why?" he asked him.

"Well, for one, I been standin' here for five fuckin' minutes and you been actin' like you don't see a nigga. Second, you sittin' in front of...what the hell is this place?"

Gunplay twisted up his face and looked at the sign above the store that Trigga was sitting outside of. It read *"Très Bébé"*.

"Tavi told me about this place a while back. She said I could order Keesh some shit to help her relax and sleep better before the baby gets here. I ordered all this shit to surprise her and they texted me to let me know it came in."

"Okay..." Gunplay started. "So why the hell you sittin' out here lookin' like yo' stomach knottin' up or some shit?"

Trigga sighed and looked around them, wondering if he should tell Gunplay what was on his mind. He wasn't the type of man to talk about his feelings or vent to others, mainly because prior to now, he hadn't had much to tell. He lived a simple life and never had to deal with emotions like he was currently feeling, before.

"I'm good," he said finally, deciding to keep his worries to himself. He already had to deal with the vision of Keisha getting ran through by another nigga who might have gotten her pregnant. He didn't want to give Gunplay the same visual.

"Nawl you ain't, nigga," Gunplay said, sitting down next to him. "Keesh told Tavi and she told me what was goin' on wit' y'all before she left. Man, we gone get dat nigga and dat's all you need to focus on. I mean, I hope da baby yours but you neva know. Maybe she should get an abort—""

"Not happenin'. I wouldn't make her kill her child just because it ain't mine. It's just hard to deal with this shit right now."

"I know how you feel my nigga. I ain't gone lie, I couldn't do dat shit. If a nigga fuck my bitch, I'ma drive her ass up to da clinic ASAP. Bad enough she fucked another nigga, now I gotta deal wit' his baby? Hell nawl." Gunplay shook his head from side to side, his long dreads splaying over his face.

Trigga glanced over at him with his eyes slanted in bedlam as he felt his chest tighten up once he'd heard Gunplay's words. His words come out tempered but volatile as he began to clutch his fist tight in an attempt to bridle his anger and not start swinging.

"Nigga, she ain't just fuck another nigga. He *raped* her. Dat's the difference. She ain't just give up da pussy. She ain't have no choice but to deal with it but I can't get dat shit outta my head."

"I feel ya. But look at it this way...my nigga, wasn't she *his* bitch before she was yours? So, yeah, he fucked her but it ain't like it's no shit he ain't had already. You can't be mad."

To Trigga, Gunplay's words were tinged with sarcasm and there was just something about the tone of his voice that vexed him. Trigga jumped up from the flimsy chair with so much force, it was as if he'd been propelled from it. It fell backwards against the glass wall of the store behind him, frightening the few patrons inside as he stood.

"The *fuck* you just said, muthafucka?" he roared at Gunplay who was watching him with a shocked expression on his face. He stood up as Trigga continued to glare at him and shrugged.

"I was just tryin' to say dat—"

"First off, you gone stop referring Keisha as a bitch and, second, you say dat bullshit again making it sound like Keisha willingly gave him the pussy and you gone regret it. I promise you, my nigga, I'ma chin check yo' fuck ass right here, bad leg and all," Trigga threatened with his fist balled tightly, still ready to swing.

A shadow passed over Gunplay's face and his bottom lip flinched as he thought on what he was about to say next. A few people were casting curious glances but then hurried off in the opposite direction as if they were afraid to see what the outcome of the confrontation would be and wanted to make sure they weren't around for it.

"Trigga, my nigga, as you already know, I play by goon rules too and I ain't neva been scared of any nigga. Dat includes you, homie," Gunplay said in a low guttural tone as he pushed his chest up and braced his body, preparing for a confrontation. Then he continued.

"You over here trippin', you know what you was getting yourself into when you started fuckin' with dat bit—chick, na'mean? Now, shit fucked up and I feel you but don't come rappin' sideways out your mouth just 'cause a nigga keepin' it one hunnid wit'cha."

"Nawl, I don't know what you mean, 'cause right now to me it sounds like you got larceny in your heart for a nigga. You know how I feel about Keisha and yeah, the shit hurts, but you not making it better. That's my wife now, so yeah a nigga heated. So what's up, nigga?!" Trigga said with his jaw twitching, pointing an angry finger only inches away from Gunplay's face initiating a fight.

Gunplay took a tentative step back as if he was positioning himself to swing first.

"My nigga, fo' real, fo' real, you don't want none of this, plus you ain't in no physical position right now with your leg fucked up. It would be too easy..." Gunplay said with a crude sneer. There was no fear in his heart.

"Don't underestimate me, son," Trigga said with a full Brooklyn accent and rolled his shoulders.

Just then there was some commotion, throngs of people began to part like the Red Sea. They both looked up and Trigga moved to pull his strap but stopped when he saw two security guards escorting a young black teenager, wearing tight jeans and a Mohawk haircut, dyed red at the top with several tattoos dotting his face. They passed, followed by a murmur of infusive voices as people gawked at them. Gunplay turned back to Trigga.

"Man, get out your feelings. It is what it is. There is a big chance Keisha getting ready to have this nigga's baby. Remember you told me you shooting blanks and can't have no children? Don't get mad that I'm saying what you thinkin'."

Trigga flinched when Gunplay repeated the one thought that had been running through his mind, although he'd been too hurt to voice it again or to tell Keisha. After they were attacked on the first night he'd met her and he was shot in the groin, the doctor had told him that he would probably never be able to bear children. When Keisha got pregnant, he thought it had been a miracle until he discovered that Lloyd had been raping her. Now there was no doubt in his mind that the baby was not his.

Gunplay continued to speak as Trigga retreated into his thoughts, but then he said something that brought him back to reality.

"...then on top of that, your own brother, Mase, bragged about fuckin' her while she was high or some shit. He said she bit his dick. The baby got his damn condition, might be his kid!"

"You lying nigga!!" Trigga said and grabbed Gunplay by his shirt collar and pushed him up against the store window. The sound rattled like thunder, making a few people turn in their direction as, simultaneously, Gunplay reached for his banger and pressed it against Trigga's rib cage.

"I'ma make you a crippled paraplegic, wearing a shit bag or worse, my nigga, if you don't get your dick beaters off me," Gunplay threatened with steel in his voice, fully intent on pulling the trigger.

Click!

He cocked the gun, prepared to wreak havoc on Trigga's body. But Trigga was unmoved, with not even an ounce of fear in his body.

"Nigga, you keep Keisha's name out your muthafuckin' mouth or I guess we gone be both wearing shit bags," Trigga growled under his breath menacingly, and clutched the collar tighter on Gunplay's shirt.

That's when Gunplay felt the cold steel of the 16 shot .9mm pressed snuggly against his belly and flinched. He suddenly realized that Trigga had actually pulled his banger first, beating him to the draw. They were both at a deadly impasse as people traversed by, some staring, others paying only the slightest bit of attention.

Finally, Gunplay spoke and it was the voice of reasoning.

"Man, what we gone do? Let this fuck nigga, Black, make us kill each other and he get away?"

"Possibly, if you keep this shit goin'."

"Tender dick ass nigga, get out yo' feelings. I was just keeping it real with you," Gunplay explained and put his strap back in his pants.

Trigga clutched him around his neck tighter before releasing him and placing his banger back at his side.

"It's time for you to get da fuck outta here," he informed Gunplay coolly, while giving him an icy glare. "No need for your assistance."

"Man, Trigga, why you actin' like—"

"Ain't shit else to be said," Trigga interrupted him.

Gunplay returned his stare with a glower on his own as he watched Trigga turn and walk off into the distance. It wasn't until Trigga was in the car and had pulled off that he was reminded he forgot all about picking up the things for the baby.

Balancing his roles as goon, husband and father-to-be were proving to be more than he'd expected. Things were going to have to change and it needed to happen soon.

KEISHA & TRIGGA 4

SIXTEEN

"Listen, nigga, yo' ass gotta go," Lloyd told Austin after meeting with Jasheem, the new connect that would be supplying Lloyd's team...courtesy of Austin.

"Lil' cuz, I know you ain't feelin' some type of way just cause a nigga pulled a few strings for you?" Austin laughed as he walked outside behind Lloyd. "You called me here because you needed my assistance. So I assisted. You had some issues with your product and I hooked you up. Don't worry...it ain't like I feel that you owe me or nothin'. We fam so it's all good. Sheem is as loyal as they come—"

"Nawl nigga, we ain't fam. I asked for your help and you come here and pull some sheisty shit," Lloyd interrupted.

"Fuck you mean sheisty shit? Nigga, I'm trying to help you."
"Fuck outta here. Yeah, help me by stuntin' in front of my workers, telling them you got better product, talking like you're superior to me. It sounds like you got some other shit going on. Let me find out, nigga."

"Find out what? You know my resume impeccable, I play by goon rules! Yeah, a nigga was stunting but in Texas, you already know how we rock. We do everything big," Austin said puffing up his chest and doing everything short of popping his collar.

Something sinister passed through Austin's dark eyes as he stared at Lloyd. The sun was starting to set which cast a shadow over them as both cousins stood in a stand-off, both with their hands near their strap, ready to go if the situation called for that level of violence.

A thought occurred to Lloyd as he watched Austin glaring at him with his eyes and stance giving away his true thoughts of superiority over him. The only reason Lloyd hadn't killed his ass already was because he was blood. Any other nigga on the streets would have been lying in a ditch somewhere with his balls, teeth and fingers missing had he tried to pull the stunts that Austin was pulling. He was a street nigga just like Lloyd, and he knew exactly what he was doing. He might have been acting dumb to what he was doing, but he wasn't a fool by a long shot.

Fuckin' around with Mase mentally retarded ass got me slippin' on the bullshit this nigga tryin' to pull, Lloyd thought to himself. *This nigga gotta go.*

"Well nigga, you ain't in Texas. You in the A, in my mufuckin' city and from here on out, stuntin' and talking to my workers trying to big up yourself at my expense ain't happenin'. They off limits. My operation brings in millions of dollars. Now if you really wanna meet somebody, I will introduce your ass to Ground Patrol," Lloyd said with a sinister sneer.

"Fuck is dat? Ground Patrol?" Austin asked with an incredulous frown.

"Bunch of hungry ass niggaz that do err'thang a nigga asks them. They part of my EPG mob and they will slump your ass in a heartbeat. Nigga, I take trappin' serious so watch yourself."

"Man, you're trippin'. After all I do for you and you gone accused me of some bullshit like that? Nigga, you must think you the only nigga eating. I came to your city and give you a plug, that should show you the kind of caliber nigga I am," Austin boasted.

A trucked passed by fumigating them, spewing black smoke, as they stood near the street across from a trashed littered parking lot. There was light chill in the air as the two merciless goons glared at each other, each one trying to compose himself in the midst of their very thin patience steadily winding down.

"All it shows me is that you came here with a connect. So that gives me reason to believe you might have had another agenda anyway, other than buying my club without my consent."

"Fuck you mean, your consent and I had an agenda?" Austin crossed his arms in front of his chest and narrowed his eyes at Lloyd.

"Okay, let me explain," Lloyd said, walking up close to Austin and looking him straight in the eyes, the Timb boots he was wearing giving him a few extra inches. "You from out of state so fo' real, fo' real, nigga, you s'pose ta' be paying protection fees just to be walkin' yo' ass round my city. But on the strength you my cousin, a nigga ain't taxing your ass! But now you gotta go. Period."

"Or what, lil' cuz?" Austin asked with his jaw clinched tight as he glared at Lloyd.

"Or I'ma have to help my auntie dress your ass up in a black suit for your own funeral like I do all the niggas. What brand suit you want, nigga? Sean John still what y'all niggaz wearing in Texas? Or you want some skinny jeans?"

That was it, Austin had had enough of Lloyd's antics. He stopped in his tracks and balled his fists up tight about to swing on his cousin, thus jeopardizing his plan.

"Nigga, you got me fucked up! I bought a club here. I got a connect here and I'm damn sure staying here and ain't a bitch gone stop me." Austin was raging mad. His nostrils flared with indignation.

"Now, how did I figure you was going to say some stupid dumb shit like that? You Texas niggaz got balls now but y'all country as fuck and slow," Lloyd said nonchalantly as he stopped in his tracks, taking out his iPhone. He punched in some numbers, glanced at his watch, and then looked around impatiently.

"Fuck wrong with you, nigga? I'm dead ass serious. I'm staying here, opening up shop and no bitch ain't gone fuck with Austin Montegro." He said his full government name with his head held high.

For some reason, Lloyd looked at him for a second then roared with laughter. He laughed so loud and hard that his sides hurt as he held his stomach.

"Fuck you laughing at?" Austin asked stone faced.

"See, I told you. I knew yo' ass had a hidden agenda. Too bad," Lloyd laughed some more.

Vexed, Austin was seriously contemplating choking the shit out of him as he strode closer. "What's so fuckin' funny?" he raised his voice.

"YOU!"

Just then, three cars pulled up, tires screeching. Austin went to grab his strap but he stopped when he felt the icy cold barrel of a gun at his temple.

"Don't even try that shit," Lloyd told him in his ear.

Austin's eyes moved back and forth as he watched each car door open up and more than ten niggas holding AKs and shotguns jumped out, with an assortment of other weapons. Some of them had bandanas wrapped around their faces, repping the EPG signature colors. Every single one pointed at Austin. Lloyd sneered at him with a gloating grin that looked more sinister than anything Austin had ever seen.

"Meet Ground Patrol, nigga. Some of these cats is street orphans I help raised. I feeds 'em. They do every fuckin' thing I tell them. They earn their stripes with a body count," Lloyd took a step closer as they approached and added with a snicker. He couldn't help it because of the pure shocked expression on Austin's face.

"Now, this is what's gone happen is GP is gonna escort yo' ass to the airport. I'm lettin' you live just cuz I got love for my aunty. But you only get one pass, nigga. You bring yo' ass back to my city and I'll light yo' ass up. My niggaz already got the order to bust on spot if they see anybody who even lookin' like yo' ole pretty ass. Ya feel me?"

"Da fuck?! Black, you trippin' man!" Austin shouted, thinkin' about NeTasha who was still back at the hotel waiting on him. "I got shit back at my hotel I need to get. Nigga, my money, jewelry...all dat shit still in there!"

"You leavin' all dat shit there, nigga. Don't worry 'bout it. Matter of fact, I'ma let my goons pick what they want as payment for dealin' wit' yo' ass and them not getting the pleasure of killing your punk ass, nigga."

Austin frowned and tried to turn to look at Lloyd, but he pressed the gun further into his head. "So you just gone rob me? Take all my shit? Dat's where we at now, cuz?"

"Don't fuckin' 'cuz' me, nigga! You was gone move in on my territory! Tryin' to set yo' ass up in my city and take over like I'm lame or some shit. Get yo' ass in the muthafuckin' car and I don't give a fuck what you got goin' on 'round here, I see yo' ass, you a dead man. Feel me?"

"It's all good, cuz, but you know this shit ain't over," Austin threatened as more and more of Lloyd's goons exited the cars.

"Oh, you rapping slick, talkin' sideways out your fuckin mouth like you still ain't respecting a nigga's gangsta."

"Man, I—"

Before Austin could finish the statement, Lloyd nodded his head and gave the order.

"Smash this nigga's ass," Lloyd said with his lips pursed like he was considering spiting in Austin's face.

The entire crew rushed him like a pack of hungry wolfs. The first threw was a shot to Austin's jaw, the punch nearly lifting him off his feet. Then he was struck in the back of the head with the butt of a shotgun, causing his legs to buckle like the Earth had suddenly shifted under his feet, sending him staggering. From that point forward, they began to beat him unmercifully as he fell to the ground, not even attempting to fight back.

Several spectators walked by gawking; this really wasn't anything new in the hood. People mostly looked on to make sure it wasn't one of their loved ones.

A crack head in need of a hit of dope, meandered over. She was dressed in blue jeans, a tattered Obama T-shirt and a grey baseball cap that used to be white. She pretended to scrawl her face with sympathy, but really she was just praying that some loose change or dollars had fallen out of their pockets during the fight.

Then suddenly to her disbelief, she heard the skinny, tall dude say, "Don't lump his ass up too bad, we got to take him to the airport, his ass needs to get past the security there."

By then, Austin was keeled over on his back trying to squeeze under a small rusty Toyota car seeking refuge from the ass whipping.

"Let me get dat up off ya, homie," Lloyd told him as he reached behind Austin and grabbed his banger that was in his waistband. There was blood oozing from Austin's mouth and nose, his lip was busted.

"I'm sorry it had to end this way, cuzzo," Lloyd said sarcastically as someone climbed onto the old Toyota and jumped down on Austin's stomach causing his head to snap back, striking the concrete. A wheezing sound came out of his lungs. The air had been knocked out of him and at first, it took a moment for Lloyd to figure out what the fuck was going on as the beat down continued. Just that fast, Austin had a mouse under his eye; he was in a pathetic state. If they beat him much longer, he was going to die.

"Okay, that's enough, the nigga got the picture," Lloyd said then looked over at the thirsty looking crack head. "Keep it moving, bitch, before your ass is next!"

"Boy, pah- less, I'm lookin' for my dog Scrappy," the crack head said throwing up her hands in contempt. She had a face only a mother could love, as she continued to glance back at the ground.

"Fuck outta here bitch, you lookin' for some dope to smoke. Kick rocks," one of Lloyd's hoodlums said.

"How you gone tell me wha' da' fuck to do? Y'all need to leave that man alone, y'all gone kill him!" the crack head sassed with one hand on her boney hip, looking like a mental patient as she occasionally let her eyes scroll downwards, then she did a double take at something shiny on the ground.

Suddenly, a beer bottle come whistling by her head, just barely missing. Then someone fired a shot directly at her that miraculously missed. That was all it took. The crack head took off running like she had been fired from a cannon. Hyped up like a pack of hyenas, a few of Lloyd's crew were about to give chase.

"Y'all fuckin' chill, niggas. Stop it!!" Lloyd yelled and rushed over. He actually had to physically grab a few of them to stop their pursuit. That was the only hazard about working with a bunch of young, hood niggas from the projects; they were 90's crack babies, stuck on GO if need be with the attention span of a pigeon.

Quickly, Lloyd refocused his attention back on Austin. There was a bloody tooth on the concrete. Austin had a painful scowl on his face and he was in excruciating pain, struggling to catch his breath. He was still making the loud wheezing sound. When Lloyd yelled at him next, more and more people were starting to gawk at them. A few cars slowed down as they passed. Lloyd figured it would only be a moment before the cops came.

"Nigga, get yo' ass up and stop making dat fuckin' whining noise like a bitch! You ain't hurt," Lloyd yelled and watched Austin spit out a tooth from his bloody mouth as he groaned in pain.

More and more, people started to gather around looking; it was like a carnival in the hood.

"Man, put this nigga in the car. Y'all take his ass to Hartsfield-Jackson. If he tries any fuck shit, shoot his ass and dump him on the side of the road. Make sure he gets his ass on the plane headed back to Texas."

As Lloyd happened to look up, it was a cop car turning the corner headed straight for them.

"Ohh shit, there go the law," someone exclaimed in a panic voice.

Suddenly, there was the metallic sound of metal hitting concrete, sliding across the pavement. Somebody had tossed their banger next to a car right where Lloyd and Austin were standing; it was in clear view. Even though Austin was in pain, he had enough sense to scoot away from the gun. Everyone in the hood know you didn't have to possess a stolen or hot pistol with a body on it to be charged with possession. Just the mere fact you were in reach of it was enough to catch a case. The cops even had a legal term for it called constructive possession.

Lloyd just happened to glance down and notice Austin's movement as the cop car cruised by real slow, two white man askance inside. They each donned mirrored sunglasses with pink irritated faces that displayed their disdain for young Black men, true to form southern rednecks. There was about to be a shootout if the cop car stopped. For some reason, Lloyd held his breath and felt his thorax quicken along with his pulse like an adrenaline rush, as his finger toyed with the pistol in his pant pocket.

The car passed. He along with several members of his crew released a deep sigh of relief that was only short lived because Lloyd went ballistic.

"Who in da fuck tossed this muthafuckin' banger over here?" Lloyd yelled spraying spittle at everybody. He turned, glancing at Crazy Mike who had recently come home from prison.

Crazy Mike stepped forward with his brawny shoulders hunched, eyes cast downward, the palms of his hands pressed down on his blues jeans as he nervously stroked his pants legs.

"It was me, dawg. I panicked. I'm fresh out on parole—"

"Nigga, so what, yo' dumb ass gonna get me a fresh case?!"

"Sorry."

"Nawl nigga, you know better. You got a violation coming for that shit." Lloyd turned to his enforcers. "Give this nigga a hundred to the head, a Pumpkin head deluxe, and break one of his fuckin' arms," he ordered.

"Come on man!" Crazy Mike droned with apprehension and dread.

In gang terms, a 'Pumpkin head deluxe' was the most severe violation you could get other than death. It meant that you were willingly punched in the face and head a hundred times, and you couldn't do a thing to block the punches. Afterwards, the unwilling participant's head would uncannily resemble a pumpkin. The arm breaking was just as brutal. One of the enforcers would hold him and break the arm over his knee swiftly until the bone snapped, contorting backwards. Lloyd's rules were barbaric but extremely effective. He was feared by many and respected by all in his crew.

Crazy Mike was escorted off in a black Dodge Chrysler to be taken to get his beat down. The entire time, he grumbled and complained like he was thinking about bucking his punishment.

"Nigga, I peeped the move! Your ass ain't in bad condition. When the cops drove by this bitch, it looked like you was thinkin' 'bout runnin. So run yo' ass up in that fuckin' car and get ghost!" Lloyd barked at Austin, then scanned the streets again.

Austin gathered himself, standing on wobbling legs. One good ass whipping was good enough for him. Them Ground Patrol niggaz combined with the wrath of Lloyd's anger had showed him enough. They were nothing to be fucked with.

He was still slightly wheezing and panting when he sat down in the car, positioned between two of Lloyd's goons. Lloyd couldn't help but chuckle when he looked inside the car and noticed Austin with a sour grim expression. He could see Austin's tongue prodding around inside his mouth, tracing his gums, searching for missing teeth and any damage done.

"Nigga, don't forget what I said, charge it to the game. Don't come back here for shit or I'ma dress your punk ass up, I promise."

"Yea, okay," Austin said, then looked at Lloyd long and hard as he mopped at the blood flowing from his mouth, with the back of his hand. For a fleeting second, Lloyd thought he saw treachery laden in his cousin's eyes. He then tossed the thought out of his mind as the cars pulled off in a caravan, three deep.

Lloyd didn't know it just yet, but he'd made one of the biggest mistakes of his life by not killing Austin.

***

Austin's eyes roamed back and forth, as four of Lloyd's men walked with him through Hartsfield-Jackson airport. They'd left the AKs and shotguns in the cars, but Austin was certain that they had something on them.

"Nigga, the fuck? You tryna hold my hand or some shit? I can walk by my damn self," Austin grumbled as he snatched back from one of the men next to him who had placed his hand on Austin's upper arm. The man responded by pulling him closer and the next thing Austin felt was something hard pressed up against his ribs.

"Don't get yo' ass blasted right here, fool," the man threatened. "Try somethin' and I'ma let loose on yo' punk ass."

Austin clamped his mouth shut but a smirk crossed his face in spite of his situation. One thing he knew for sure was that there was no way that Lloyd was going to keep him out of the city no matter what he'd told his goons.

"Damn, can a nigga take a leak or some shit?" he asked after the one holding him handed him what he suspected was his plane ticket and boarding pass.

He had another in his hands which he held out for another man standing to Austin's other side. He appeared a little younger than the others but not at all less deadly and merciless. When he looked at Austin, Austin could see the same blatant disregard for his life in the man's eyes that all of the other man wore in theirs.

"You can do all that shit once Twon sees you get your ass on the fuckin' plane. Now get the hell on," the first man said gruffly, pushing Austin forward.

The one who went by Twon followed closely behind him as they walked towards the security checkpoint.

"I'm not goin' to give you no problems, nigga," Austin told him. "I'm ready to leave out this bitch. I got shit to do."

"Shut da fuck up and get to walkin', nigga," Twon sneered. "I don't give a fuck about what your bitch ass gotta do, fuck nigga."

Austin gave him a look and made a mental note to make sure that he took care of Twon personally once he made it back to Atlanta, and continued to walk forward. After making it through security, Austin made it to the board the plane just in time, with Twon on his heels watching him the entire way.

As soon as he sat down in the seats, he looked out the window and waited for takeoff but his mind was rolling a mile a minute. Lloyd may have been able to get him out for now, but Austin had implants all around the city that Lloyd didn't even know of. As soon as he touched down in Dallas, he was going to make a few calls to set things in place.

If Lloyd thought he had gotten rid of him, he was sadly mistaken. The only way Lloyd could stop what he had going would have been to kill him. And Lloyd had fucked up his only chance.

SEVENTEEN

"Have you lost your rabid ass mind? Why would I want to fuck your bucktoothed, chainsaw mouth, beaver lip, ugly ass brother?" Keisha snapped as she turned away from the kitchen sink where she was washing dishes with a sharp butcher knife in her hand, causing Trigga to take a hesitant glance down at her hand.

"It's just what I heard and there has been so much shit going on, it's frustrating and you ain't talking to me, your ain't telling me nuthin," Trigga said in frustration.

"What do you want me to tell you? And where are you getting this foolish shit from?"

"I heard it. The streets be talking. You never answered my question," Trigga said and took a step towards her. The knife was still in her hand.

"Ugh, what is there to answer?" she sassed, frustrated, with a jerk of her neck causing her hair to feather over her delicate forehead.

"Did you fuck him, give him head and bite his dick?" Trigga threw the words at her like a verbal assault.

"He tried to FUCKIN' rape me!!" she shot back, eyes ablaze with furry. The knife in her hand was only inches from his stomach.

"So you sucked his dick?"

"No, I bit his damn dick when he tried to put that bitch in my mouth!"

Trigga smacked his forehead with the palm of his hand, in exasperation. As he pushed closer, the knife brushed against him.

"So you did give him some pussy too and sucked his dick?" Trigga accused as he pulled her by her arm tightly.

"Ouch!" she snatched her arm away. "What the hell you mean, I gave him some pussy too, you act like you talkin' to some sloth-hoe-dumb-bitch and for your information, I didn't willingly fuck Lloyd either." The words incorrectly slid out her mouth.

"Either?" he frowned incredulously. "So you did fuck my brother, huh?" he persisted melodramatically.

"Trigga, pah-leeeaaaase, stop this madness! I never fucked your brother. He tried to rape me," she huffed as her hand reached to her forehead messaging her temples like she had a migraine headache coming on.

"Why you never told me about it... why am I always the last to know who has been beating up in your guts? FUCK!" he yelled and punched a hole in the wall. She flinched uncontrollably and nearly stuck him with the knife out of reflex. Trigga couldn't help but notice it.

"Beating up in my guts? Really nigga?!" Keisha scrawled at him in disbelief. She had had it up to the max with his antics.

"How in da' fuck could you bite my brother's dick without him fucking you?"

"Would you like me to show you, stupid ass?" she responded.

"So that is where we at in our relationship now? We got married and you got all types of fuck shit going on in the closet," Trigga said angrily as he rubbed his hand.

"The only thing I got going on is what's in your imagination, in your crazy ass head. You're taking this whole thing out of proportion."

"How? You fucked around with my brother and now you're pregnant with a baby that ain't even mine!"

In his anger, Trigga had let the words accidentally slip out his mouth about the baby.

"You never let me explain..." It suddenly dawned on Keisha what he had just said. "Hold up, nigga, what did you just say about the baby not being yours?" Her brow crinkled, lips pursed across her face, as she took a step towards him with the knife held at her midriffs and raising like she was ready to attack him.

Trigga wet his lips with a dry tongue, as he summoned the courage to speak from his heart, something that he had been holding back from her.

"Keesh...remember the time we got ambushed by Lloyd and I got shot in the groin?" he asked. She didn't answer, she continued to stand motionless with the knife poised in her hand as she looked at him with eyes slanted.

He continued. "... the doctor told me... he told me... I couldn't have children—"

Her jaw dropped and the knife slipped out of her hand and clung to the floor as suddenly her legs went wobbly. She grabbed hold to the kitchen counter and began wailing, crying her heart out. Trigga was overcome with grief with his heart on his sleeve, as he watched painful sobs rock her body. He reached out to her to embrace her, to hold her in his arms, to tell her he was sorry for what he had said.

As soon as his hands touched her shoulders, she spun around and attacked him like a pole cat, and scratched him across his hand and neck drawing blood.

"You knew this all the time!! You set me up for this! Why? Why?" she sobbed uncontrollably. "We're married, expecting our child, your child. Now you do this to me, why?! Why?!" She crumbled to the floor in a ball of raw emotions.

Trigga fumbled his words, his thorax quickened, his mouth suddenly dry as sand paper. He certainly wasn't trying to hurt her like this. He squatted down ignoring the excruciating pain surging in his leg. Gently, he laid his fingers against her soft cheek, wiping at her tears affectionately. She swiped at his hand again.

"Stop! Leave me alone!" she cried harder. Her pensive sobs wrenched his soul pitifully.

"Keesh... bae, I'm sorry. I never meant to hurt you."

She scooted away from him. "You could have told me this before we got married. Instead, you wait for all this shit to happen then drop it on me."

"No, no, and the only reason I didn't tell you was because there was a chance," he persuaded, attempting to take her little hand. She pulled it away.

"How could there be a chance if the doctor said you couldn't have children?" she yelled.

"He told me more than likely I couldn't have children but there was a chance."

She looked up at him with a tuft of unruly hair on her delicate forehead, eyes red, misty with tears, drivels of snot running down her nose. She mopped at it with the back of her hand and spewed.

"I'm packing my stuff to leave. I'll probably go stay with Tish or somebody," she said, folding her arms over her breasts confidently like her decision had been made.

"What about our marriage, the baby, our love? That should mean something," Trigga said with a stricken face like a plea for sympathy.

"What about it?? You, Lloyd, and Mase have assaulted me, put me through the ringer, made me—the victim—look like the damn criminal. I haven't done a fucking thing wrong."

"Me?! How am I making you look like a criminal?" he asked as he reared away from her.

"You're accusing me of fuckin' Lloyd and your brother and on top of that, we both know if this is Lloyd's child, and I doubt it is, you are the one who would be left with the responsibility. Can you raise the baby like it's yours?" she said with a trembling bottom lip, her face wet with tears, her accusation strong, penning him to a wall of his own insecurities.

Trigga didn't answer, and didn't really want to. The hard truth of the matter was he was fully intent on murking Lloyd and his hatred was so strong for Lloyd if Keisha gave birth to his child, his conscious would be killing him and as that child grew older, especially if it were a boy, there could be some disharmony. Then what would happen when the boy became a man and eventually he found out that Trigga had killed his real dad?

Trigga pondered Keisha's last words, giving them more thought. He wanted to love the child, he should love the child like his own, but could he? That was his dilemma.

"Answer the fuckin' question?" she yelled at him with bloodshot red eyes sparkling with tears.

He hunched his shoulders. "I dunno… I mean… sure, I can love the baby like its mines," he said, not looking her in the eyes.

"You lying nigga!" she shouted with hurt in her voice. "You men and your fuckin' egos, and fuckin' pride, that's what's going to get you killed."

"Why you sayin' dat? Why you talkin' like that, Keesh?" he grumbled, then winced in pain. The position he was squatting in was hurting his leg. He sat down on the linoleum floor next to her.

"None of this shit would have happened to me, to us, if you would have just taken me away, instead of chasing behind this punk ass dude, Lloyd. It's your ego, your pride, the same ego that wouldn't let you love an innocent child, yours or not."

"I can love the child, mines or not, and I can love you," Trigga said in a shaky voice laced with uncertainty.

"Prove it!" she said, and latched onto him grabbing his shirt yanking him close.

"How?" Their faces were only inches away.

"Take me away from here, far away. I don't wanna do this anymore. I don't wanna be shot any more or terrified, waiting up nights afraid you're not coming home, afraid the next time he catches me I'm going to die... pregnant." The dam of emotions erupted again and Keisha cried harder, causing tears to dangle off her chin.

Trigga pulled his eyes away from her and stared up at the ceiling fan. He could feel his heart racing in his chest. She was asking a lot of him. Queen had paid him handsomely and his brother too. Money that he would have to pay back if he abandoned the mission. This was exactly what Gunplay was trying to warn him about. Trigga knew he had to stand his ground, be stern with her.

"I got business to handle, that ain't happening," he said with enough manly vigor to frighten a child.

"Fine. If you can't do it, I'm packing up my stuff and leaving," she issued a stern caveat.

Instantly, Trigga's stern demeanor fell when he heard her threat. He had never thought that they would get to the point where Keisha was serioius about leaving and, as much as he hated it, he was ready to give in. Suddenly, he was reminded of what Gunplay had said about him being a soft dick ass nigga.

Maybe I am, Trigga thought to himself.

"But...we married, you can't just walk out and leave," he rebuffed somberly.

"At this point our marriage is merely a piece of paper that can be balled up and thrown in the trash because it obviously means nothing to you. If you did, you would stop this madness, and stop chasing after Lloyd's crazy ass and focus on us, your family, and our marriage."

"Fuck!" he scuffed angrily.

Silence lulled...

From somewhere a clock ticked as time merged with his thoughts.

Just that fast, her slick ass has turned the tables, he thought, stealing a glance over at Keisha and the slight swell of her belly as she watched him, waiting for an answer.

"Okay," he said like the word was hard to get out his throat.

"Okay, what?" she asked sitting straight up.

"Okay, I'm retiring, getting out the game. I want my family more than anything," he said with his hands clasped in front of him, eyes distant, looking straight ahead like he was seeing something only he could see; Gunplay's image, in his mind's eye, calling him a 'soft dick, sucker for love ass nigga'.

She leaned over and hugged him. "Thank you baby," she said delivering wet kisses on his cheek and neck, then pulled away and added, "What are you going to do about Mase?"

"What about him?" Trigga asked suspiciously as he pulled away from her.

Her features softened as she caressed his chest. "After all, he is your twin brother and no, I can't stand his ass, but I can tell you still love him after all he did to you."

Before she could finish her statement, Trigga nodded his head "no" at her. There was no love between him and his brother, maybe pity.

"Go see him and ask about me, he will tell you the truth. Get this out your system, him out your system, then come back home to me and let's pack and go to your hometown, New York."

Her voice was sweet, melodic as a love song. It nestled in that place where femininity has taken refuge in stubborn masculinity, and he found himself resisting the overwhelming urge to scoop her off the floor in his arms and take her in the bedroom and make passionate love.

"Yea..." Trigga swallowed the dry lump in his throat.

"Yea, what?" she asked in rhythm.

"I'ma go see him before we leave, but I don't know if it's going to be good. I do know that I need to get him and this out my system like you said," he gestured with a spread of his arms.

She leaned forward and rested her head on his shoulder, caressing his arm, then giggled girlishly.

"What's so funny?"

"You."

"Me?"

She reached down and stroked his erection, causing the bulbous mushroom head to show an outline through the thin basketball gym shorts he was wearing. He smirked uncomfortably.

"How about I pick you up and take you in the bedroom so I can hit dat ass. Why don't I long stroke it from the back, just like you like it?"

"I can do better than that. How about I just take the dick out right here and ride you like a stallion," she teased without waiting for an answer.

Pulling his shorts down, she stroked him with so much vigor that his eyes rolled to the back of his head. She then hoisted up her skirt. She wasn't wearing any panties. Teetering at first with his large hands balancing her, she eased on top of him and, together, they enjoyed making love to each other until she creamed all over him.

Afterwards, satisfied and saturated in sweat, they lay on the floor with Keisha on top of him, his penis still inside of her as they both breathed hard like they had run a 10k marathon.

"I'ma get up and take a quick shower, and visit my slimy ass brother for the last time. Then you and I are bouncing to the N.Y. We leaving furniture and everything in this bitch."

"Seriously?" Keisha asked with her eyes wide, not even thinking about the fact that he said he was going to visit Mase.

Trigga nodded his head and kissed her one last time.

"Get ready to go. I'll be back soon and then we're out for good."

EIGHTEEN

With his heart beating at a quickened pace, Trigga slowly walked down the halls of the hospital. Trigga had spent so much time in the hospital recently that it was a place he despised. It was like visiting a morgue or a tomb for the living. There was always the perpetual smell of disinfectant and fear. The linoleum floors were buffed and waxed to a gloss and embellished with gloomy, wary faces.

Trigga was headed to the room that he was told housed the man he'd formerly called his brother. According to the doctor who spoke with him upon his arrival, Mase was in critical condition. He'd gone through four unsuccessful surgeries since he'd been there and had at least two more to go before everything wrong with him could be corrected.

As Trigga came closer to the room, he thought back to the time when he'd been in the hospital, much like Mase was now, fighting for his life. The difference in their situations was that Trigga had been there because of Mase's betrayal. Now Mase was in a similar state because of his own foolish, greedy decision.

Turning the corner into the room, there were two huge burly cops walking straight for him. Trigga had his nine in his pants. The first thing that crossed his mind was the warrant for his arrest for missing court. Up ahead was a vending machine. He patted his pockets and veered straight for the machine. Oddly, the cops slowed and paid him extra attention. As they neared bringing with them the loud spatter of police walkie talkie radios, metallic sounds of guns, handcuffs and an assortment of keys, Trigga held his breath...

The cops passed and he let out a subtle sigh of relief then placed several quarters in the machine, getting a water for himself as he looked around. He didn't want to walk into a trap.

***

Gingerly, Trigga entered the room, a beacon of limpid sunlight shined across the floor. From somewhere in the room, a mechanical sound droned with a loud hum.

Whoosh...Whoosh...Whoosh...

Trigga could feel the hair on the nape of his neck crawl. The first thing that Trigga noticed was all of the medical equipment in the room, lining the wall.

Trigga walked past the first bed. Initially, it looked like a balled up white sheet sprawled up in need of tending to, but as he passed, he noticed the elderly white man, a ghostly husk of his former self. His head was bald, with a face shriveled up like a shrinking skull with sparse, gnarly, gray eyebrows.

"Shit, man!" Trigga said loudly, covering his nose with his hand.

From somewhere in the room, there was a malodorous smell, akin to rotting flesh. Trigga resisted the urge to pull his shirt over his nose.

Whoosh...Whoosh...Whoosh...

The morbid sound grew louder. There was a thin, white curtain divider in the room that separated the patients' beds. From somewhere, Trigga could hear the music from *The Price Is Right* game show. With a few more rushed steps, he walked up and pulled the curtain back, unveiling more of the of the huge machines, lights and gadgets adorning it. A tangent line raced across a what looked like a black and gray television screen. There was a huge plastic tube sprouting from the apparatus along with several wires. Trigga's eyes followed the wires...

Whoosh... Whoosh... Whoosh...

His legs nearly buckled. He felt an emotion that he couldn't explain rise up in him, and he felt a tightening sensation in his gut causing him to take a step backward.

Mase had tubes everywhere...in his nose, in his mouth, in his arms. His chest was rising and falling in sync with the machine.

Whoosh...Whoosh...Whoosh...

It didn't take long for Trigga to figure out that one of the machines Mase was hooked to was what is called an iron lung in the hood. Mase wasn't breathing on his own.

With trepidation, Trigga walked closer. Directly overhead was a small TV mounted to the wall with a chain attached, and a game show was on. Resisting the urge to walk out, Trigga trudged on. Then he saw him. Gaunt eye and ashen face, his body was emaciated and frill, with sunken cheeks. There were only a few patches of hair on his head. Trigga stutter stepped as a timorous chill ran down his spine. Upon close examination, Trigga noticed one of his eyes was missing along with the entire right side of his face. It was nothing more than grisly bone thin weathered skin; he looked like a horror creature in a walking dead movie.

Trigga leaned closer as the mechanical breathing machine continued to resonate loudly throughout the room. He couldn't tell if Mase was asleep or awake. Trigga leaned forward at Mase's face...

Whoosh...Whoosh...Whoosh.

"Boo!" Mase said, startling his brother.

Trigga damn near jumped out of his skin and reinjured his leg in the process, as he moved backward, hitting his leg on the side of the nightstand table, nearly losing his balance.

A mechanical gurgle came with a protracted "Whooshing" sound as Mase laughed.

Trigga stroked his injured leg feverishly and responded, "I see you have not lost your sense of humor."

"Hell nawl... I am lucky to be alive...didn't figure ... you would come."

"I had to come, needed to get some shit off my chest," Trigga said grabbing a metal folding chair and straddling it backwards.

"The last time I saw you, you was in bad shape, and it didn't look like you would make it," Trigga said looking up at the TV.

"I'm still fucked up. Doctors say I'm going to be paralyzed for the rest of my life from the neck down. I lost an eyeball and I don't have real lungs to breathe with, due to Lloyd and his Goon shooting and stabbing me up pretty good. Hell, I can't even wipe my ass or scratch my nose."

"Was it worth it?" Trigga asked casually. There was a newspaper in the trash can. He retrieved it, and then spied the door checking for any unwanted guest as he unfolded it on his lap.

"Fuck nawl, it wasn't worth it!" Mase snorted with a mechanical *whoosh* of his breathing apparatus causing the tangent wavy lines to move faster.

"So why did you do it? Why fuck with Lloyd? I mean, man, I can forgive you, but the shit you did was premeditated. You got me down

LEO SULLIVAN & PORSCHA STERLING

here to Atlanta to kill me," Trigga said and turned the paper to the sports section.

"You... Ma... y'all ain't never... loved me," Mase snorted through the tube like he was gasping for air.

Trigga looked up from the paper at him. "Nigga, I spilled blood for you. Loved you like my own life. We came in this world together. Out the same womb, same fucking day, son."

"No... you always... showed off... always outshined me... to impress other people... especially mama ... the girls."

From somewhere in the hospital, the P.A. system blared along with the murmur of hospital sounds.

"So you happy now?" Trigga said to be spiteful as he turned the page looking for the basketball section to see what the New York Nicks had been up to.

"You damn right... I'm happy... a priest paid me a visit the other day. He used to work in death row... was around dudes... worse ... off than me..."

"But did they sell their souls to the devil like you did?" Trigga asked.

Mase ignored him. "He said if I confess my sins... believe in Jesus... I can still make it to heaven," Mase managed to say with a snarky voice.

"So did you confess your sins?"

"Yep, sorta," Mase responded.

"Speaking of sins, did you try to take advantage of my girl, Keisha?"

Mase laughed a derisive cackle that sounded like somebody with asthma blowing into a water hose.

"Keisha, you talkin' 'bout... that coke hoe... that Lloyd used to let her keep his stash?"

"That was the past."

"I fucked her... we rain a train on her...one time she was ... so high she... bit my dick."

"She said you tried to rape her."

"That is what you want to hear..." Gasping long sips of air, he continued. "I fucked your girl...she sucked dis dick... get over it." Mase managed to turn his head and glowered at Trigga with one evil eye.

Trigga peeped the move. Mase was on some misery loves company mood and an in light of the fact he would be preeminently paralyzed for life, along with a lot of other fucked up shit, Trigga bit his tongue and was willing to walk out the room and let his pathetic ass brother wallow in his own sorrow.

Just as he folded the paper back up and raised preparing to leave, Mase spoke as if panic stricken.

"Yo...you don't wanna... ta' hear da... rest of my sins... the big one that God is... gonna get me in heaven with."

From the short sentence alone, Mase was winded. The lines on the machine's screen began to zig-zag faster.

Trigga almost smirked as he thought about Mase's juvenile tantrums. He was pissed about something. In reality, Mase was nothing more than a child in a man's body with an I.Q. his shoe size. Mase was bitter because Trigga was getting ready to leave him and good riddance, it would be Trigga's last time ever seeing him his hateful twin brother again.

"Okay, tell me the sin that God is going to let you in heaven for, because when I leave this will be my last time ever seeing your miserable ass ever again," Trigga said and couldn't help but smirk with a gloating grin.

Whoosh... Whoosh... Whoosh...

Mase's volcano eyes smoldered with insatiable hatred as he prepared to deliver the final blow to Trigga's heart. He knew that Trigga still mourned the loss of their mother like it was yesterday, and he had a tattoo on his arm of her of endearment to prove it.

"Remember dat time...Remember... I found mama... and I told you she had fell down the stairs... and broke her neck."

Mase had a lunatic look on his face and as his breathing increased, the mechanical sound got louder. The smile died on Trigga's face as he suddenly stood stolid, stiff as a board. His face was rigid with concern and his heart was beginning to thump like a bass drum in his chest, as his pulse quickened. The blood drain from his face.

I know this nigga ain't getting finna to say what the fuck I think he is, Trigga thought to himself.

"Yes, I remember," Trigga replied in a hoarse voice. He balled his fists so tight his knuckles popped.

With a fiendish scrawl, Mase raised his head above the pillow and stared at Trigga with one eye and a demonic evil as the tubes ran from his nose.

"Ha, ha, I pushed... dat bitch... down the stairs..."

The syncopated beeps of the machine got louder as if enhanced by Trigga and Mase's confrontation. Mase took one look at his twin brother's sour disposition and saw the gratification he had been searching for, his need for any iota of revenge. Trigga was beyond devastated. All the blood had drained from his face. This time it was Mase's turn to laugh.

"Heeeeeee, heeeeee, heeeee..."

Whoosh...Whoosh... The lines on the machine moved even faster.

Trigga abruptly turned and stormed over to the TV, and turned it up loud. The old white man in the next bed stirred, but didn't turn in their direction.

"What you do that for?" Mase asked with his good eye darting around in his head as he was still smiling.

"So nobody can hear us," Trigga said and snatched the pillow from under Mase's head.

Mase's laughter abruptly stopped.

"Man...wh... what you doing??" Mase stuttered.

"I'm finna do something I should have done a long time ago," Trigga gritted.

"What, puff up my pillow? Make my stay at the hospital...betta?".

"No...get you into a graveyard, ASAP." Trigga raised the pillow over his face.

"But I was just playing!"

Ignoring his words, Trigga placed the pillow over his brother's face, ignoring a solitary tear that cascaded down his cheek. Mase was the last blood family that he thought he loved.

Mase began to thrash weakly with only his head. A muffled sound of "stop" came from his mouth, but Trigga pressed harder and the tears ran down his face until suddenly Mase stopped moving and breathing. The episodic beeps and intermediate chimes on the large machines died in a carnage of stifled silence that merged with the hospital noises. The tangent white line on the KGE machines went straight.

Trigga removed the pillow and wiped at the tears on his face with the back of his hand. He turned to leave and the lured face of the white man in the next bed was looking at him scornfully with ghostly gray eyes, as his boney fingers clutched and unclutched the white sheets. He was supposed to be comatose and brain dead but for a finite moment in time, his eyes held Trigga's with the accusation of murder. Trigga picked up the pillow prepared to murder him too, a witness to the crime. He walked over, placed his hands, waving at the old man gesturing.

No response. Maybe he was blind.

His expression was suddenly blank, impassive.

A nurse's aid walked into the door; a buxom black woman, short with mammoth breasts. She was humming a tune, bristling when she entered. Trigga dropped his head to conceal his face, and tossed the pillow like it was a hot potato and walked out.

As the elevator dinged opening, Trigga stood anxiously waiting until he heard a scream. He wondered was it the nurse discovering Mase's lifeless body.

NINETEEN

Rapper Yo Gotti's song blared from the loud speakers, as Lloyd and his crew strode in, right past security and several club staff. The stage light flashed a kaleidoscope of colors as an assembly of gorgeous, drop dead dancers gyrated to the beat. The heavy scent of Loud was in the air. Instantly, pandemonium erupted just as Lloyd had planned it. The muscle bound bouncer ran up accosting them.

"Hey, fuck wrong with y'all? You gotta get patted down and go through the metal detectors just like everybody else." The bouncer made the crucial mistake of grabbing one of Lloyd's henchmen.

Wham!

One of the crew swung, hitting him square in the jaw, and the entire crew of about seventeen deep, jumped on the guard and began pummeling him as the rest of the security staff and club patrons watched.

Lloyd strolled up to the new manager of Diamonds strip club, formerly known as Pink Lips. The manager was a tall, regal slender guy, fastidiously dressed in a black suit coat, blue bottom down shirt and jeans. He wore a thin goatee and baldhead with thin intellectual bifocals that made him look more like a college professor than a club manager. Lloyd knew him from Austin. Austin had flown him in from Texas to run the club. The guy was actually a wizard when it came to running business. His name was Clay Benson.

"What's going on, Black?" the manager asked after making a beeline straight over to Lloyd.

"Nigga, you know what this is, I'm taking over the club. My attorney will be getting with you ASAP!"

The guy's face dropped like a basset hound as he wiped his baldhead with the back of his hand. He was beginning to perspire as he glanced over to the other side of the club. Lloyd's crew was stomping the shit out the bodyguard as patrons looked on aghast.

Lloyd read the manager's Clay mind. "Nigga, I heard you was a wizard at laundering money and avoiding taxes. I'ma give pay you double for working with me," Lloyd said as the lights of the club strobed his face a cluster of blue and red.

Clay raised a brow then cringed when one of Lloyd's man stomped the bouncer's head hard on the marble floor, causing blood to squirt. Several women screamed. From across the club, Lloyd raised a hand for them to stop beating the poor guy; they were about to catch a case.

"Yea nigga, we on some East Point Gangsta shit hard up in here. You join me and I'ma feed ya."

Clay fidgeted as he watched his security attend to the bodyguard laying on the floor in a puddle of blood. Several of them looked over in his direction for advice. Clay gave them a shrug and asked Lloyd with a stiff chin as if he was trying to keep his fortitude in the face of harm, "And what happens if I don't want to be a part of your crew?"

Lloyd shot him a repugnant stare and rubbed his hands together, as he spoke to a redbone with a banging body and long purple hair flowing down to her ass. She flirted.

"Heyyy Black, you gone sponsor a bitch tonight?" she cajoled.

"Hell yea, holla at a nigga later." As she passed he hit her on her ass. She smiled and waved.

"You was saying?" Lloyd turned back to Clay.

"What happens if I don't take you up on your offer?" Only that time he was watching Lloyd intensely as his bouncer was being carried off the floor.

Lloyd smiled and waved at a couple of females. "Nothing really other then I'm going introduce you to Ground Patrol like I did Austin, and we gone get you outta here on the first thing smoking."

Clay's jaw clinched tightly. Lloyd continued, as Clay began to nervously look around the club as if thinking of a quick exit plan.

"Have you talked to your boss, Austin?"

Clay didn't trust his voice to speak, he just waggled his head, "No". They both know he was lying.

"Okay, you got about an hour. Go call your boss ask him about me. Take me up on the offer and we good."

"And?" Clay asked wide eyed, his fear, suddenly palpable, etched on his face like he was standing in front of a firing squad.

"Man, can't we talk this over, I mean I feel like you just—" Before he could finish the sentence, Lloyd shoved him so hard he nearly stumbled.

"Nigga, go call Austin, let him know what the business is!" Lloyd yelled about the music. Clay was about to say something, but then thought better of it and stalked off to go call Austin.

They sat in the VIP section popping bottles, making it rain with big head Benjamins, as about every stripper and bad bitch in the club crowded around the VIP section trying to get in.

The big bootie redbone that had greeted Lloyd earlier was head down, ass up, bouncing her shapely ass making it clap in his face. As Lloyd sipped on a cup full of muddy codeine, mixed with a Sprite, for some reason his conscious was deeply troubling him. For one, there had been a lot of disharmony and grumbling amongst his clique. Even some of Lloyd's most loyal members had been missing for days.

Annoyed, Lloyd glanced at his Rolex. The manger Clay still hadn't made it back yet with his answer and he had given him an hour to come up with a decision.

The song ended and the stripper turned around, her hair sprawled in her face. Her supple breasts, coral pink nipples like bullet heads. She stood bowlegged, curvaceous with her pussy shaved as bald as a baby's ass.

She reached out and feathered Lloyd's cheek and stuck her tongue out showing him one of her sex faces, as a green light bathed her body in a hue. He stroked her breasts and pitched a perky nipple. She giggled and danced closer, leaning forward and whispering, making sure her lips and tongue seductively brushed against his earlobe.

"You still gone sponsor me, baby? Take me home later and I'll suck dat dick all night long just like you like it." Lloyd was barely paying attention to what she was saying when he reached over to grab a wad of money off the table. Just as he passed her a stack of bills and told her to come back later, she frowned at him with a look of rejection. The truth was his mind was elsewhere; something was wrong and for the life of him he couldn't put his finger on it.

The iPhone in his pocket suddenly vibrated. He looked at the caller ID and got excited. It was a call he had been waiting for.

"What's good??" he yelled into the phone as he placed a finger in one ear to hear better, just as a stripper walked up and tried to push up on him. She was slim with a pretty face. But she had a severe overbite like she still sucked her thumb. He shooed her away from him.

"I got an address where Trigga is staying with Keisha," the voice responded. Lloyd sprung from his seat so fast he knocked over a $5000 bottle of Louis XIII liquor One of his crew scrambled to pick it as they looked at him.

"You lying," Lloyd yelled into the phone as he walked away from the table bumping into people.

"I ain't lying, I just left there. Trigga's leg is fucked up like a nigga hit him with a Chopper."

"Give me the address."

"Give me my money first. It's one million for both of them, correct?" the voice responded.

Lloyd shook his head dismissively and responded, "Yea, yea, what is the fucking address?"

"Money first, nigga."

"Man, that fuck ass money don't mean nothing to a nigga. Where you want me to meet you at?" Lloyd said agitated, just as another stripper paddled up to him. She was caramel complexion with hazel eyes, a sensuous gap between her thighs and a big ole round donkey booty.

"Hey baby!" she caroled with a smile, with perfect ivory teeth and the face of an angel. Her breasts were small but perky and ripe, protruding like a cantaloupe.

He felt his dick jump in his pants and threw up a finger as if telling her to wait a minute. That was when he looked across the room. He saw Clay on the phone all animated, talking to somebody. It looked like he had been spying on Lloyd the entire time.

"Send me the address and I'll give you half then and the rest after. You got my word."

"You know Trigga is hot about the baby not being his," the voiced returned.

"He will be okay. I'm finna eradicate that problem when I kill both of their asses. Now give me the fuckin' address or I'ma add you to that list," Lloyd barked on the phone and gestured for the caramel stripper to come forward, as she stood to the side with her arms crossed over her breasts. She walked over in her six-inch spaghetti lace stiletto heels, and stood in front of him audaciously wearing a sexy grin. Lloyd reached over and squeezed her breasts, kneading it like he was sampling exquisite fruit.

"I'm getting ready to handle some business. When I come back—"

Before he could get the words out, the redbone that he had been talking to early eased up between them.

"Damn, don't tell me a bitch 'bout to lose her sponsor," she sassed with her hands on her wide hips. Lloyd couldn't help but crack a grin as he suddenly looked between both of them. The caramel complexion chick wasn't intimidated at all, as she stood like a prized stallion.

"How about I sponsor both of y'all? I'll be taking over this club. After tonight, this bitch belongs to me. Y'all gone fuck with a nigga or not?" he boasted.

Both females exchanged giddy glances and replied they were game.

"Yes," they replied in chorus and both hugged him.

That was the sole purpose of working at a strip club; to be freaky, make money and hopefully catch a baller. They had accomplished that. Lloyd was that nigga.

He spied his Rolex. "I'll be back later. Can y'all get some Mollies and Loud?" They both nodded their heads 'yes' in unison.

"I'll be back in about an hour," he said and walked off back over towards the VIP section.

Before he could make it, Clay, the club manager met him. For some reason he was smiling like he had just won the lottery.

"I talked to Austin. He is pissed but he wants me to take the offer. He said he didn't want any drama," Clay said, extending his hand for Lloyd to shake it, which he did.

"What you mean, he don't want no drama?" Lloyd was baffled.

Austin was the most vindictive nigga he knew. When they were children, Austin would fight over video games when he lost and wouldn't let it go until he won, even if it took months for him to master the game.

Clay was still smiling. "He said there are no hard feelings and you can keep the club, just pay him back the money he invested. The liquor license and insurance came close to a half a million."

Lloyd almost laughed out loud had it not been for his mind thinking about murdering Trigga and Keisha. Lloyd muttered under his breath, "As long as I owe dat nigga he won't ever be broke."

"What you say?" Clay asked.

"Nothing, yea, tell the nigga once I get situated I'll break bread with him." Clay smiled brighter.

Lloyd glanced at his watch again. You could tell his mind was elsewhere. He began to frantically wave his henchmen over. Clay panicked, thinking he was calling them over for him.

"Wha...wha... what did I do? I told you we good, I wanna work for you."

"Man, you're good. Get the paperwork ready," Lloyd said with a pat on the back. "Just don't fuck over me, my nigga, or I'ma kill you and dat's on everything I love." With that, Lloyd walked away.

With a sigh of relief, Clay took out his phone and began to urgently text someone.

A rush of men, all members of Lloyd's crew, walked over and surrounded him like a quarterback in a huddle. Only these niggas were goons.

"We just found out where this nigga Trigga staying with his bitch. We getting ready to go Chopper City his fuck ass, and the pregnant bitch too. We gotta make an example out both they ass. Since the streets have been watching, and this nigga done ran up in several of my trap houses and slumped some good niggas, we gon' make his ass pay. The hood needs to know, East Point Gangsters ain't nuthin' ta be fucked wit'."

A loud clamor of roars, and boisterous rowdy voices erupted throughout the club as they all shouted obscenities of what they were going to do to Trigga and his pregnant bitch, Keisha as they headed for the door on their way out.

***

A crescent moon hung from the sky, ominously, in the dark night. A light chill tinged the air as nocturnal noises chirred along with the pulsating beats coming from inside the club.

They headed out the club like a small military band of thugs organized with deadly intent. They were all parked in a mini caravan of vehicles, Cadillac SUV's, Benz's and other luxury cars. Big Hank, Carlos, Tank and Mars were going to ride with Lloyd in his Bentley. Just as they walked into the parking lot, for some reason it was eerily quiet. Normally it would be festive with dudes sitting on top of their cars, parking lot pimping, and females galore.

Not that night.

Lloyd didn't pay the slightest attention to them when he rushed over popping his trunk, prepared to take out the AK-47 and AR-15. None of his crew was really strapped except for a few hand guns.

Big mistake!

In the hue of semi darkness, Lloyd just so happened to be bent over, reaching down inside his trunk, when all hell broke loose. It sounded like hells furry and the night was lit up by high power weaponry as a barrage of shots rang out. Grown men wailed in agony. Lloyd felt what he thought was water slap his face, as several bodies dropped in front of him. It dawned on him what was going on; they were being ambushed.

He looked up as Big Hank's head exploded just like a grapefruit, spraying blood, bone and matter. They were open seasoned. Someone had set him up good. Walked him right into an ambush like a sitting duck. All around him his men were dropping like flies. They didn't have a chance.

"Fuck!"

He had no choice but to duck down and run for cover. In the process, he leaped over several bodies of his men, who were all either dead or dying. He sought cover behind a tricked out Chevy on 26-inch rims, as he looked over by a garbage dumpster which was where most of the shots were being fired from, or so he thought.

"Look behind that car right there, dat fuck nigga didn't get hit. Where he at?"

Lloyd's heart slammed against his rib cage. He knew the voice all too well. It belonged to Block, one his workers. He had once caught him being too buddy buddy with Austin. Now it all made sense. Block and several of his workers had formed a coup and went rogue.

"Shit," he cursed under his breath, as he stayed crouched down low at the back of the vehicle. He wiped his face with one hand, which was smeared with blood. He heard footfalls fast approaching. His heart beat faster. They were searching for him.

In the parking lot to his right, he heard someone groaning and moaning in pain. He strained his eyes in the darkness as his heart beat in his throat. He removed his 9.mm; it was no match for a gang of dudes with assault rifles that could destroy a car. He was thinking about pulling Tank closer to him out of harm's way, when several feet walked up. A voice whispered.

"That's Tank, Lloyd's homie," Shawn said with a hint of excitement in his voice. He was only seventeen years old.

"I know, bust his ass! We killin' all these niggaz, ain't no coming back from this," Block said with heightened enthusiasm as he bounced on the balls of his toes looking around frantically.

Lloyd crouched down lower. All Block and his goons had to do was look at the back of the car. Lloyd was in plain sight.

Tank continued to groan in pain. He had been hit in the neck with a Chopper, blood running from his body like a river.

Shawn placed the barrel of the AK-47, pressing it tightly to Tank's head.

KAY-BOOM!!!

The assault rifle exploded with a sonic boom, with an impact so strong it decapitated Tank's head leaving a football size hole in the concrete.

"Dat fuck nigga around here somewhere." They turned in Lloyd's direction. He slid under the car on his back, in a nick of time.

"That nigga got to be around here somewhere!" a voice said.

Just then, the sound of police sirens could be heard. Lloyd heard the sound of hard toe shoes coming up the pavement briskly.

"Did you get him?" The voice belonged to Clay.

"Nawl, but that nigga around here somewhere," came a response from a voice Lloyd vaguely recognized.

"Man, Austin is going to be mad as a muthafucka. How y'all let him get away? What we gone do now?" Clay asked gravely as his feet shuffled back and forth.

"Well, it's officially war with us but you good. That nigga don't even know you masterminded this shit so play it off. Just rock his ass to sleep when you see the nigga again, you're good," Block said.

"Okay, will do. Get out of here, the police sound like they're getting close," Clay said and rushed off. Lloyd could hear the sound of running and car doors opening, speeding off.

With a ringing in his ear and blood splattering his face and clothes, he scrambled from under the car. The parking lot was littered with bodies, some of them still alive. Something panged his heart. He wanted to stop and help, but he couldn't; he needed to keep moving.

He hopped into his whip just as people began to rush out the club doors, stampeding to their cars so they could leave. Just as he pulled up to the main entrance of the club, his car was bathed in limpid bright lights. Blue lights flashed. He wiped at the blood on his face with his shirt and crunched down in his seat, prepared to be pulled over.

When the lights continued to speed past, Lloyd let out a sigh of relief. Sliding up slowly, he peeked out the front window and saw that he wasn't being watched. Slowly, he eased away down the road, thankful that, once again, he'd been able to escape a terrible fate, but promising himself that he would be back soon to finish off the ones who had betrayed him.

TWENTY

"Keesh, are you ready? We gotta get out of here," Trigga asked once he walked into the house.

He was trying his hardest to keep himself cool but inside, his heart was bleeding. The only person in the world that he had always expected to be on his side until the day he died, was now gone. And he was the one who had sent him to his grisly end. No matter how much Trigga loved his brother, the bottom line was that Mase had gone far beyond the point of no return and there was no way things could have ever been the same.

But, on top of that, Trigga was also trying to cope with the fact that he still didn't know what he was going to do about Keisha and the baby. Was it possible to love a woman and to hate her child? The more that Trigga told himself that things would be fine regardless, the less he was beginning to feel that way. He sincerely didn't know what to do, but he did know he had to get the fuck out of Atlanta. That was a necessity.

"Maurice, I'm trying, but we have too much stuff to take with us...and what about our furniture?" Keisha asked, walking into the living room where Trigga stood with her hands full of clothing and bags.

Trigga let his eyes slide over her for a moment before speaking. She was still as beautiful as she was the day he fell in love with her. Even more so with her pregnancy glow. He felt a pang in his chest when he looked at her bulging belly, and then dragged his eyes away quickly, hoping that she couldn't read his thoughts through his eyes.

"We aren't taking any of this shit with us. Keesh, just grab the things important to you and let's go," Trigga told her, avoiding her stare. "And stop that Maurice shit. Nobody calls me that."

When he finally let his eyes rest on hers, he noticed that she was looking at him intensely, almost as if she could see through to his soul. A feeling of anxiety washed over him and he averted his gaze away from her and walked to the kitchen, fully aware that she was still watching him.

"Baby, what's wrong?" he heard her call behind him, but he didn't answer because he couldn't. Instead, he grabbed a sharp butcher knife from out of the kitchen and bit down hard on the inside of his cheeks in an attempt to keep his emotions at bay.

With the knife in his hands, Trigga walked out of the kitchen and over to where Keisha stood, watching him with her hands at her side. He lifted it high in the air and began slashing up the couch next to her.

"Trigga! What the hell are you doing?" she asked, her voice high with the surprise that she felt.

In that instant, she was certain that the weight of everything had finally gotten to him and he'd gone mad. There was no other explanation for the reason he was gutting up brand new furniture with a butcher knife, as if he'd lost his mind. But then, Trigga dropped the knife and reached inside, pulling out handfuls of money...and bags of dope.

"Go get those duffle bags out of the closet," he told her as he started pulling out the contents of the couch with both hands.

Keisha watched him with her mouth wide open. "Where the hell did you get all of that from?" she asked him.

"You don't wanna know," Trigga replied, quietly.

All of the money and dope that he had stashed came from Lloyd's trap houses that he'd raided when he was trying to flush him out and find Keisha. Trigga wasn't a dope boy but he wouldn't have any problem trading the dope for cash once he was back in New York. This, along with the cash that he had saved, provided him with more than enough money to pay Queen back for failing in capturing Lloyd, and also gave him enough to start a legit business so he could keep his promise to Keisha.

Without asking any further, Keisha took his word for it and walked down the hall to grab the duffle bags. When she came back, Trigga had retrieved all of the contents out of the furniture. It was more money and drugs than Keisha had ever seen. She started to feel a churning in her stomach as she stared at all of it. When she felt Trigga's eyes on her, she turned to him and saw him watching her intently, as if trying to read whether or not she was still tempted by everything in front of her. Truth was, she was tempted by it. But she wasn't dumb enough to indulge. Especially not while carrying her baby.

Handing the bags to Trigga, she sat down on the only chair that wasn't in shreds, and watched him pack up each bag.

"Mase is dead," Trigga said matter-of-factly as he dumped handfuls of the money into one of the bags.

His eyes weren't on her, but she could see from the way he kept clenching and unclenching his jaw that it was bothering him. She'd known something was wrong right when he walked in the house. His eyes were drooped at the ends in grief and they sparkled the way eyes did when someone was holding back tears.

"I'm sorry...did you get to see him?"

Trigga nodded his head and then rubbed at his nose.

"Yeah...I was there when he died," Trigga said softly.

Then he looked up at her, his eyes crystal clear but there was a shadow behind them that told Keisha everything that he meant when he said that statement. Yes, Mase was dead. And Trigga had killed him. She looked away from him and shuddered.

"A'ight." He sighed as he stood up after closing up the bags. "You ready?"

Keisha shook her head and stood up. She walked over to Trigga and wrapped her arms around his neck, pulling him into a passionate kiss. He resisted for a second, his body still tense and seeming on edge, but after a couple seconds of feeling her in his arms, he relaxed and began to explore her warm mouth with his prodding tongue, leaving no parts untouched.

Without saying a word, Trigga's body spoke to her and Keisha pulled away and then dropped carefully to her knees as he watched. She unbuckled his pants and pulled him out slowly. He was already getting hard just from feeling the heat of her hands. He clenched his jaw and closed his eyes, relishing the feel of her warm, wet mouth, when she slurped him in and began flicking her tongue over his swollen mushroom head as she deep throated him.

"Shhhhhiiiiiittt," he moaned as he grabbed her gently by the back of her head and pulled her forward.

The smacking and slurping noises she was making as she serviced him with perfection, almost sent him over the edge. His toes were curling up in his shoes. She worked him like a pro, making sure to be liberal with her saliva, to the point that her mouth was gushing with a combination of its natural juices and Trigga's as well. He tried to pull away when he was about to orgasm; Trigga had a thing about coming in her mouth. But Keisha grabbed him hard and sucked down on him to prevent him from moving.

"Keesh...shiiiiiit, fuck!" he cursed as he let go between her cheeks, releasing all of his thick liquid.

Keisha swallowed it down easily, enjoying the taste of him on her tongue. When she stood up, Trigga was looking at her as if she'd grown angel wings out of her back. His eyes were blinking slowly as if they were heavy from both euphoria and fatigue. Keisha smiled, knowing she'd managed to please him, releasing a little of his stress and getting his mind off what had happened with his brother, even if only for a little while.

"Get your ass in the bed and take all this shit off," Trigga ordered in a raspy, throaty tone that made Keisha get wet instantly. He roughly pulled at the tank top that she had on, nearly ripping it off of her himself.

"Hurry up," he added, smacking her on the ass. Keisha didn't hesitate to turn around and walk down the hall, tearing off her clothes all along the way.

She was already in the bed, naked as the day she was born, with her legs wide open and giving Trigga an eyeful of everything that was his, when he walked in licking his lips. Dropping his pants and boxers to the floor, he kicked them off and pulled his t-shirt over his head, keeping his beautiful gray eyes focused on her mound and the pink button in the center.

Leaning down between her legs, Trigga pulled his lips into an 'o' formation and totally covered her nub and sucked on it gently, knowing that this was what Keisha liked the most. She arched her back into his face and started grinding her hips, pushing her pussy into his face and decorating him with her sweet juices.

Just as he was about to bring her to an orgasm, he stopped and replaced his tongue with his dick, running his throbbing, fat mushroom over her clit in an up and down motion to totally soak it in her juices before slipping inside. Both of them sucked in a sharp breath when he entered inside.

Keisha clutched at the sheets and arched her back, wanting to fully give herself to him. Trigga pushed down hard at her knees, needing to take more. After countless moments of thrashing, moaning and grinding, they both collapsed on the bed, panting to catch their breath as they held each other.

"We gotta get ready to go," Trigga whispered in her ear, although the last thing he wanted to do was move out of this perfect moment. He had the only person in the world that he loved in his arms and she was pregnant with the baby that he would learn to love as his own. With God's help, anyways.

"Baby, you need to rest," Keisha said, yawning loudly. "We can leave in the morning. A few hours won't make a difference."

She nestled into him just as Trigga closed his eyes and drifted into a much needed sleep.

TWENTY-ONE

"How you like me now, muthafucka?!" Lloyd said into the recording he was making on his iPhone for his beloved cousin, Austin, who had tried, and failed at murdering him.

Wearing a mask, embroidered with the EPG sign on the side, Lloyd was standing in the middle of Clay's living room making a video that he knew would send a clear message to Austin, as if he needed another one to prove that Lloyd wasn't to be fucked with. After laying low in the cut for what felt like hours, Lloyd finally got what he wanted when he saw Clay's car pulling out of the parking lot of the club. Lloyd pulled out right behind him, but stayed far enough back not to be seen, as he followed him home.

Clay was so engrossed in the conversation he was having that he wouldn't have noticed Lloyd even if he were right behind him. Whoever he was talking to had his full, undivided attention.

"Must be talkin' to that nigga, Austin, and fillin' him in on your lil' mistake," Lloyd said to himself as he stroked the handle of his Glock .9.

He was so furious about what had transpired at the club, he didn't even bother calling anyone to help him with what he was about to do. With niggas trading sides and shit, he didn't know who he could trust other than the niggas he called his 'orphans', his Ground Patrol. But since he needed them to help him with another plan that he had for later on, he decided to handle this one solo.

As soon as Clay stood up outside of his front door, jingling his keys in the lock, Lloyd came up behind him and clocked him over the head with the butt of his weapon, knocking him straight to the ground like a sack of bricks. He went down easy but was still conscious enough to scoot his ass through the entrance of the house as instructed by Lloyd, who commanded him at gunpoint.

Now, Clay was strapped up in a chair with blood leaking from the crown of his head as he awaited his punishment while Lloyd talked shit into the video.

"You thought you was smarter than me, huh? Well, listen fuck ass nigga, I got'cho lil' girlfriend right here and I'm about to teach both y'all muthafuckas a lesson on what happens when you fuck wit' Black!" Lloyd spat.

Walking over to a bookshelf, Lloyd positioned the phone in a way that would allow the camera to catch the angle, and then grabbed his gun off the table.

"You got something you wanna say, nigga?" he asked Clay as he held the gun to his head.

Tears, sweat and blood were running profusely down Clay's face as he breathed heavily with the terror of a man who knew that his end was near. After moving his lips in a flapping motion for a few seconds, he finally sucked in a breath and prepared to speak. But before he could get a word out, Lloyd lifted his hand and brought it down with all his might, right against his mouth, knocking loose about three teeth in the process.

"Don't nobody give a fuck what you gotta say, muthafucka!" Lloyd yelled out. Then he turned to the phone and pointed, talking to Austin.

"Listen, my nigga. You ain't here so yo' boy here gone have to get the punishment for your violation." Lloyd turned his attention back to Clay who was crying loudly. He grabbed a towel off the table next to him and stuffed it in his mouth to stop the noise. The last thing he needed was for someone to hear his pathetic howls and call the police before he was able to finish the job.

"Now, this right here is what I call a Pumpkin Head Deluxer Than a Muthafucka!" Lloyd said and then stopped, as if thinking whether the name was good enough.

After thinking for a few seconds, he shrugged and decided to go with it. Then he wrapped himself up with saran wrap, making sure to only leave an opening so that he could see and breathe, and began to beat Clay repeatedly in the head with his gun, unmercifully. The entire time he pelted him with the gun, he counted the hits, making sure that he was keeping track. By the time he got to fifty, Clay's head was covered in blood and he was nearly unrecognizable. He was drooped down at the neck and unmoving. Lloyd was covered in his blood.

"Nigga, is you sleep?" Lloyd asked, temporarily stopping his punishment. "We only halfway through. You hanging in there?"

He kicked at Clay's feet and heard a low grunt, so small that he'd almost missed it.

"SHIT!" Lloyd cursed. He had been halfway hoping that Clay was dead so that he could stop. He had other things to tend to and, truth be told, he was sore as fuck from delivering the blows to Clay's head.

Usually his team delivered the punishment and he just handed out the orders. It had been a while since Lloyd had actually carried out a punishment for himself.

"Man, fuck this shit...I got things to do!" Lloyd muttered.

He wiped the bloodied gun and dropped it at Clay's feet, then picked up another one that he'd laid on the bookshelf where he'd placed the phone. After placing a silencer on the barrel, he pointed it at Clay and let off ten bullets all over his body, making sure to send the last one right through the dome. Placing the gun back on the bookshelf, Lloyd walked over and started shuffling his feet and throwing up gang signs, doing his celebratory EPG dance around Clay's dead body and making motions at the phone, in a gloating manner.

"Now," Lloyd started as he took off the saran wrap and threw it down on the floor. "I'm going to hunt down all the rest of them niggas that you persuaded to join up wit' yo' fuck ass and I'm handing out the same punishment. So you might wanna call them niggas and tell them to get the fuck out my city if they want a chance."

Lloyd, still wearing the mask, positioned himself right in front of the phone and spoke in a low tone.

"But as for you, cuz, there ain't no mercy being given to your ass. I'll be comin' to find yo' ass personally," he muttered and switched off the camera.

He cleaned up and gathered his cell phone and gun from the house, then walked out, covered by the cloak of night. Although he had succeeded in what he'd planned to do, his spirit wasn't settled. He'd started a war with his cousin while in the midst of another war. With niggas on his squad steadily turning their backs on him to link up with his enemy, he had to move fast to put out one fire so he could focus on the other.

As soon as Lloyd got into his car, he scrolled down to the text that had been sent to his phone about thirty minutes ago. It had the address of his next destination and forwarded it to his Ground Patrol team. He had to act quickly because he was running out of time. What he was learning with every passing second was that he couldn't underestimate Austin. Although he was better at hiding it, Austin was just as ruthless and cunning as he was. If not more.

***

KEISHA & TRIGGA 4

Lloyd gave the signal and all twelve of his men took off with their weapons in hand, surrounding the perimeter of the large home that he'd been told that Keisha and Trigga were living in. A moment that should have given him nothing but pure satisfaction, infuriated him. All this time he'd been looking for this tall ass pretty boy who had taken his side bitch, killed his cousin and looted all his trap houses and here he was, only about fifteen minutes from EPG headquarters, tucked away in a country ass part of Lithonia.

He snorted as he walked up on the home that Keisha was now living in. It looked like the perfect home for a square nigga to live with his square bitch, a nice middle class home on a nice chunk of land.

Gotta give it to a nigga, Lloyd thought, *he tryin' his damndest to turn a hoe into a housewife.*

"Let's go," Lloyd said quietly and all of the men took aim and started pelting the house with shots, focused on destroying all life inside.

Without waiting for another command from Lloyd, they took off doing what they knew to do next. Although the weapons had silencers, they still had to move fast and get out. When Lloyd walked in, the first thing that he noticed was the couched slashed open. He continued walking, searching for the master bedroom, although his mind was on the tattered sofa cushions.

Da fuck was that about? he thought to himself as he gritted his teeth and pushed forward.

Everywhere around him, his men were piling into rooms with their guns drawn and pointing around corners, following his orders to kill anything that moved. But deep down, Lloyd hoped that he was the one who could deliver the kill shot to both of them. He was greedy but for a good reason. The two of them had done all they could to ruin his life and, at this point, he didn't care about anything else other than ending theirs, if they hadn't already.

"Is that the master?" Lloyd asked quietly to one of his men who was standing next to a closed bedroom door. Lloyd's heart leaped in his chest and started thumping with excitement when he nodded his head 'yes'.

Stepping to the side, Lloyd pushed the man out of the way, forcefully taking his position as he stood at the door, AK in one hand and grabbed the doorknob with the other. A devilish smirk crossed his face as he nudged it open, ready to blast at anything that moved. This was the moment that he'd dreamt about and it couldn't have come at a better time. After busting nearly a dozen caps in Clay's ass, he was on a high that only came when he was bodying niggas. He was more than ready to continue the rush he got from a fresh kill.

Lloyd pressed his finger against the trigger and bullets emerged from his chopper at top speed, whirling through the air in a circular motion, crushing everything in its path. Lloyd couldn't help but laugh as he pulled as hard as he could on the trigger, as if the force of his tug would inflict more pain.

Satisfied that he'd completed another job well done, Lloyd released the trigger and lowered his weapon. But, even in the dimly lit room, he could see that something was wrong. Trudging over to the bed with his weapon drawn, he grabbed at the tattered, bullet-ridden sheets and snatched them up.

"WHAT DA FUUUUUCK?!" Lloyd yelled out as he looked at the empty bed.

Keisha and Trigga were nowhere in sight.

***

Gunplay sat in the cut watching...as Lloyd and his men charged into Keisha and Trigga's former residence, lighting it up with bullets. He watched in silence with a menacing look on his face, knowing full well that Keisha and Trigga were not inside. Trigga had called him hours ago to tell him that they were leaving and he needed to come to the house to get some jewelry and clothes that she had left over there.

"Ain't this some shit," he whispered under his breath as he watched.

There was a snitch and he knew exactly who it had to be. The only people who knew where Trigga and Keisha lived were him, Tavi and one other person.

Careful to not to bring too much attention to himself, he crept down the road, far enough to maintain a safe distance but close enough to see what was going on. There he waited until Lloyd and his crew began to pile back into their cars and pull out of the gated driveway.

With a clenched jaw, Gunplay pulled off behind them. He knew niggas like Lloyd and he knew how they operated. If the snitch had told him that Keisha and Trigga would be there, Gunplay was willing to bet that Lloyd would be on his way to give the snitch a major ass whooping or worse since he'd been unsuccessful at getting rid of them for good.

He followed Lloyd's car all the way until he got to an apartment complex and turned in. Gunplay was about four cars back and slowly followed behind but stopped when he saw a female duck out from behind a group of bushes, holding a duffle bag in one hand, and shoot off down the street towards where a city bus waited on the counter. He squinted, something about her seeming familiar.

That's her muthafuckin' ass!

His thoughts scattered as he tried to decide whether to run up on Lloyd or to get Tish. At the last second, he decided that Tish was the better option being that he was along and Lloyd was accompanied by at least five other niggas who were riding in the whip with him, all of them toting heat.

Gunplay slammed on the gas and pulled right in front of Tish, blocking her path. She stopped too late and ran dead into the side of his burgundy red Cadillac.

BOOM!

The force of the hit made Tish's body propel backwards and the weight of the duffle bag sent her crashing down to the ground. In a matter of seconds, Gunplay was out of the car, his .9mm in his hand as he walked over slowly to where she lay, scurrying to get up off the ground. The city bus began to creep away, leaving only a few people on the street walking around. Once they saw Gunplay walking fully strapped, they took off running without bothering to look back.

"Stop! Please—I didn't do anything!" Tish begged with tears coming down her face.

Gunplay leveled his banger with her head and put his finger on the trigger.

Click.

"Bitch, what da fuck you mean?! Yo' greasy ass told dat nigga exactly where Keisha and Trigga lay their head. If they had been there, they would be dead fuckin' with you! I wish I could make yo' ass suffer but that ain't my style."

Gunplay was ready to squeeze the trigger. He'd already spent too much time in the same spot and didn't want to risk running into the police.

"No, I didn't! I was just tryin' to get his money! I knew they weren't there because Keesh texted me and told me they were leaving. I swear! Check my phone!" Tish cried.

Gunplay wavered as he thought about what she was saying. It seemed believable that she could have been playing Lloyd just to get a pay day. He eyed her over the barrel of his weapon. She looked pitiful; mucus and tears were running down her face as she pled for her to have mercy.

"That sounds like a true story," Gunplay told her in a calm tone. "And had I been Trigga's lovey, dovey ass, I might have let you go. But unfortunately, that ain't my style."

Biting his lip, Gunplay squeezed on the trigger, sending a bullet straight through Tish's skull. Afterwards, he grabbed the duffle bag she'd been holding, jumped in his ride and pulled off, his eyes searching furiously for a spot where he could ditch the car that he'd stolen a few days back and find another.

He had to call Trigga and tell him what he'd discovered about Tish. He also had to let him know that he had to kill her so he could break the news to Keisha. She wouldn't take it well but he had to do what he had to do. Whether Tish had meant well or not, the fact of the matter is that you never make a deal with the enemy, even if it is to save your own ass.

TWENTY-TWO

"How long are you going to love me?"

"Longer if you keep giving me head like you did last night," Trigga responded.

Keisha nudged him in his side, making him waver slightly in the road. Laughing, Trigga steadied the car and then glanced at her. She had her bottom lip poked out and her arms crossed.

She's such a fuckin' crybaby, Trigga thought, smiling to himself.

"Oh, you were bein' serious?" he asked, glancing at her out of the corners of his eyes.

"I thought I was," Keisha grumbled.

Trigga checked his watch. They were making good time. He'd been driving ever since the day before and now they were almost to his apartment in the city. When Keisha told him they needed to wait and leave until the morning, he wanted to but he had a nagging feeling that he needed to get his wife out as soon as possible. So, after taking a fifteen-minute power nap, they got on the road and took off, heading back to his home.

Keisha slept the majority of the way, leaving Trigga as a prisoner in his own thoughts. He was thankful for the silence. It gave him time to think on what he really was facing when he got back into the city. Not only would he have to deal with Queen's wrath, but he'd have to figure out how to welcome a child into the world that was conceived through one of the worst periods in his life, and he also had to deal with his buried feelings concerning killing his only brother. If ever a nigga needed a drink, it was now. The weight of the world was on his shoulders.

Then there was the matter of his manhood being questioned. The only thing he could think of was that he was being a tender dick ass nigga, just like Gunplay had called him, for allowing Keisha's demands to stop him from going after the one nigga on Earth that he would trade his own life for in order to end his. Every time Trigga thought about the fact that so many innocent people had been killed in his journey to get at Lloyd, he began to get heated all over again. Even as he looked at Keisha, the only thing he could feel at times was his anger with her stepping in and making him feel like less than a man, by encouraging him to retreat when he should have pressed on and gotten the job done regardless to what she had to say about it.

"I'll love you until the day I die," Trigga told her honestly.

Keisha cut her eyes at him and relaxed somewhat. But there was still more that she needed to get out.

"Even if the baby isn't yours?"

And there it is, Trigga thought to himself once he heard her words.

He'd been waiting for her to ask that question or something similar. He knew it was coming. She needed confirmation from him that he'd always be there no matter what.

"Keesh, even if the baby isn't mine, I'll love you. I'll love you until the day that I die. I said that and I meant it."

"What about the baby? Will you love it too?"

He paused and thought back to the many men whom his mother had dated while he and Mase were younger. Not one of them loved them although they had no issues fucking with their mother. There were a few of them who were nice, but nice wasn't love. And they would really only be nice to Trigga because he was the one easier on the eyes, the smart one...the athletic one.

Trigga thought back to how it felt being in the presence of a man who he knew wasn't his father, but wishing that he'd only treat him in that way so he could know how it felt. It never happened and soon enough, he stopped wishing for it. He would see his mother bring home a man and he'd see him exactly for what he was: a user. Someone coming to take from his mother what he wanted and give nothing in return. They could only fake their affection for her children for as long as they could fake their affection for her, and sometimes not even that long. But Trigga wasn't faking his affection for Keisha. He sincerely loved his wife. So wouldn't he love her child, regardless of who the father was?

Before Trigga could answer her question, his phone rang. Thankful for the opportunity to escape her questioning, he reached down and grabbed it.

"Hello?"

"Uh...is this Maurice Blevins?" a male voice said on the other line.

A frown passed over his face as he wondered whether to say something more or just hang up. Not once recently has good news come to him from anyone calling him by his government name.

"This—this is Officer Burns, by the way. And I'm calling with good news," he added in a rushed tone.

Trigga exhaled heavily, noticing for the first time that Keisha had been watching him with wary eyes.

"Hey Burns, what's up, man?"

"Well...er, I—I, uh, well, I wanted to just let you know that I'm still grateful for what you did. You know...by not killing me and all." He let out a dry, nervous chuckle as Trigga continued to hold the phone silently, wondering what it was that he really wanted.

"Anyways, you had a warrant for your arrest, as I'm sure you know from the voicemail I left you last week. I was able to get it lifted. So you're all clear here," Burns finished.

Trigga's lips formed a straight line as he nodded his head graciously. "Thank you. I appreciate that."

He shot a look over to Keisha who was staring out the window with her hands folded in her lap.

"Anything else?" he asked, hoping that Burns caught his drift.

"Uh...no, that's all I had to say. So—"

"So there isn't *anything else* you wanna tell me?" Trigga asked again while praying that Burns would understand that he wanted to know anything that the officer might have heard regarding Lloyd or his crew.

"Nope! That's pretty much it. I'll give you a call if I hear anything else about that other business you inquired about. You know...concerning 'you know who'. Have a good one!"

And with that, Burns hung up the phone, leaving Trigga frustrated with Keisha eyeing the side of his face, undoubtedly ready to pick up their conversation where they'd left off. Trigga dropped the phone in his lap, suspicious that Burns was lying.

"This is our exit," Trigga muttered, pulling off the interstate.

"You ain't gonna answer my question?" Keisha gawked at him as he avoided her eyes.

"Keesh, anything dealing with you or any part of you, I will love. Happy?"

The frown on her face told Trigga that she wasn't, but he didn't have the patience to start fussing with her over something that they would have to wait for months to get a direct answer on. Who knew who the father of her child was? Only God Himself. The only thing they could do is wait.

Keisha stared out the window and tried to act like she wasn't amazed by everything she was seeing. She had never been to New York, although she'd always wanted to go and had even begged Lloyd a few times to take her. He'd always promised he would but something would always come up. Something concerning Dior, and she would be left out in the cold, as usual.

She rode in silence watching as Trigga drove past buildings taller than her eyes could see, swerved past taxis and crowds of people, larger than she'd ever seen. Everyone seemed to be busy going somewhere extremely important, completely and utterly fixated on their own problems, issues and thoughts, not at all caring about anyone or anything around them. Keisha wished that she could have the problems and issues of a normal person instead of being the reluctant wife of a killer.

"Here we are," Trigga muttered as they pulled up to a building.

It looked expensive. That's the only word that Keisha could think of to describe it. As Trigga passed by the rows of cars in the covered parking garage, Keisha eyed the rows of expensive cars as if finally realizing just how much money Trigga really had. She knew he wasn't broke, but things were definitely being put into perspective for her. Finally, Trigga pulled into his designated parking space and turned the car off.

"Home sweet home," he said, looking at her.

Keisha glanced at him and shot him a small smile. As Trigga stared at her, the thought occurred to him that he hadn't been back in his spot since before he and Keisha had become a couple. Digging far back in his mind, he tried to recall the state he'd left his condo in last but came up blank. So, for the second time in less than thirty minutes, Trigga resorted to prayer and prayed that the last chick he'd had over there didn't leave her shit at his place anywhere that Keisha would find before he did.

Following Trigga's lead, Keisha stepped out of the car and strutted behind him in her high heels and Balenciaga bag wearing a Chanel dress that she'd bought before getting pregnant but could still fit. Her pregnancy did nothing to stop her shine when it came to her sense of fashion and, although Trigga eyed her like she'd lost her mind when he saw her place her feet in the heels, she also saw the way that he couldn't keep his eyes off of her once he saw her walking around in them.

"Good to see you back, Mr. Bivens," the doorman said when he saw Trigga walked in. Trigga nodded his head to greet him but, by that time, the older white man's eyes were already focused in on Keisha, who was behind him looking around at the inside of the building in awe.

"Hello ma'am," the man greeted her. Keisha waved and gave him a smile then stepped on the elevator with Trigga.

Trigga pressed the button to go up to the penthouse and then set the duffle bags down on the floor as the elevator rose.

"You live in the penthouse?" Keisha asked him, trying not to sound as impressed as she was.

Trigga nodded as if it were nothing.

The doors opened finally, right into his condo. Keisha walked in slowly taking in the sight of it all, as Trigga sat back watching her nervously. This was the first time that she'd been able to see a piece of him. This was his home, where he lived before he'd even met her, and his most sacred of places. Not many women had been welcomed in this spot but Keisha was different. He loved her and he couldn't help but feel a little anxiety at the way that she was walking slowly around, inspecting every little thing.

"Make yourself at home," Trigga said easily. "It is your home now."

Without causing too much attention to himself, Trigga slipped into the master bedroom and checked under the bed for panties or anything else that women liked to leave when they were at a man's spot. As if they didn't realize that they were walking out with a bare ass when they left in the morning.

When he stood back up, his eyes settled right on Keisha's face as she stood in the doorway watching him with a smirk on her face.

"Checkin' to make sure none of your fans left anything?" she asked, giving him a knowing look.

"Naw, checkin' to make sure ain't no cobwebs and shit."

"Yeah, whatever nigga," Keisha laughed and rolled her eyes.

Trigga walked up on her and grabbed her by her waist, smiling as he looked at her.

"Ain't no bitch livin' who can hold a candle to mine," he said, kissing her gently on the lips.

Keisha smiled and returned his kiss, then pulled away.

"Good," she said and then turned around to walk to the bathroom in his bedroom.

"And by the way, the panties that you *weren't* lookin' for are hanging from your ceiling fan. Whoever you was messing with before me must have been a freak. We gettin' a new bed tomorrow..."

Keisha continued talking as Trigga tried to relax after feeling all of his muscles tense up. Her voice was drowned out when she closed the bathroom door behind her and he was finally able to achieve a mild sense of calm. Frowning, Trigga looked up above his head but there wasn't anything there.

Bullshittin' ass girl, Trigga thought as he laid down on the bed and closed his eyes.

Keisha turned on the shower and started loudly singing the words to "I'll Beat That Bitch With a Bottle" as if sending Trigga a covert message in case he needed one. Snickering, Trigga turned to his side and started to drift off to sleep, feeling completely content with his life for the first time in almost a year.

It was good to finally be home.

When Keisha walked out of the bathroom after taking a shower, Trigga was knocked out on the bed. The sight of him finally getting rest made her smile. It had been forever since she'd seen him this peaceful.

Walking over, her eyes fell on his toes. It suddenly occurred to her that she had never, ever seen Trigga's feet. He always made sure that if he didn't have on shoes, he was wearing socks. When he came out of the shower, he could have been naked but he always made sure his socks were on. Being home seemed to make him more relaxed because he was lying in the bed with his bare feet exposed, showing off something that she hadn't realized he had until that moment. Webbed toes.

"Wow," Keisha whispered as she leaned in with her brows lifted to get a close look.

Trigga stirred and she tried to move quickly away but it was too late. He saw her.

"Man, Keesh, get the fuck away from my feet. Damn...you ain't 'posed to ever look at a nigga's feet. Who does that shit?" he grumbled, rolling over and tucking his feet under the covers.

"Don't act like that. It's cute," Keisha laughed. She walked over and sat next to him on the bed and leaned into his face.

"I know you're not ashamed of your lil' webbed toes."

Trigga grabbed the pillow from under his head and batted her with it, knocking her gently against the head. Keisha fell out laughing, although he looked genuinely upset.

"I thought I could trust you so I relaxed but nooooo, your traitor ass walks in and looks right at my muthafuckin' feet. Then got the nerve to get a damn close-up."

"It's cute!" Keisha repeated.

"Ain't," he rebuffed. "All the men in my family on my mom's side have webbed feet. It's a curse and ain't shit cute 'bout it."

"Well, I think it's cute. Maybe our baby will have webbed feet," she said, more to herself than to him.

"Umph," Trigga grunted and rolled over. "I'm sleepy, babe."

Keisha walked out of the room with a smile on her face, still amused at the fact that she'd discovered something about Trigga that he'd kept hidden for so long. But Trigga was anything but amused and knew that it was now unlikely that he would be able to sleep. Keisha mentioning the baby sent his mind spinning back to an issue that he'd been trying to push away from his thoughts.

Sighing heavily, he flipped over onto his back and closed his eyes. Muttering to himself about how he needed to get his head together, he willed himself to go to sleep and stop thinking about the baby. He was completely unaware that Keisha was standing at the doorway watching him and thinking about the exact same things.

TWENTY-THREE

Days later

Austin grinded his teeth together as he thought about the video that Lloyd had sent him of his torture and subsequent murder of Clay. When he had first been sent the video, he was in front of the top men of his crew getting an update on things that had happened while he was in Atlanta, as a cute, big booty shorty who was in nursing school tended to his wounds.

It hurt him like hell to sit and pretend like watching the video didn't affect him. Clay was one of Austin's most trusted friends, and he'd put him in the way of danger without properly preparing him or warning him. Something had told Austin to tell Clay not to go back home the second that he called to relay the news that he'd missed out on killing Lloyd.

Lloyd was like a cockroach. Hard as hell to kill. Even if you cut off his head, the muthafucka still survived. The only way to get rid of him was to extinguish him fully and completely, and then watch him die to make sure the job was done. He had to be put in a situation where there was no way out. Austin had to beat him at his own game. Lloyd always seemed to be ten steps ahead of everyone so it was hard to touch him. But the thing was, there was a nigga that was always ten steps ahead of Lloyd and also wanted him dead, probably more so than Austin did.

Now, having fully recuperated from the damage inflicted on him by Lloyd's goons, Austin was almost ready to get his plan back on track and get rid of Lloyd for good but he had to make sure that this time he had planned everything out perfectly so that he wasn't the one left at a disadvantage.

Pulling out his phone, he pressed 'call' and dialed a number that he knew from the moment he saved it, he would have to use.

"Yeah??" the person on the other line answered in a short, rushed tone as if Austin had called right as he were in the middle of something.

"Ay, man, you don't know me but I have a plan to get rid of all of your problems," Austin began. "My name is Austin. I'm Black's—"

"I know who da fuck you are. How da fuck did you get this number?" Trigga interjected.

Austin smiled, for some reason finding humor in the situation although he knew that it would be difficult to get Trigga to trust him.

"NeTasha gave it to me."

The line went silent. After waiting for a few seconds, Austin continued.

"We have a common enemy. Black is tryin' to get at you and, from what he told me, he's tryin' to get yo' ass first. I don't know all the details about why da fuck he want you so damn bad but I do know he got a two million dollar bounty on you and yo' girl's heads. I also know that he got a snitch workin' with him. Somebody close who been giving him info. They gave him the address to yo' crib in the A and him and his crew went and demolished that shit, thinkin' y'all was in there."

Trigga bit the inside of his cheek as he listened to Austin talk, the whole time thinking on what he'd said about Lloyd having a snitch. Only a few people knew the address to where he and Keisha had lived and one of them had been working with Lloyd. He thought back to the day he came home from the hospital with Keisha and saw Gunplay with a duffle bag full of money. He seemed nervous when Trigga spotted it.

I ain't goin even front with a two-million-dollar reward a nigga mama will turn on a nigga so it could be any damn body. Feel me?

Those were the words that Gunplay had said to Trigga that day. Could it have been him?

"So you want me to work with you to murder yo' own cousin. How da fuck do I know I can trust you?" Trigga muttered into the phone.

Austin's smile grew even wider. He had the perfect answer for him, one that he knew a nigga like Trigga wouldn't be able to ignore.

"Because if I was workin' with Black, I could have ended this when I saw Keisha in the mall. You were nowhere around. I could have killed yo' chick but I didn't because this ain't my beef. The only thing I want is to get back at my cousin for some grimy shit he did and to take over Atlanta. You not standin' in the middle of me doin' what the hell I wanna do so I don't give a shit 'bout whatever the hell beef he got with you, na'mean?"

Trigga heard everything that Austin said but his mind was still lingering on one thing.

"You saw Keisha?"

Austin tried back to hold in his laugh. It became obvious when Trigga asked how he'd gotten his number that Keisha must have not told him about their encounter at the mall, which is why he knew that tidbit of information was the piece he needed in order to gain Trigga's interest and possibly earn his trust...at least enough of it to do what he had to do. He knew right away that a lovesick nigga like Trigga wouldn't be able to ignore the fact that he hadn't been around to protect Keisha when Austin had first seen her.

"Yes, but I didn't do shit because, like I said, that's not my beef. Now, Tasha's ass had to go once I found out that bitch had fucked you after tellin' me she was a virgin. But Keisha is none of my concern."

Trigga's mind only lingered for half a second on Austin's revelation that NeTasha was dead. His real focus was on Keisha and why she'd never mentioned any of this to him.

"But anyways, back to business...I need to get rid of this nigga and I know you do, too. As they say, the enemy of my enemy is my friend. We can help each other get a one up on this nigga."

"Naw'll fuck that," Trigga told him, shaking his head. As much as he wanted to agree and listen to the plan, he'd made a promise and he needed to stick to it. He was out of Atlanta and Lloyd needed to be out of their lives. Queen's beef wasn't his, the same way Lloyd's wasn't Austin's.

"Another nigga will be down there to handle his ass for Queen. You can work with him when he gets there."

And with that, Trigga hung up the phone. Austin dropped his cell in his lap and clicked his tongue against his teeth. The call hadn't gone as planned but he wasn't worried. Although he didn't know him personally, the vibe that he got from Trigga was that they were more alike than they knew. He had a feeling that he would call back.

TWENTY-FOUR

Looking up at the majestic and luxurious home in front of him, Trigga hung up the phone and stepped out of his car. The armed guards stationed around the entrance nodded their heads at him in greeting, but their faces were grim. They knew full well that Queen would not be happy to see Trigga if he didn't have good news.

"She's expecting you already," one of the men told him, opening the front door to allow Trigga to enter.

Trigga nodded his head, his lips forming a straight line as he walked in.

The inside of the home was anything someone would image a woman by the name of 'Queen' to call home. No expense was spared and, many times before, Trigga had roamed the halls of the home wondering if he would ever take part in the family life and move into something similar with his own wife and children. Each time he'd shook his head 'no' as soon as the thought entered his mind. But this time was different. Now he had a wife and a baby on the way and the way he'd planned out his life had changed.

"Mr. Maurice!" a small voice called out to him as he walked down the long hallway to where he normally met with Queen.

Stopping in his tracks, he turned and was greeted by a beautiful sight. Queen's eight-year-old daughter, Italy, was standing in the middle of the hall, looking up at him with a big smile on her face. She looked just like her mother in every way, down to the long black hair that hung down her back in soft curls, but she had her father's blemish-free, chocolate skin-tone.

"Ay, Lee-Lee, what's up, lil' mama?" Trigga greeted her with a smile.

"Mr. Maurice, nobody calls me Lee-Lee anymore!" she laughed, her voice sounding like a wind chime.

"HEY!" another voice called out. "I didn't know you were here!"

Italy's twin brother, Rome, had peeked out to see who his sister was speaking to and was not running down the hallway. Trigga chuckled to himself as he watched him run down the hall and stop right in front of him with his hand out. Reaching into his pocket, Trigga pulled out a crisp hundred-dollar bill and placed it in the palm of his hand.

"You didn't forget," Rome beamed, looking up at Trigga.

Trigga nodded his head. "Of course not. How could I forget your entry fee?" he asked, playfully punching Rome in the shoulder.

Rome looked just like his father but had his mother's demanding and entitled personality, commanding that Trigga pay a hundred-dollar fee any time he entered the home. It was something he had started when he was four years old and used to demand one dollar. His fee had grown exponentially over the years.

"Trigga...this way," a voice thundered out from behind him. "Rome and Italy, go do what I told you to do."

The sound of their mother's voice made both children do an about-face and rush to do as she'd instructed. Clenching his jaw, Trigga turned around and looked at Queen who had a blank look on his face that he couldn't read. When it came to her, he never knew what to expect. Although Trigga had worked with her many times throughout the years, she made it very clear that there were two sides to her. There was Queen, the friend, mother and wife, and then there was Queen the head of The Queen's Cartel. But, as he looked at the expression on her face, he knew that this was not Queen, his friend. This was Queen of the Cartel, the same one who had visited him in Keisha's apartment and strapped her up in the corner. She meant business and Trigga already knew that she would not be receptive to what he needed to say but he also knew that he had to say it.

***

"Dre," Queen said, speaking to her husband that stood by her side as she sat at her desk. "Did this nigga just tell me that he wasn't going to complete the job but that he also couldn't give me back any of my money?"

Exhaling sharply, Dre sat on top of Queen's desk and nodded his head. "Yeah, dat's exactly what this nigga said."

"See, that's what I'm not understanding," Queen started as she stood up and sat next to Dre. "I paid you and your stupid ass brother to do something. You didn't do the shit and now you're tellin' me you can give me back some of the money but you can't give me back the half that I gave to Mase. Why?"

"What I'm tellin' you is that I'm out this shit. I have a wife and she's pregnant. You asked me to see to it that Lloyd and his top men who were involved in the Juwan's murder were killed and that's what I did, except for Lloyd. He's the only one alive but I will give you back half of the money you paid. I can't give you back whatever Mase was given...he's dead and the money is gone," Trigga informed her.

Standing with his hands behind his back in prison stance, Trigga looked away from Queen and towards Dre. Out of the two, Dre was the one Trigga knew best and worked with the most. In fact, Dre was the reason that he even worked with Queen to begin with. Initially, Dre had employed him to be Queen's bodyguard and shooter. But, never one to work under a boss, Trigga eventually decided to go solo and take on jobs for Queen whenever she needed someone she could rely on to get the job done.

Looking at Dre, Trigga could tell from the way he nodded his head that he understood what Trigga was saying about wanting to pull out of the job because of it being too much for him now that he had a wife and a child on the way. If ever a man existed that loved a woman the way that Trigga loved Keisha, it was Dre. His entire life, since Queen had turned sixteen years old, had been about protecting her but also allowing her to be the woman she needed to be.

That said, Trigga also knew that Dre and Queen had a very hard rule: Dre never came against Queen's decisions when it came to how she managed The Queen's Cartel, unless it dealt with something concerning the safety of her or their children. He allowed her to spread her wings and run things as she saw fit while he provided the overhead protection that she needed. He understood Trigga's stance, but he wouldn't object to whatever Queen decided.

"Our friendship is the only thing that is keeping you alive," Queen spoke finally and Trigga knew it was true. She'd ordered him to kill men for far less than what he was doing by refusing to assassinate the man responsible for the murder of her own brother.

"Kill Lloyd or give me the money back. *All* of the money. That is your only choice," she said with a tone of finality, signaling the end of the conversation. Standing up, she walked around to the other side of her desk and sat down. Her head dropped and she began to read over some papers, silently dismissing him from her presence.

Clicking his tongue in his mouth, Trigga looked over at Dre who was giving him a wide-eyed expression as if to say 'you got off easy. Hurry up and leave'. Trigga nodded his head and turned around to make his exit.

As he walked down the halls, he thought on the details surrounding what he had to do. He had no choice but to call Austin back and hear him out. If what he said really checked out and he was willing to help Trigga get rid of Lloyd so that he could take over his city, it might be the quickest way to do what he needed to do so that he could move on in peace.

The only problem now was figuring out how in the world he was going to tell Keisha.

TWENTY-FIVE

"I don't understand why this bitch says 'jump' and every nigga in ear range leaps their muthafuckin' asses in the air! Who gives a fuck about Queen? We can just leave! That bitch doesn't run the world!" Keisha fumed after hearing Trigga's explanation of why he was getting ready to get in the car and take off back to Atlanta.

It had only been a few days and it had been the best couple days of her life. For once, she didn't have to worry about Trigga leaving in the middle of the night and wondering if he would come back home. They spent their days like a normal couple, having sex, watching movies, shopping for groceries...simple shit that they'd never been able to do. And now, here was Queen messing all of that up for them.

"It's not about that, Keesh," Trigga told her through his teeth, feeling himself getting angry. "I gave my word and I have to do it. I didn't even want to ask her about that shit but I did anyways!"

"Why can't you just give her Mase's half of the money and yours too?" Keisha pouted as she laid back on the soft sofa cushions. "You don't have enough money to do that?"

"We have the money," Trigga told her, putting extra emphasis on the 'we'. "But it's money that we'll need so I can pull out of the streets for good. I have more than enough to give her what she wants but I can't put my family at risk when I'm in the middle of doing some new shit!"

Keisha rolled her eyes and exhaled loudly. She knew she was being unfair and she already knew the outcome of this conversation. Trigga would be leaving and there wasn't a thing that she could do about it. The fact was, one of the reason's she loved him so much was because he was a man of his word with a strong sense of duty. He was a man's man, a true street thug and he followed the rules of the streets. Those rules were rooted in the law of loyalty and he couldn't betray Queen no matter how much he wanted to.

"Just trust me. Let a nigga lead sometimes...wit'cho evil ass," Trigga added with a chuckle.

Kneeling down in front of her, right between her legs, he reached out and grabbed Keisha by her chin and pulled her so she could look right at him.

"Let me do what I have to do so you can live how you want to. The only shit that you worry about is this. You don't have to worry about another bitch, no outside kids...I ain't no fuckin' junkie...I'm not whoopin' yo' ass, even though you make me wanna strangle yo' disrespectful ass sometimes—" Keisha gave him a look. "—But the point is, you ain't got shit to complain about but this. Let me get this simple shit out of the way and then we can live."

"Okay," Keisha agreed quietly.

She wrapped her arms around her belly and it was almost as if her child knew her thoughts and kicked in reply. Gasping, Keisha grabbed Trigga's hand and placed it on her belly in the same spot she'd felt the kick.

"Did you feel that?!" she exclaimed when she felt it again.

Looking up, she saw a dark shadow pass through Trigga's eyes but, a second later, it was gone. Hoping that he wasn't thinking of the paternity of the baby, Keisha wanted to ask him what that was about but before she could, he smiled and she pushed away her worries.

"Yeah, I felt it," he told her. He ran his hand over her belly a few more times and then lifted up.

"There is something I want to ask you."

Still poking at her stomach, Keisha nodded her head without looking up. It was the most amazing feeling to feel her child kicking so hard in her stomach. She'd felt flutters and thumps before but it had never been so forceful as it was now. It was almost as if the baby was telling her to stop fussing and let Trigga go handle his business so he could get back home to them.

"Did you see a nigga named Austin in the mall with NeTasha a while back?"

Freezing in place, Keisha thought back to the incident that had occurred in the mall with NeTasha. She hadn't told Trigga about it when she got back because as soon as he walked in the door, he started going off about how he'd heard that she had sex with Mase and she forgot to bring it up.

"I saw NeTasha with some guy. I don't know who he was. And, yes, I did confront her because I saw that she had been blowin' up your damn phone. So OBVIOUSLY, her ass didn't learn when I beat her ass the first time!" Keisha shifted her weight to one side and placed her hand on her hips.

"Keesh, I don't give a fuck about that female shit y'all got goin' on! The nigga she was with was Black's cousin! Did he know who you were?" Trigga asked her in a way that snatched the 'stank' right out of her attitude.

Keisha's eyes opened wide as she realized what he'd just said. Although he hadn't talked to her about much concerning what was happening with Lloyd, he had mentioned to her about Austin and asked if she'd known or heard of him. She hadn't at the time but Trigga filled her in on enough for her to know that, although he looked nothing like Lloyd, he was just as vicious, terrifying and deadly.

"H—he..." she paused and lifted her eyes to the ceiling as she thought back to that day and the way that Austin had looked at her when he repeated her name. Something had clicked in his eyes and he'd watched her from that point on in a way that made her feel as if he knew something she didn't know. Then his eyes had rested on her belly...the child that Lloyd had told everyone was actually his and not Trigga's.

"Yes...he knew who I was," Keisha said finally.

A soft frown formed on Trigga's face and a glassy, glazed over look entered his eyes. For some reason unknown to her, the look affected Keisha in a way that made her feel guilty, as if she'd made a major blunder by not telling Trigga about this before.

"What did he say?"

"He didn't say anything. He just looked at me and then said 'not my beef'. After that, he grabbed Tasha and walked away. She seemed afraid..."

"NeTasha's dead," Trigga told her quietly. "He killed her for lying about her history with me."

Keisha's head snapped up to search his eyes for any kind of hint that what he'd said was a lie. When she saw that he was completely serious, her eyes filled up with tears.

"It's my fault...I shouldn't have said anything. She asked me not to!" Keisha dropped her head in her hands as she cried. "I—I saw that she was afraid but I was afraid and I said that I knew she was calling you and—"

"Keesh, it wasn't your fault. What happened to her was because of her own decisions," Trigga said, trying to calm her although he was on edge.

If Austin had wanted to, he could have ended her life then and Trigga wouldn't have known shit about it. Now more than ever, he knew he had to go do what he had to do. He didn't know Austin to trust him but he seemed like the type of nigga who only involved himself in someone's shit if it benefitted him personally. At the moment, it benefitted Austin to link up with Trigga to get rid of Lloyd. He gained nothing by killing Trigga or Keisha, which is why he hadn't bothered her when he had the chance. With everything that happened when it came to street niggas, Trigga had to go with his gut and his gut was telling him that he needed to give Austin a call back.

Reaching up, Trigga wiped the tears away from Keisha's eyes and kissed her lips.

"I have to get going. I'll get someone here to be with you so you won't be alone and I promise I'll be back as soon as I can."

Nodding her head, Keisha laid down on the sofa and stared off into space. It was obvious that she had a lot on her mind. And so did Trigga. He breathed in deeply and grabbed his phone as he walked down the hall into the bedroom door and then closed it behind him. After scrolling to his received calls, he clicked on the last number that called him pressed the call button.

"Hello?" Austin said on the other line, using a tone that made Trigga feel as though he'd expected his call.

"I'll be there," Trigga told him. "I'll call when I touch down."

TWENTY-SIX

"Yo ass is stank as fuck!" Lloyd laughed as he squatted down and eyed Karisma.

She was on the floor scooting along with her saggy diaper trailing behind her. Reaching out, he poked at it and made a face, twisting up his lips as he looked at the diaper. Humored by his expression, Karisma smiled when she saw it. LaToya sucked her teeth loudly and walked over, scooping Karisma up into her arms.

"And yo' ass need to learn how to change a diaper," LaToya remarked as she walked over to the table, grabbed a clean diaper from out of Karisma's diaper bag and the walked to the sofa so that she could change her.

"You so pwetty! Ain't you so pwetty!" LaToya baby-talked as Karisma cooed and giggled.

The little girl was starting to grow on her, which was a major thing being that she'd never really wanted to have kids. But Karisma was hard not to fall in love with. Even though she had the devil for a father, she was a happy baby, always smiling and giggling about something.

Lloyd watched their interaction with a half-smile on his face. This was how he'd always wanted things to be. Him, his bitch and his child all in the house together, living as a happy family. Unfortunately, Dior and Kenyon had to fuck all that up for him.

It's okay though, he thought to himself. *Because both of them backstabbin' muthafuckas is dead. I need to set some time aside to do the Eastside Swang on their muthafuckin' graves.*

"She's like new!" LaToya said, hovering Karisma in front of Lloyd's face.

Grabbing her around the waist, Lloyd twisted LaToya around and make her sit down on his lap, kissing her on the lips.

"Ay, what you think 'bout doin' this fo' real, fo' real?" he asked her.

LaToya rolled her eyes and leaned over to place Karisma on the floor by their feet. She took off instantly, crawling in the direction of one of her toys that was scattered around the living room.

"Do what 'fo' real, fo' real', Black?" LaToya repeated, mocking him.

Lloyd reached over and squeezed her ass. "I mean, this family shit. Like, me and you...and mama over there. You know, you let a nigga beat up in them guts officially."

LaToya rolled her eyes once more and slid off of Lloyd's lap.

"That's the best way you can say what you tryin' to say?"

"Toy, don't start this shit!" Lloyd stood up and looked at her as she sat in front of him with her arms crossed in front of her, resembling a spoiled brat. A sexy ass one, at that.

"Start what, nigga? You only want me around because you need somebody to take care of the baby! If you hadn't 'sent her mama on vacation'—" She used air quotes. "—I wouldn't be here playing babysitter. Now you just tryin' to lock me down for good so you don't have to worry about it."

"Man, Toy, kill that shit. I don't need your ass to help me take care of my daughter! Ain't shit out here I can't do," Lloyd shot back, his black face twisted in anger.

"Oh yeah? Change a damn diaper then!" she huffed.

Running his tongue along his top row of gold teeth, Lloyd smirked at LaToya, fully realizing what was wrong with her. It had been a few days since he'd gotten up between her thighs and he knew that's where the attitude was coming from. Why else would she be spitting all that bullshit about him not really caring about her? She needed a sample of his anaconda dick to put her ass to sleep so she could wake up in a better mood.

"Ay, put Karisma in the crib. It's time for a nap," he told her, pulling her up from the sofa by her arms. "Everybody need to take a nap."

"What?! I'm not sleepy," she said grabbing Karisma from off the floor. The little girl yawned as if she already knew what was coming.

"Yo' ass is cranky so we gone see." He smacked her on her ass and watched her walk away.

When LaToya walked into the bedroom, Lloyd was already on the bed naked as the day God made him, stroking his big, thick black dick.

"You want me to suck it, daddy?"

LaToya licked her lips hungrily in anticipation of what was about to happen. Lloyd chuckled as he watched her. He knew that this was exactly what she had needed. He hadn't even done anything yet and she was already getting her act together.

"Yeah, come suck me up real quick."

Before he could say anything further, LaToya was in his lap, sucking him up like a pro with her hands inside of her short shorts, fingering herself.

"Get on top of it," Lloyd demanded when he couldn't wait any longer. Her head game was all that but he wanted to feel some pussy.

When she sat on top of him and started grinding, he lost his entire mind. Flipping her over, he pushed her ass up in the air and got behind her beating it up from the back, just like he liked. They both came in minutes and LaToya collapsed on the bed, breathing heavily as Lloyd lay beside her, deep in his thoughts.

"Ay, I wanna keep you around for good," he told her, thinking over his life. He didn't want to admit it but parts of him missed having Dior's crazy ass around.

Before she betrayed him and started fucking with Kenyon, she was the truth definition of a ride or die and did any and everything he needed. He missed having someone real by his side. Someone he could always count on to pray at night that he made it home. He wanted a family.

The same type of shit that fuck ass nigga, Trigga, 'bout to have with my baby and my bitch, he thought to himself.

"I'll stay," LaToya said, sleep falling upon her. "Just don't fuck around on me and we're good. I don't play that shit."

Lloyd tried to suppress laughter at a woman telling him what the fuck to do with his dick. Dior hadn't been able to do it, and he actually loved her. LaToya was bugging if she thought she had what it took to change a nigga.

"A'ight, baby," he said, pulling her into his arms. "You got it. Whatever you want, a nigga will do."

'I don't play that shit', Lloyd mocked her in his thoughts. *Get da fuck outta here with that bullshit.*

TWENTY-SEVEN

A cool autumn breeze caused a ripple through the trees, making the leaves blow and mix with the strewn trash that lightly littered the small parking lot. Trigga watched the combination of leaves and trash begin to swirl like a miniature tornado as he stood halfway outside his rented black Dodge Changer with one foot in and the other inside the vehicle and the motor running. He was prepared to mash out in the event the there was an ambush. He kept his .9mm aimed at his possible victim's head. He wasn't taking any chance, even at the expense of enraging Austin.

"Nigga, this how you playin'? Gone get me to meet you here in a fuckin' abandoned shoe store parking lot and ambush me?!" Austin roared with his hands raised high as he had been told to do by Trigga...or else get shot.

"Yo, I told you from day one I didn't trust you, nigga. So just keep yo' fuckin' hands up in the air!" Trigga demanded while waving the banger, causing the thick Cuban link diamond bracelet on his wrist to sparking in the moonlight.

A blue Chevy Impala posted on the side of the street, began moving forward and did a slow creep; which wasn't part of Triggas's plan. Instantly, the sound of a cartridge being engaged into an assault rifle could be heard from inside the black Charger. Trigga had recruited one of his most trusted homies to come to Atlanta with him for the dangerous mission. UGod, was perched in the backseat with the tinted window partial down and the AK-47 barely visible, sticking out the window. Just enough to where a passing spectator couldn't see the enormous weapon but enough for Austin to know the high powered assault rifle was aimed at his head and, for that, he was furious. Truth be told, he was also in fear of his life; Trigga had the ups on him.

"Man, that shit was all on the news where I tried to get my crew to body Lloyd's bitch ass! And I sent you the video of him killing my dude, Clay, and the pictures of us as shawties. Clay was my nigga! I just want the club that I spent all that damn money on and to take over the trap houses I had niggas serving my work out of!"

The tone of Austin's voice was near a frantic plea as he lowered his hands.

"Nigga put yo' muthafuckin' hands back up!" UGod barked from the backseat of the car.

He was a bear of a man, at 6'6 and two hundred and forty pounds. He wore a thick scrappy beard, with tiny, beady hazel eyes, that looked like they were set too close together in his skull. He wasn't the most attractive man but he was intelligent and not much got pass him. His expression was always stoic, unemotional like he just didn't have a care in the world because he didn't. That day he was in Atlanta to do a job: kill anything that moved.

Trigga scratched the stubble underneath his chin as he thought over the events that had lead him up to this point. Austin did have a valid point, however. Trigga had heard the news of the massacre at the club and Lloyd was lucky to have gotten away with his life. Remembering the photos of Austin and Clay as children at the neighborhood YMCA in basketball uniforms with their arms around each other's neck in a brotherly hug, Trigga could see their bond and strangely it reminded him of his brother.

But still...

"Nigga, how I know you ain't trying to set me up? Dat fuck nigga, Black, got a two-million-dollar reward out for me and my lady," Trigga mentioned, then noticeably flinched when he heard a noise. It was the sound of the wind pushing a beer can across the concrete parking lot behind him.

"Man, I want this nigga dead and gone just as much as you do—"

"Hold up! If that Impala come thru here one more time, I'ma wet your ass up. I ain't fuckin' playin' wit'cha!" UGod exploded from the backseat.

Bewildered, Trigga didn't have a clue what he talking about until Austin spoke in an urgent voice.

"Okay! Okay! Them just my people. They checking on me. That's on everything I love. I told them to watch my back."

"Well, they bouta get your fuckin' back blown out! You better tell 'em to bounce. If I see dat muthafuckin' whip one more time I'ma jus' start blasting!" UGod yelled and swung the door all the way open.

He stepped out intentionally so whoever was in the passing car could see him looking in their direction.

"Fuck! Man, sorry about that," Austin said apologetically and began to wave frantically for the car to keep going.

Trigga was taken aback but grateful by how keen UGod's sense of awareness was and also to the fact, he hadn't really paid that much attention to the vehicle until then.

"I see you finna make a nigga wet your ass up all ready. You must have not checked my resume," Trigga said, he was slightly vexed. "Now speak. What's your plan?"

"Okay..." Austin began, relaxing when UGod lowered his weapon. "Lloyd is a sucka for pussy. Any bad bitch with a fat ass and a pretty face. On the night he was at the club and I tried to have him killed by his ex-lieutenant, Block, Clay had already sent some stripper bitches at him to set him up and get him into a hotel. One of them was answering to Redd and the other Ronisha."

"Well, what the fuck happened?" Trigga asked with a frown, then shifted his position on his feet; his leg still bothered him at times.

"The nigga got a phone call or something and left early. It just so happened that Block and the crew was in place but they still missed," Austin said with dismay and closed his eyes for a minute. He was still regretting the death of Clay.

"So what does that have to do with me being able to get at his ass?" Trigga asked.

"Man, I don't trust this nigga." UGod commented all of a sudden; Trigga ignored him.

"Tonight, he gone meet up with both of the chicks, Red and Ronisha, at the Best Western Hotel in Buckhead. They gone put a mickey in the nigga drink then call me when it's time to move. They will be in room 313. It's easy," Austin said with a shrug.

"If it's easy why in the fuck can't you do it? Why you need us?" UGod said taking the words right out of Trigga's mouth.

"Because this nigga Lloyd got a crew call Ground Patrol and they the truth! A bunch of ruthless ass young project niggas that's always somewhere close. They would recognize me or my dudes on sight."

Just as Austin said that, his phone started chiming.

Trigga walked over briskly with his banger at his side. "Answer it and place the call on speaker phone."

Austin looked at the caller I.D. causing his eye brows to knot up. He answered the call:

"Yo, what da fuck?!" he said into the phone.

A husky voice returned. "Nigga, you good? Why you wave us off?"

"Yea, I'm good! And don't bring dat muthafuckin' car back round here. I'm with my niggaz. We finna take over this fuckin' city. I'll call y'all later on."

He disconnected the call.

Suddenly something occurred to UGod, "If you can't get close to da nigga how in the fuck is Trigga supposed to?"

"This nigga, Trigga, done ran up in about a half dozen of Lloyd's trap houses and done murked a gang of niggas. I figured if he couldn't do it nobody can and, not just that, I got a hundred thousand dollars on the backseat. You can take it. It's all yours if you can pull it off," Austin attempted to persuade them as he looked between both Trigga and UGod.

Trigga glanced inside the car and there was a Gucci bag on the floorboard.

"Man, let's kill this pretty ass nigga, take his money and go back to the Apple," UGod said causing Austin take a hesitant step back, like he was thinking of reaching for his strap.

"No...I can do it. I have an idea," Trigga said with his mind percolating. Then he walked over and took the money out the vehicle.

"Fuck, you robbing a nigga?!" Austin gawked at him.

"Nope, I'm making sure I get paid up front, nigga. Just ask anybody about Trigga. My word is bond or else you would have already been leaking on the pavement dead, na'mean?"

Austin couldn't help but agree as he watched Trigga stroll back over to the car with his duffle bag full of money in one hand and gun in the other. Seconds later, he and UGod were gone.

***

They were seated in parked cars, side by side, in the back of the parking lot on the opposite end of the hotel as inconspicuous as possible. The radio was on V-103, the quiet storm. UGod couldn't stop snickering and giggling at the get up that Trigga was wearing; a big ass wig and a maid's uniform of some type.

"My nigga this shit ain't funny," Trigga said and crossed his legs as he peered out the window.

"It may not be funny to you but, nigga, you got pigeon legs! And wearing dat goddamn wig, you looking like some of these chicks I used to guard when they went out on Halloween night dates from those muthafuckin' online ads."

Trigga just looked at UGod, shaking his head.

UGod laughed some more; in fact, he laughed so hard his sides hurt.

"Yo, Yo, they just called." Austin gestured with the wave of his hands. However, unlike UGod, he wasn't smiling; he had too much to lose. If this failed, he was at a loss as to what to do next. It was as if Lloyd had eyes in the back of his head, they had to be careful.

Trigga stashed the 22 caliber throw away in his apron and hopped out the car headed for room 313.

***

The FBI sat in an unmarked white van during their covert operation. They had been investigating Lloyd for months, even before he had beat his last charge and got out of jail on a technicality. Persistent as a pack of hungry wolves, the Feds were finally ready to indict him under the federal Rico Kingpin Act, which stood for Racketing, Influence, and Corruption Organization. It carried a life sentence with over a five-million-dollar fine, if convicted. The Feds felt they finally had enough evidence to convict Lloyd and put him away for life. It just so happened that they were there, outside of the hotel, on the same day Trigga had come to murder Lloyd. They had also followed him there.

An agent with platinum blond hair and a long beak nose was in the vehicle with three other agents and coincidentally peered, through night binoculars, up at room 313 when Trigga walked by dressed as a maid and walked around the corner to the elevator. There was a total of eight agents staked out and ready for the big takedown that night.

"Damn, that big bitch walks like her damn feet killing her," one of the agents commented, causing giddy laughter to ensue afterwards.

***

Room 313

"Oh shit! Suck dat dick! Lick them balls, fu...fu...fu..fuck!" Lloyd stammered as one of the girls, maybe Redd—he couldn't remember her name—had her finger slid deep in his ass gyrating and tstroking his prostate. Ronisha, the younger of the two, was lying on her back, butt naked underneath Redd, eating her pussy like she was a delicacy.

All of a sudden, Redd pulled Lloyd's dick out of her mouth, a dribble of saliva and pre-cum dangling off her thick bottom lip. Then she reached over on the nightstand and handed Lloyd his drink.

"Hey, bae...drink some more. I want you to cum in my mouth," she tried to talk straight but Ronisha was on the brink of giving her an orgasm.

Her eyes rolled to the back of her head. She couldn't help it, she spread her legs wider as Ronisha drove in and plowed her tongue deeper.

"Sheeeiit!" Redd cried out in ecstasy.

The entire orgy experience turned Lloyd on. His dick was hard as a rock as Redd masterfully played in his ass. Just as he was about to take another swig from the drink, he saw something floating on top. It was green...in fact, it looked like green slime. It was right around the time he started to feel light-headed.

"What the fuck is this?" he asked, staring inside the glass so hard he looked cock-eyed.

Both girls exchanged muted glances.

Ronisha slid from under Redd and quickly stood up, causing her small perky breasts to sway. She was the one that had mixed up the concoction for the drink but, at the time, she had been high as fuck off Loud.

"Oh, it's just dirty glasses," she said with a bob of her head a she looked inside Lloyd's drink. She reached out and stroked his penis. He was rock hard.

"We ordered some ice. Just waiting for room service now."

They both nodded their heads at the same time.

There was a soft knock at the door, causing Lloyd to jump to attention like he had been dosed with a bucket of ice.

Ronisha rushed over to the door just as Lloyd was telling her 'no' while, at the same time, reaching for his banger.

Not even noticing his actions, Ronisha opened the door.

***

Trigga waited with his heart racing in his chest after he knocked on the door and, for the first time in his life, he had a gut feeling he had made a tragic mistake. For some strange reason, he thought about Keisha.

The door opened with a *whoosh*. Cool air hit him in the face, along with the sound of the hotel air conditioner whirring.

Hidden in the dim of the hotel light, Trigga detected movement. Vaguely, he made out the image of bodies moving.

"Who is that?" came a man's voice.

A voice he recognized all too well. It was Lloyd.

"It's the maid. She's here is with the ice," the chick said, she was completely nude. They already knew about the lick and that Trigga was coming dressed as the maid. She opened the door wider and stepped to the side.

With the gun positioned under the ice bucket, Trigga went into action.

He walked into the room, just as Lloyd tried to get up from the bed with his banger in his hand and his stiff penis swinging. He aimed at Trigga.

But he was too late.

The drugs had him too slow and, even as he tried to fight it, he still recognized that something was wrong. He managed to fire his gun, bullets hit the ceiling as Trigga fired back repeatedly at him, at point-blank range. Each shot was more deadly than the next until, finally, his body dropped to the ground.

The women scrambled to grab their clothes and scurried out the door, barefoot and screaming.

***

"What the fuck was that?" one of the F.B.I. agents anxiously asked, pointing up to the room. But it was dark and the smog was heavy, making visibility difficult.

"I don't know but we need to get the fuck out of here. Our guy has a reputation for gang land violence and murder. Let's take him into custody. NOW!"

The agent gave the order over his radio and they all got out of their vehicles with guns drawn and ran towards the stairs and elevator to get to room 313.

***

"Finally, I got your bitch ass," Trigga gritted as he stood over Lloyd with his body riddled with bullets.

One shot was to his neck, causing blood to spew in a jet stream, soiling the brown carpet. The front door was wide open and Lloyd's gun lay next him on the carpet, out of reach.

Spitting up blood, Lloyd coughed violently.

"That fuck ass bitch set me up...drugged a nigga and now you show up. How much money you want? Tell me what you want to let me walk out of here!" Lloyd croaked.

Trigga bent down, squatting, as he placed the gun to Lloyd's head, the barrel was still smoldering from the shots he had just fired.

"I want your life. I want to take you out of here and to make sure there is no more Lloyd on this Earth. Nothing of yours left on this planet," Trigga said with a raspy voice as he cocked the gun at Lloyd's temple.

Lloyd laughed a dry cackle and spit up more blood.

"There will always be a Lloyd as long...as long your new bitch...AKA, my old bitch, has my baby in her stomach. Nigga...I'ma always be alive—"

Pop! Pop!

Trigga shot Lloyd in the head. The small 22 caliber sound resonated in the small confines of the room.

Suddenly, Trigga thought he heard the elevator door ding, signaling that it was opening and it brought him back to reality. He quickly picked up the empty ice bucket with his prints on it and, just as he was exiting the room, he thought he heard footsteps. He looked over the hotel balcony and saw a platoon of what looked like undercover police, racing across the parking lot. Right as he took off walking, someone shouted for him to get out the way. Instantly, he recognized the badges as they raced right passed him. They were Federal agents. Trigga managed to take the back stairwell and exit back to the car where UGod sat, waiting. Austin stood up, delivered Trigga a curt nod then dapped him up and they each went their separate ways.

As soon as the car pulled off and made it safely onto the expressway, UGod turned to him and said, with a dead serious expression.

"My nigga, I sure don't want to be your enemy. You went up there and got that nigga...then escaped past a fuckin' army of cops, too. I thought it was a wrap for you for a minute."

Trigga reared his head back on the head rest and tried to enjoy his victory. But, for some reason, Lloyd's last words echoed in his head.

As long as your new bitch, AKA my old bitch, has my baby in her stomach, I'ma always be alive...

TWENTY-EIGHT

Keisha awoke in excruciating pain in the dead of night. The first thing that she did was reach out for Trigga, but when her hand fell on empty space, her heart dropped to the pit of her stomach. Twisting around in the bed to free her other arm, she wrapped one arm around her belly, the source of the pain, and ripped the covers from off of her legs with the other.

She could feel a warm sticky feeling between her legs and a feeling of dread washed over her as she felt around on the damn sheets, her mind trying to make sense of what was happening to her. Moaning lightly, Keisha reached out to turn on the light next to her, biting her lip to assist in bearing the pain. But when she switched on the light, nothing could have prepared her for what she saw next. The sheets were dotted with spots of blood and a wet substance. She was losing the baby.

Opening her mouth, Keisha let out the loudest, most terrifying scream as she cradled her stomach in her hands and cried out for help. Within seconds, her bedroom door burst open with so much force that it was a miracle it had managed to stay on the hinges.

"What is wrong?!" Carolina ran in with a confused look plastered across her face.

Carolina was Queen's mother-in-law whom Queen had 'volun-told' to watch after Keisha while Trigga was away. Trigga had asked if Queen would stay with her, a request she quickly declined, but sent her mother-in-law instead.

When her eyes settled on the bloody sheets on the bed, Carolina gasped and ran to Keisha and snatched the phone off of her nightstand.

"Hello, 9-1-1? I need an ambulance immediately! The address is…"

As Carolina spoke, Keisha's eyes clouded over with tears as she rocked gently from side-to-side, wrapping herself around the girth of her stomach with her arms. Tears ran down her cheeks as she cried and prayed to God to spare the life of her child. No matter who the father was, not once had she ever hoped or wished for her baby to be harmed. It hurt her to her heart to think that she could possibly be losing it.

"I need to call Trigga," Carolina stated anxiously as she snatched the silk wrap off her head and started scrolling through the contacts in Keisha's phone. She put the phone to her ear and sat down next to Keisha, rubbing her back and forth on the back.

"It will be okay, mama," she said to her in a gentle tone that immediately gave Keisha some sense of calm. "Just breathe and relax. You have to do that for the baby. It will be alright."

Trigga picked up the phone and Carolina started to fill him in on everything as Keisha tried to block out her words. She closed her eyes and tried to think of what it would be like to hold her healthy child in her arms, to escape this moment of helplessness and go right to the period where she would finally experience the joy of being a mother.

"Keisha," Carolina called softly to her, pulling her out of her blissful reverie. "He wants to speak to you."

Reluctantly releasing her belly, Keisha reached out with one hand and grabbed the phone from Carolina. Taking a deep breath, she put it to her ear but she couldn't manage to say a word.

"Keesh, I'm on my way, baby," Trigga said in a calm tone that had an urgent, crispness to it at the same time. It was as if he was forcing himself to be composed, although his nature was fighting against it.

"Keep calm and wait for me. I'll be there before you know it. Everything will be fine. I love you."

"I love you too," Keisha said back and then dropped the phone to her side as she collapsed into tears in Carolina's arms.

***

As the medical staff ran through the hospital pushing her on the stretcher, Keisha gritted her teeth and squeezed the metal rods to her side, trying her hardest not to scream out loud in painful pleas for someone to knock her out and stop the pain that she felt.

"Breathe, baby, breathe!" Carolina's voice hovered somewhere above her head but she couldn't quite place it.

Every image passed in front of her eyes in flashes that seemed to uncannily coincide with the tremors of pain that ripped through her body. Unable to hold back any longer, Keisha held on to her belly with both hands and screamed out in agony and anguish, praying that the life inside her would not be lost.

And then everything went black.

When Keisha came to, she was in a hospital bed housed inside of a bare room, except for the television mounted on the egg-shell walls. The episodic beeps of the machines around her, invaded her consciousness and assisted with pulling her out of her dreams. Shifting slowly, Keisha looked to her side and saw Carolina lying back in a chair next to her bed. Her eyes were closed and her hands were clasped in front of her as she slept peacefully, seeming almost angelic.

There was a tube coming from Keisha's nose delivering oxygen and another in the bend of her arm that was connected to an I.V. situated beside her. Her mouth felt clammy and dry. Looking around the room, which held a strong and almost repugnant odor of disinfectant and ammonia. Keisha located a pale pink jug of water and reached for it. Just as her fingers connected with the handle, a tall, chocolate-skinned Black woman with a long, black ponytail walked in wearing a white coat.

"You're awake," she noted, looking into Keisha's face.

Walking over to the table near her bedside, she grabbed the jug of water and poured Keisha a cup full. Silently, Keisha grabbed the cup with shaky hands and readied herself to hear the bad news. Was her baby gone or was something else wrong?

"I actually came in here to check and see how far you've dilated." Noting the relieved expression on Keisha's face, the doctor continued. "Your baby is fine but he will be delivered tonight. Either by C-section or we will induce you to hurry everything along. But first, I want to check your progress at this point to see if we can move everything along naturally."

"Okay," Keisha whispered but her mind was on Trigga.

She checked the clock on the wall. It was about four hours after when she last spoke to him. Was that enough time for him to catch a plane back? Would he be back in time to see the baby be born? Or, would it be better that he didn't show up being that there was a huge possibility that it wasn't his to begin with?

Wrapped up in the deep complex corners of her mind, Keisha didn't even realize the daughter was done examining her until she felt her pull her hand out from between her legs.

"You're already about seven centimeters dilated. Only three to go! You may be able to have this baby on your own."

The doctor smiled and Keisha flinched subtly. She knew exactly what the doctor meant when she mentioned Keisha having the baby on her own, but her statement was too close to the reality of Keisha's situation. If she had the baby and it turned out Trigga wasn't the father, she felt as if there was a real possibility that she would really be left having a baby on her own.

***

"Ay, man, what's up?" Trigga spoke into the phone as he hustled out of the exit of LaGuardia airport, his eyes searching back and forth for a cab.

Raising his hand in the air with the phone tucked between his ear and shoulder, he watched with a deep frown on his face as two cabs sped by and stopped a way behind him to pick up two other lighter-complexioned customers. The old saying regarding how hard it was for a brotha in New York City to find a cab was true. It was damn near impossible.

Walking over to where a white man stood with his hand out to flag down a cab, Trigga stuffed his hand in his pocket and turned his attention to the person on the phone.

"Ain't shit. Just wanted to tell you that I'm back home now. I left after I handled that shit I told you 'bout concerning ole girl," Gunplay said, alluding to Tish. "Anyways, you in the city?"

"Yeah, man. Just got here, racing to the hospital. I sent you a text earlier about what was goin' on with Keesh. Anyways, what you up to?"

Trigga scanned the streets as he spoke. He saw a cab approaching and watched as it slowed down to pick up the man next to him. As soon as it came to a stop, he jumped up and ran to it, opened the door and sat down. The white man who had hailed the cab made a face as if he wanted to say something but then changed his mind when he got a good look at the deep scowl on Trigga's face and found something better to do. After rattling off his destination to the driver, Trigga tuned back in to Gunplay as he continued.

"Tavi got me over here at her mama's crib and I'ma 'bout to nut the fuck up if Mom Dukes keep talkin' dropping all these damn hints 'bout us gettin' married and shit. The only reason I'm still sittin' over here is because she cooked and a nigga hungry as fuck. You know Tavi ass didn't cook shit the whole time we as in the A, my nigga."

Gunplay groaned and Trigga laughed, although he could relate. Keisha didn't cook either but he didn't mind it because he had no problem with making a meal, although he would never admit that to Gunplay. That was the type of shit that you only told your girl and nobody else.

"Anyways, you good, nigga? That's why I really wanted to call. I was tryin' to catch you before you got to Keisha," Gunplay informed him finally.

Sighing heavily, Trigga ran his hand over his face and then nodded his head.

"Yeah, I'm good. I got this shit regardless of what the outcome is. Even if he's not, I'm gonna raise shorty like he mine," Trigga replied.

"Yeah...sounds good."

Immediately, Trigga began to feel himself get furious.

"What the fuck do you mean by that?"

The cab driver shot a tense look in Trigga's direction as he swerved through traffic, determined to hurry and get him to his destination before he snapped.

"Calm down, nigga. Damn, shawty be makin' you nut up fast as hell," Gunplay told him. "All I'm sayin' is that I know they type of nigga you are so I know what you gonna do but I also know how niggas think. You ain't no bitch ass nigga so I know you gone handle yours. But on some real shit, I just wanted to know where your head was 'bout this whole thing because it's hard as hell hatin' a nigga and then seein' his ass every day when you look at your chick's baby, na'mean."

Gunplay had a point and it was something that Trigga had thought about the entire two hours that he was on the plane back to New York. He knew that he could make his actions line up with what Keisha needed him to do but he had no idea how he would feel. He could say how he would feel all day but some things you don't know until you're experiencing it.

The cab stopped and it was at that moment that Trigga realized that they were in front of the hospital and Gunplay was no longer on the phone. He was so in his thoughts that he didn't even remember when the call ended. Stuffing his cell in his pocket, he pushed eighty dollars into the cab driver's hand and muttered for him to keep the change before sliding out of the car.

Running his face over his hands, he let out a sharp breath and walked onto the elevator, pressing the button for the maternity floor. On the elevator with him was a young, black woman in scrubs. She lifted one eyebrow as she looked at the anxious expression on Trigga's face.

"This your first baby?" she asked him.

Turning towards the sound of her voice, Trigga nodded, giving her a quick once over. She had a gentle, friendly face and was young but didn't appear to be coming on to him, even though she was definitely interested in what was going on in his mind.

"Yeah," he replied curtly and averting his gaze.

"Just be there for her. She'll say all kinds of things to you but don't pay any attention to them. Just do whatever she needs and do it quickly. It'll be over before you know it." She smiled with him as the elevator doors opened and then patted him on the shoulder and walked out.

Trigga walked out behind her and stopped at the locked double doors as she walked in the opposite direction. He picked up the phone on the wall and waited for the receptionist to pick up.

"Hello, how can I help you?"

"Hi…My name is Maurice Blevins. I'm here to see my wife. Keisha O'Neal-Blevins. She's about to have m—my son," he said firmly into the phone.

"Oh, you're just in time, she's been asking about you! I believe they are telling her to push right now! Come on back!"

Before Trigga could even wrap his head around what was being said, the lock on the doors clicked, allowing him entry. With each step that Trigga took, his heart thump louder than a drum. Never before had he been afraid of anything but Keisha changed that for him when he fell in love with her. His life changed dramatically because, for once, he knew what it was like to lay awake at night and be afraid because the person you care about more than anything is not there with you and you can't be sure that she's safe. Now another person was coming into the world and the fear he felt would multiply from one to two.

He looked to his right and saw a short blond woman sitting at the receptionist's desk frantically pointing at a room only a few doors down from where he stood. She was saying something to him but he couldn't make out the words, everything was a blur and the only thing he could make sense of was the burning feeling in his chest; the tension he felt as he neared the room, hoping like hell that his wife was okay.

Trigga pushed open the door to Keisha's room and walked in, his thoughts merging immediately as his eyes settled on the sight in front of him. The doctor, a Black woman, was seated between Keisha's legs which were gaped wide open with her knees up, and her arms were damn near up to the elbows inside of Keisha's innermost part. Two nurses surrounded her, watching intently with their eyes on every single thing that was occurring as if they were being taught a lesson. Carolina was on Keisha's side with her hands to her mouth and tears in her eyes as she watched the birth. An anesthesiologist sat near Keisha's side, running her hand back and forth along her back, instructing her to push and then breathe.

And then, finally, Trigga's eyes settled on Keisha. She was beautiful and soaking wet with sweat. Her long, black hair was drenched and plastered onto the side of her face as she gritted her teeth and tried her hardest to give birth to her son.

Their son.

"Keesh," Trigga called out to her as he walked to her side. "You can do this baby. You can give life to our son."

Although she was in an enormous amount of pain, seeing Trigga and feeling his presence near her gave her an inkling of calm and subdued the anxiety that she had felt in his absence.

"I can see the head!" the doctor shouted as she stared down between Keisha's legs. "Stop! Okay, one more big push on the count of three. One...two...three...PUSH!"

Trigga placed his hand over Keisha's as he tried to resist the urge to leave her side and peek down at the baby to see if he could see any traces of himself. It wasn't the time. Keisha was still grunting and moaning as if she were about to be pulled apart and he had to be there for her.

"Okay...one more push is all we need! You're doing a great job, Keisha! Count of three...One...Two...THREE...PUUUUSSSSHHH!"

"AARRRRRGGGHHHHHH!" Keisha yelled and pushed with everything she had in her.

It was the last piece of energy that she had left and she prayed it was enough because she didn't have any more to give. Collapsing on the bed, she fell out, nearly in a daze and shivering from the cold sweat that covered her.

Then it dawned on her. There was no sound. Her baby wasn't crying.

Her eyelids started to flutter as she felt energy from somewhere returning to her body and she lifted up, her heart beating ferociously in her chest as she waited anxiously for her son to make a sound to let her know that he was okay. She looked over to where the nursing staff was working, doing things to him that she couldn't see because their bodies were covering him completely.

"What is..." she started and then looked up at Trigga for answers.

He was standing, his eyes on the activity as he watched from a higher view, taking in everything that was happening before his eyes. As Keisha looked up at him, she saw that his eyes had filled with tears. She watched as his jaw clenched and unclenched before one lone tear slid down his cheek. He brushed it away gently.

"Trigga, is he..." Keisha asked, her voice interrupting his thoughts.

Caught up in emotion, he looked down at her and shook his head, unable to speak.

"He's fine...he..." Unable to finish his sentence, he pointed over to the baby and that's when she saw it.

Keisha couldn't make out much but she saw one thing as she peeked through the bodies that surrounded him, almost covering his little body. But in the middle of the crowd, she made out his tiny little feet, batting around in the air in distress as he fought to understand what was going on with him and why.

Keisha smiled at the exact moment that he opened his mouth and allowed her to hear the most beautiful sound that she had ever heard in her entire life. His cry.

"WAAAAAAAAAA!!"

Tears slid down her face as the doctor walked over and lifted him up in the air and brought him over to where she sat waiting with her arms out, wanting nothing more than to hold him.

And to kiss his little webbed toes.

TWENTY-NINE

"You have a visitor," a voice said from behind Keisha's back.

She woke up with a start, not even knowing, until that moment, that she'd fallen asleep. Instinctively, she jumped up and reached for her child, Cameron Maurice Blevins, who had been lying next to her last she remembered. Once she noticed that he wasn't there, she turned around and saw that Trigga was holding him in his arms. He was wide awake, looking at his daddy with the widest eyes she'd ever seen on something so small.

Cameron was only a couple days old and was already so alert, his beautiful gray eyes monitoring everything around him. He had been born early and had a few medical issues, but he was strong. There was nothing weak about him.

"Who?" Keisha asked once she finally thought about what Trigga had said.

Before he could answer her, three big burly men walked in wearing all black with weapons at the hip, among many other places. You couldn't see the heat they were holding, but one look at them let Keisha know that they would never in life pass through a metal detector. They were strapped like the United States Army. Keisha shot a nervous glance at Trigga but he wasn't paying too much attention to anything other than the small child in his arms that was reaching out for his face.

"Trigga, I—"

Before Keisha could finish her sentence, in walked Queen in all her splendor, dressed like a model for the Balmain clothing line, sparkling like a star with each step. She was a sight to make even the most beautiful woman feel subconscious about her appearance, perfectly put together as if she woke up runway ready.

At first glance, it was hard to believe that this was a woman who sat at the head of an empire so powerful and vicious, that she'd never met an enemy that had a chance at defeating her. But once you looked into her eyes, you could see that she wasn't as gentle as she looked. She had a merciless stare that stayed whether she was smiling or not. Everything about her aura screamed that she was not to be fucked with.

And in case someone thought that none of those threatening things, which came natural to her, were enough to deter them from trying her, she had a man at her side that looked even more cruel and heartless than she did. This was Keisha's first time seeing Dre, the man who she'd only heard about, who was the only man able to be on the receiving end of Queen's love. The first time that Keisha had heard from Trigga that Queen was married and had children, she called him a liar so many times that he had to swear on his mama's grave that he was telling the truth before she believed him. It just seemed so unthinkable that any man would be able to break her into someone capable of love and passion. But when Keisha looked at him, she saw that he was just like her.

Dre was a handsome man, with a similar build to Trigga, only not as tall. But his presence made him seem like a giant, as he stood next to his wife, holding her hand. That simple act of affection had Keisha blown as she observed them. It was so odd and so loving at the same time; seeing two people, who didn't think twice about killing another, showing such an act of love for each other ...there was something about it that almost took her breath away.

"Keesh, this is Queen and Dre," Trigga introduced them.

Queen shot Trigga a look and a sheepish expression crossed his face, followed by a small smirk. He cleared his throat and looked back to Keisha who was now frowning as she tried to figure out what was going on. Dre had a sly grin on his face as his eyes went back and forth between Queen's vicious side-eye and Trigga's awkward expression.

"I mean, this is Queen and Dre...Cameron's godparents," Trigga corrected himself.

Keisha lifted one eyebrow at Trigga who gave her a wide-eyed look and shrugged as if to say "What you expect me to do?".

When Keisha glanced back over to Queen, her entire countenance had changed. The threatening gaze was gone and was replaced by one of pleasure and awe, as she peeked over Trigga's shoulder and stared at Cameron. She released Dre's hand and held out her hands, palms up, to her side.

Without missing a beat, one of her security guards squeezed a bottle of hand sanitizer and delivered the contents in her hand. The other men snickered at the look on his face as he followed her unspoken order, obviously not pleased at all to be the one on sanitizer duty. With a flick of her wrist, she dismissed all of the men and they filed outside of the room, closing the door shut behind them.

Keisha watched as Queen stepped over to Trigga and reached out, plucking the baby right from his hands without asking, which Keisha had become accustomed to her doing. Queen never asked for anything and no one ever said anything about it.

Holding Cameron in her hands, she rocked him gently back and forth, smiling and laughing at him as she talked to him in a calm, tender voice. Cameron cooed in her arms, fully enjoying her song and dance. Dre, obviously catching the bewildered look on Keisha's face as she watched Queen's transition from coldhearted-bitch-killer to doting god-mommy, walked over and smiled down at her.

"Queen wants to have another one but that shit ain't happenin' no time soon. Rome and Italy are giving me hell. Both of them niggas got her muthafuckin' attitude, turning all my shit on my head gray," Dre joked as he ran a hand over the top of his head.

"Ay, fam, I know what you mean," Trigga joked walking over to where Dre stood and extending his fist for dap. "This lil' nigga ain't even been here a full day and his lil' ass tryin' to tell everybody what the hell to do."

"Well, Queen's ass is gone spoil him, that's for sure. Keisha, don't be afraid to tell her to give you back your damn child. Matter of fact," Dre swiveled around on his feet and looked at his wife. "Queen, bring dat baby over here! I don't want your ass gettin' anymore ideas."

Queen scoffed at Dre and rolled her eyes before turning her attention back to Cameron. Keisha looked back and forth between her and Dre, for the first time seeing them in their natural state with their guard down. They were a regular, loving couple just like her and Trigga but they'd found a way to make it work. They were able to live the street life in a way that fit them, but they didn't let many people inside to see this precious side of their relationship when they let down their defenses so they could just be who they really were.

"You okay, baby?" Trigga asked, bending down so that he could look her in her eyes.

Sensing that this was turning into a personal moment between the two, Dre walked away and let them have their privacy, as he moved up behind Queen and looked over her shoulder into Cameron's smiling face.

LEO SULLIVAN & PORSCHA STERLING

"I'm good...I—I just...I don't want to change you," Keisha found herself saying suddenly, tears coming to her eyes as she felt the overwhelming love that she had for Trigga swelling up in her heart. "I don't want you to be unhappy because you changed because of me. When we met, you were the person you are and you've never stopped being that. I don't want to make it seem like you have to be a different person to be with me."

Pulling her hands in his, Trigga looked her square in the eyes, his own eyes twinkling with sincerity as he spoke.

"Keesh, I'm a different man because of you. You're not changing me; I'm making a decision based on my present circumstances. Before you, I didn't give a shit if I lived or died. I operated with no fear because I ain't have shit to lose. Now I have a lot to lose and I can't risk puttin' you in danger for that."

"But..." Keisha started, glancing over at Queen and Dre as they spoke lovingly to each other in hushed tones.

"Stop right there. Don't compare what we have to their shit. Queen and Dre were raised in the streets. They were brought up and trained to live the life they are living. Queen's father was the biggest dealer in Harlem. She couldn't live a normal life if she wanted to, the streets are all she knows," Trigga informed her with soft eyes.

He reached out and ran his finger along the outline of her jaw and then shook his head.

"I don't want a chick to be my rider, although you make a damn good one," he added when she frowned at him. "I want somebody who can take my mind off all this foul shit and put me at ease when I come home. In my mind, ain't shit lovely about bodying niggas for fuckin' with my wife. That works for Dre because he has no choice...ain't shit he can do about changin' Queen. But I want to be able to come home and lay with my chick without worrying about some bold ass, finna-be-dead nigga tryin' to bust down my damn door, ya feel me?"

Keisha nodded her head gently and took a deep breath, feeling relief from Trigga's words. She was willing to do what she had to in order to make him happy but, secretly, she thanked God that he wasn't making her do it. Ever since hearing Lloyd was dead, she'd enjoyed being able to relax without feeling like she had to look over her shoulders.

"Here you are," Queen said in a flat tone as she walked over to Keisha.

She held out her hands and dropped Cameron in Keisha's arms but had a reluctant look on her face. Once Keisha had Cameron in her arms and pulled him close to her chest, she looked up just in time to see Queen roll her eyes at Dre.

With a smirk on his face, Dre ignored her and looked directly at Keisha.

"Thanks for letting Queen's greedy ass—" Dre stopped when Queen nudged him and then he began to laugh as she scoffed at him. "Thanks for letting my wife and I spend some time with you and Cameron."

Queen exhaled sharply and then, looking at Keisha, began to speak.

"I know we don't know each other very well, but Trigga has been working with Andre and I for almost ten years and I trust him with my life. If you need anything, just let me know," she said, staring right into Keisha's eyes. Then she paused and rolled her eyes upwards as if she were thinking to herself.

"For Cameron, I mean…if you need anything *for Cameron*, let me know," she corrected herself. "I don't do all that talking and gossiping shit. My time ain't for everybody."

Stifling a laugh, Keisha nodded her head and gave her a gracious smile as she watched Queen acknowledge Trigga with a look and then turn to Dre. Dre knocked on the door to tell the men that it was time to go. Instantly, both he and Queen's entire demeanor changed back to what Keisha was accustomed to seeing. Dre walked out first and Queen followed behind him. But before she left the room, she turned her icy glare to Keisha and then pressed her lips together firmly, as if giving Keisha her version of a smile.

The door closed behind them and Keisha turned to Trigga with a look on her face that begged for him to explain to her what the hell had just happened. Laughing, Trigga sat down in the chair next to her and shrugged.

"Don't look at me to answer shit about Queen. A few months ago, she was ready to body a nigga for taking too long to carry out her demands and now she's our son's god-mother. I'm almost ten years in and I still don't understand her ass."

***

Cameron's god-mother made sure that he left the hospital with a five-man security team as if he were the firstborn son of Beyoncé and Jay Z. The hospital staff shot curious stares back and forth between the men and both Keisha and Trigga, as they tried to figure out what was going on when the men showed up.

"Ay, I know Queen sent y'all but you can leave," he told the men.

Unmoving, they each looked at him with blank faces as if they didn't understand what they were being told. They had been given orders and were sticking to them.

"Obviously your god-mommy has forgotten that I'm the nigga Dre originally hired to protect *her* ass," Trigga muttered to Cameron as he pulled a soft blue hat over his head.

The nurse walked in with a wheelchair in her hands as she squeezed by the men in order to get to Keisha, who was putting lip gloss on her lips in the mirror. When she saw the woman, she shook her head softly.

"I don't need that. I'll be walking out."

"You sure?" the nurse questioned with a lifted brow.

"Positive."

She made her exit and Keisha turned around to tell Trigga she was ready to go, but closed her mouth when she saw Trigga leaning over Cameron, who was lying on the bed, and whispering things near his ear. It brought her happiness just to see him with his son; the same son that he'd doubted was his, a child he thought he could never have.

"What are you tellin' him?" Keisha questioned with a smile.

"Man shit," Trigga replied back simply, nudging Cameron on the side which made him coo.

Keisha rolled her eyes and grabbed her purse as Trigga grabbed up the baby, placed him in his car seat, and then picked up the baby bag.

"Let me get that door for you," Trigga told her. "Cam, always get the door for your woman," he instructed Cameron who squinted up at his father.

Sucking her teeth, Keisha walked out the door shaking her head. Just as she passed in front of Trigga, he reached out and swatted her on the ass.

"And always make sure you tap her on dat ass when she walks out," he continued with a sexy ass smile.

"TRIGGA!"

EPILOGUE

"Ay, Yadi, you know I ain't got no issues with you hangin' around and shit but you can't be walkin' up in my office wearin' that shit. You know she ain't got no issues goin' to jail," Trigga warned Yadi as she leaned over in his face, checking out the schedule for the week.

Trigga was sitting at his large cherry wood executive desk, frowning up at Yadi who was standing in front of him as naked as the day she was born, with only tassels covering her chocolate nipples. She was a curvy dark-skinned bombshell that pulled in the most money of any of the chicks at the club, and she owed it all to her beautiful, smooth ebony-colored skin, almond shaped eyes and fat ass. Not to mention, she had the smallest waist you ever saw but everything on her was a hundred percent natural, no surgery needed. She didn't need surgery; she was just a bad bitch.

A bad bitch that needs to get her naked ass out of my office before my wife walks up in here, Trigga thought to himself as he made sure to keep his eyes on her face and nothing else.

"Trigga, I'm sorry because I know it's hard as hell for you to hear this bein' that all them bitches out there be fallin' at your feet and shit, but I'm not attracted at all to anything holding a dick," Yadi shot back as she rolled her eyes.

"That's because you ain't had a taste of the right one," Keisha chimed in as she walked in behind Yadi. "But you gonna have to take my word for it because if I catch you sniffing around mine, I'ma fuck yo' lil' skinny ass up. Now don't let me catch yo' ass in my husband's office with yo' damn clothes off no damn more!"

Yadi stepped back, putting her hands in the air with her palms up, in a state of surrender.

"My bad, Keisha, I was only checking the schedule, that's it."

"Yeah, yeah, yeah...you come back in Trigga's office like that and I'ma chin-check yo' muthafuckin' ass! You know I don't have a problem with you so don't make me have nan!"

With one brow lifted, Yadi looked over to Trigga for him to respond but he only shrugged. He wasn't stupid by a long shot and the last thing he was going to do was step in when Keisha was freely handing out ass whoopings. She'd long ago made it known that she didn't play when it came to chicks trying him.

"Don't look at Trigga because he will not save your ass if it happens again. Play with it and see what happens."

Keisha stood with her hands on her hips and watched as Yadi walked out slowly, her bowlegs making her ass rotate in just the way that niggas liked.

"Ugh, I can't stand her ass! Bitch know damn well she ain't gay. She just says that shit so she can get close to you. I don't see what the hell niggas see in her knock-kneed ass!"

Trigga licked his lips and tried to hide the smile that was creeping up on his face but he was doing a terrible job.

"She's not knock-kneed. She's bowlegged," he corrected her, knowing that it would only piss her off even the more.

"Whatever the hell it is, the shit ain't cute!" Keisha huffed and sat down on the top of the desk.

"It ain't her legs that niggas are lookin' at, Keesh. It's the way that ass shifts when she walks, that shit looks like—"

Stopping mid-sentence, Trigga ducked out of the way when Keisha swung at him in an attempt to deliver a firm backhand to the side of his neck.

"Yo' jealous ass needs to stop. Yadi been gay for as long as I've known her, which is damn near twenty years. I keep tellin' your ass that."

Standing up, Trigga walked around the desk and grabbed Keisha in his arms, then kissed her on her lips repeatedly until he felt her relax. Everything was exactly how he'd wanted it for so long. He had his wife and his son, alive and well in the city that he loved. He was out of the game and had legitimate businesses.

Sure, having a strip club wasn't ideal, but it had been Keisha's idea of how to quickly spin their money so they didn't run into any financial troubles. The fact was that although Trigga wasn't in the streets anymore, he still had lived his entire life in them. The reputation that he'd built for himself only resonated in the hood so he couldn't pull out completely. The strip club was a way to be legit but still use his connections to keep the club running. Members of The Queen's Cartel frequented the club to hang out, meet or relax after a long day in the streets. They felt safe because they knew Trigga was a real nigga and wouldn't give them a problem.

"I know what you keep tellin' me but I ain't buyin' that shit," Keisha shot back. "Anyways, when will you be done here? Cam is with Queen and I want to spend some time alone before we go get him. I know he misses me."

Trigga grabbed his cell phone and car keys then waited for Keisha to walk out of the door, making sure to pop her on the ass when she walked by.

"No, you miss him. You know Cam is havin' the time of his life over at Queen's. She probably got Aiden's big muscular ass reading him stories again like last time."

Trigga laughed as he locked up his office and thought about how Queen ordered her security team to do all kinds of things to entertain Cameron. It was the first time he'd ever seen big ass, muscular, Marine-looking niggas playing with sock puppets for a toddler and he could barely believe the sight of it, although it was right in front of his own eyes.

"Yeah, I do miss him but I think it's good that he has such a good god-mother because I have a feeling that soon we'll have our hands full," Keisha said in a way that made Trigga stutter-step. He looked at her and saw the coy look in her eyes. The corners of his lips began to slowly form a smile.

"What you mean by that?" he asked her.

Pulling her lips into her mouth, Keisha tried to hold back a grin as she reached into her pocket and pulled out three pregnancy tests. All had a plus sign on them for positive. Trigga's eyes lit up when he saw them. She was pregnant. Lightning had not only struck once, it had struck twice. Against all odds, Keisha was pregnant again.

"I love you, Keesh," Trigga told her, pulling his wife into an embrace.

"I love you, too," she told him as they stood outside of his strip club.

It's like déjà vu, he thought as he kissed all over is wife's face and thought about the moment he first realized how irresistible she was, speaking to him about her car issues while standing outside of the strip club in Atlanta. And now she was his.

If there was a God...He must really love niggas.

Thanks From THE AUTHORS!

I would like to thank God for giving me the talent to write and touch the lives of many.

Secondly, I want to thank my family, I love you all. And to my loyal fans and readers thank you so much, this has been a very long journey.

Also, I would be remiss if I didn't give a special thanks to my writing partner, the very beautiful and talented Porscha Sterling. This project wouldn't be possible without her hard work and dedication. She has been the glue that held this project together. We spent endless nights and early mornings talking, even debating, over the characters and riveting plots. I will say this...from day one, she never liked the character, Lloyd. I know I said this before but I still have to chuckle about it. :)

Also, I would like to give a big shout out to all the staff and writers at Sullivan Productions. I appreciate you all so much!! And to my brothas and sistas that languish behind enemy lines in neo-slavery, keep your heads up. It won't last always.

Happy reading! You can follow me on Facebook or Instagram.

LEO SULLIVAN

I can't say how happy I am to complete this series! It's definitely one of my favorite and I love it, however, I'm happy that Keisha and Trigga are finally in a happy place. They went through a loooooottttt! And, although I wanted to kill of Lloyd in book 2, I think everything played out the way it should have and I love how it ended.

Many thanks to everyone who took the time out to read this series! I appreciate you all! Please know we will be coming with another banger next! This one a complete, standalone novel...get ready for it!

Thank you to Leo Sullivan. You are amazing at what you do and I'm grateful to be able to write with such a talented author. You're my mentor and so much more. I've learned an incredible amount about my craft just because I've been able to work with you. And thanks, for finally agreeing to get rid of Lloyd!

To my 4-year-old, Alphonzo...mommy loves you, always and forever. <3

To the avid readers, I have a lot more in store! Please make sure to follow me and keep up with my work! HUGE shout-out to Royalty...y'all are the best group of authors out there. I appreciate you!!!!

Feel free to contact me on Facebook, Instagram or Twitter!

Join our mailing list to get a notification when Leo Sullivan Presents has another release!

Text LEOSULLIVAN to 22828 to join!

To submit a manuscript for our review, email us at leosullivanpresents@gmail.com

CPSIA information can be obtained
at www.ICGtesting.com
Printed in the USA
LVOW04s1745021216
515533LV00009B/833/P

9 781530 500321